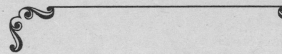

Anthony placed his fingers on the side of her cheek in the barest of caresses.

That was when he lost control.

Daphne stood transfixed by the magnetic pull of his dark eyes. She saw his mouth lower to hers in a kind of dream. She knew immediately she craved his kiss. . . .

His lips pressed against hers, then gently covered her mouth. Daphne felt the warm firmness of his mouth in every fiber of her being. Her hands came up and wound around his neck. She returned his kiss with a hunger that belied her outward calm. . . .

By Rosemary Stevens
Published by Fawcett Books:

A CRIME OF MANNERS
MISS PYMBROKE'S RULES
LORD AND MASTER

LORD AND MASTER

Rosemary Stevens

FAWCETT CREST • NEW YORK

A Fawcett Crest Book
Published by Ballantine Books
Copyright © 1997 by Rosemary Stevens

http://www.randomhouse.com

Library of Congress Catalog Card Number: 97-90886

ISBN 0-449-22727-8

Manufactured in the United States of America

First Edition: December 1997

10 9 8 7 6 5 4 3 2 1

With love for my family—
J.T., Rachel, and Tommy
and
with special thanks to Cynthia Holt and Melissa Lynn Jones
and
Anthony Joseph Perry

Chapter One

"Harkee, Harkee, Ladies and Gents! See the world's smallest tiger!" a loud male voice cried to the patrons of Astley's Royal Amphitheatre.

Miss Daphne Kendall, entering the horseshoe-shaped theater accompanied by her companion, Miss Oakswine, just missed the invitation.

"May God forgive you, Daphne, for pestering me into taking you to this horrible place," Miss Oakswine railed at her employer while the two women made their way toward their seats.

Daphne stopped herself from cringing before Miss Oakswine noticed. Any sign of weakness seemed to fuel the woman's fire, making Daphne subject to a prolonged rebuke that invariably digressed to a wide number of topics.

Instead Daphne gazed about in pleasure. Astley's boasted the largest stage in England, and at the foot of the stage was an orchestra pit. Tiers of seats and private boxes ensured the comfort of those who came to enjoy the entertainments offered.

Miss Oakswine was not one of them.

"Pshaw! I can feel my nose beginning to run from all the dreadful animal dandruff in the air. Trained horses and dancing dogs! Heaven only knows what I shall have to endure. Of a certainty I shall deteriorate over the course of the evening. And you know any sort of anxiety is bad for my weak heart."

"Perhaps if you try to enjoy—" Daphne began, glancing sympathetically at the older woman.

Miss Oakswine pulled a yellowed handkerchief out of her reticule and applied it with vigor to her long, pointy nose.

"Oh, I am sorry," Daphne said, and averted her gaze.

She was indeed remorseful, but not overly so. For the long-suffering and loudly complaining Miss Oakswine and her sneezing fits threatened to spoil the much anticipated visit to the famous Astley's.

Daphne's sorrow was rooted in the past, three years before, when her carefree parents had been tragically killed in a carriage accident. Tears threatened as she remembered her dear mama, who had shared a love of all creatures with her only child.

Daphne blinked rapidly, then a reluctant smile came to her lips when a picture formed in her mind of her papa, and how he would merrily tease that he held second place in their hearts to their beloved animals. Amid laughter, they would fall upon him with hugs and assurances that it was never so.

After her parents' deaths, Daphne had still been in a grief-filled haze when her beloved country home had gone to a distant male relative, who was the new viscount, and his large family. And while Daphne later told herself she should be grateful she was left the London town house and a large dowry, she could not help missing the freedom of the country and the cherished long walks with all her pets gamboling about at her side.

Furthermore she found living in Town with her mother's old school friend a daily trial to her patience. Employing the woman had seemed such an expedient solution to her need as a young, unmarried lady to have a companion reside with her for respectability.

When Miss Oakswine had written Daphne, expressing her condolences on the loss of her mama and papa and offering her services, seventeen-year-old Daphne had penned an immediate acceptance, hoping the lady would have the same sweet nature as her mama.

But it had not taken long for Daphne to realize her error. Miss Oakswine swept into the town house two days after the girl's arrival in London and immediately established her authority over the household. Inside of a day, she succeeded in having the exuberant, albeit clumsy, puppy Daphne had found whining and shivering outside the kitchen door, banished from its free run of the house to the scullery.

The following week the puppy mysteriously disappeared, never to be seen again.

Daphne had wept for the little fellow, but Miss Oakswine had merely twitched her long nose and declared it was for the best. In the future, Miss Oakswine apparently had decided, there would be no animal in "her" house. Over time, Daphne learned to be satisfied with sneaking food to the stray cats and dogs who always seemed to make their way to the kitchen door.

Bringing her thoughts back to the present, Daphne guided her companion to seats in the third row. Miss Oakswine tucked her thoroughly wet handkerchief back into her reticule, sat herself down, and continued her lecture."Horses! I suppose one must tolerate them, for they are necessary to getting about Town. But they are the only exception to my aversion to animals, as you should well know by now, Daphne. By the Lord! Must we sit so close to the ring?"

Daphne ignored the woman, a stratagem that had served her well over the past three years. Now that they were comfortably seated, her attention was caught by the spectacle of a series of clowns spilling out into the arena, causing adults and children alike to shriek with excitement.

One particularly exuberant boy with red hair a few shades brighter than Daphne's auburn locks, jumped up, shouting and pointing. Behind the clowns, a shabbily dressed man pulled a wheeled cage around the edge of the ring to Daphne's left.

"See the world's smallest tiger!" the shabby man yelled.

Daphne looked in his direction, and her light green eyes widened. Painted a garish bright orange, the cage contained the most pathetic cat Daphne had ever seen.

She supposed its apricot-colored fur, contrasted by darker brownish stripes, could qualify it as bearing a resemblance to the great cats of India. However, the animal lay listlessly on its side, eyes almost closed, in the manner of one who has totally given up on the world.

While the shabby man poked and prodded the "ferocious" beast, Daphne moaned in scarcely audible protest.

After staring compassionately for several moments, a growing sense of outrage propelled Daphne from her seat to follow when the man led the cage out of the ring.

Miss Oakswine screeched an objection at this unexpected turn of events. She leapt from her seat and scurried behind while Daphne made haste to catch up with the man and his cage. On the point of exiting the public area, Daphne and her unnoticed follower reached the wheeled cage.

"Sir! Sir!" Daphne called.

The man turned and stared rudely at the beautiful lady in the expensively cut dark green gown. His eyes narrowed when he comprehended the light of battle in her expression.

"I am Miss Kendall, and I wish to speak with you about your cat."

"My name's Cuddlipp, and it ain't a cat. He's the world's smallest tiger," the man responded stubbornly.

Daphne eyed her opponent's greasy black hair with distaste. Obviously, if he was not even willing to admit the cat was a cat, social niceties would serve no purpose. She decided to come right to the point.

"Mr. Cuddlipp, it is apparent the animal is in a sad condition."

"What! I gives him scraps every day or two. He's better off than wandering the streets, where I found him."

Daphne thought of inquiring how Mr. Cuddlipp came to find a *tiger* wandering the streets of London, but held her tongue. Perhaps a measure of tactfulness was called for here.

Unfortunately Miss Oakswine, who had also arrived on the scene, put no such strictures on her own speech. "Daphne, come away!" she said breathlessly, one hand pressed to her heaving chest. Inhaling a lungful of air, she continued. "Like all men, it is plain to see that common sense is foreign to Mr. Cuddlipp's nature. And what can the fate of that animal possibly have to do with you?"

Mr. Cuddlipp glared at Miss Oakswine. "I don't know who you are, lady, but you've got the longest nose and the smallest ears I've ever seen on a human."

The hairs on Miss Oakswine's head, which were prone to

stick out in every direction, quivered with her indignation. "Daphne," she hissed, "let us return to our seats immediately! People are looking our way. It will not do to be seen arguing with someone dirty as a sweep."

"Mr. Cuddlipp, I shall give you ten pounds for that cat," Daphne pronounced firmly.

"Oh, I am having palpitations," Miss Oakswine moaned.

A choking sound emitted from the man's throat. "Ten pounds? You must be daft. Anyhows, he's not for sale."

Daphne glanced at the cat, who had not moved an inch. It appeared likely to cross the threshold of death's door at any moment. Daphne felt a renewed surge of pity for the creature. "Twenty-five pounds, Mr. Cuddlipp."

The man screwed his eyes up and considered the tall, elegant female before him. Daphne returned his gaze without flinching.

Once again, though, Miss Oakswine took it upon herself to interrupt the proceedings. "Daphne, how many times have we spoken of how insensitive men are? How they are little more than animals themselves? Your very home was taken away by a man who never even offered to give you houseroom. Why you stand here and try to deal with this churl is beyond anything."

Mr. Cuddlipp's face turned red under Miss Oakswine's latest insult. "I don't wants your money, Miss Kendall. You'd be better off spending it on more cordial company than what you've got there." He jabbed a finger in Miss Oakswine's direction. "She can't be any relation of a beauty likes you, as ugly as she is."

Miss Oakswine drew a sharp breath. "You rattling sinner!" She moved as if to crack Mr. Cuddlipp over the head with her reticule.

Daphne felt a wave of frustration at her companion's behavior. She feared the opportunity to rescue the cat was slipping from her grasp.

"May I be of assistance?" a deep masculine voice asked.

Startled, Daphne swung around to face the stranger.

He was of above-average height and powerfully built. His

hair was a rich dark brown and showed a tendency to curl slightly. His skin was very white, and his mouth was firm. He was dressed impeccably in slate-gray, and a large sapphire burned darkly on the ring finger of his right hand.

But what Daphne noticed most about him were his eyes. The color itself was not unusual, being an ordinary deep brown. What was remarkable was the intensity she saw in their depths. His eyes seemed to possess a power to draw her to him and to veil just the two of them in a web of intimacy.

Daphne had experienced two Seasons since her arrival in Town, and her period of mourning had ended. She had danced and flirted with many gentlemen and would have remembered this particular one had she seen him before.

"Forgive me for intruding, Miss—"

"Kendall. I am Miss Daphne Kendall, and this is my companion, Miss Oakswine."

"And I am Ravenswood." He bowed gracefully to both ladies. "I could not help but observe that a controversy of some nature was taking place between you and this person," he said, indicating Mr. Cuddlipp.

"My lord," began Miss Oakswine, who knew her peerage and recognized at once she was dealing with the Earl of Ravenswood. Not that male members of the nobility inspired much more respect than commoners. Men were men in Miss Oakswine's view. Rather like sheep or cows. "My charge insists on squabbling with this vile man over a *cat*. She has always been foolish beyond permission when it comes to animals, but this incident surpasses her galaxy of stupidities."

The earl raised one dark eyebrow at Miss Oakswine, and she seemed to shrink. Then his dark brown eyes met Daphne's. "You wish to take this cat home with you, Miss Kendall?"

Daphne felt she had lost control of the situation, if indeed she had ever had command. She was a clever and intelligent girl and was not used to others interceding on her behalf. "Yes, my lord. But I am perfectly capable of sealing the bargain with Mr. Cuddlipp without any help, though I do thank you for your concern."

One corner of the earl's mouth twitched.

Mr. Cuddlipp entered the conversation. "And I've told you, miss, that you could not buy the tiger, so that's that."

Lord Ravenswood turned his head and glanced down his nose at the cat. To Daphne's utter amazement, the animal strained to raise a paw in his lordship's direction.

Daphne thought she saw a shudder of distaste cross the earl's handsome features, but it was gone so quickly, she believed she must be mistaken.

A rusty noise issued from the cat's throat. It was not a meow. The odd sound was more a cross between a growl and a weak tiger's roar.

"The monster!" Miss Oakswine declared. "I have never heard a cat's meow sound like that. Heaven above only knows what the animal's nature might be."

"Mr. Cuddlipp," Lord Ravenswood stated in a tone that would tolerate no argument. "You will accept my generous offer of one hundred pounds for the cat, release him from his cage, and hand him to Miss Kendall. I shall do you the favor of not inquiring of Mr. Astley as to why this particularly woeful animal was permitted to be a part of one of the entertainments, when everyone knows Astley's reputation for excellence."

There was a collective gasp.

Mr. Cuddlipp's face lit with joy over the huge sum of money.

Daphne was torn between shocked indignation at the earl's high-handed offer and relief that the cat would suffer no more.

Miss Oakswine was furious. "Daphne! You will not bring that creature into the house. I absolutely forbid it!"

But Daphne had not come this far only to go away empty-handed. She strained to keep her voice level. "I must contradict you, ma'am. This cat needs nursing, and I shall see to it in the kitchen. We shall not disturb you."

Lord Ravenswood eyed the pair curiously. "Miss Oakswine, are you by way of an aunt or some other relation of Miss Kendall's?"

Mr. Cuddlipp snickered.

Daphne felt her cheeks warming, and her temper slipping, at what must appear to his lordship as her inability to control a paid companion. The fact that this was somewhat the truth goaded her into addressing him tartly. "My lord, Miss Oakswine suffers sneezing fits around animals, and I have respected her feelings in the past. However, on this occasion, it cannot signify. The cat's very existence depends upon me."

Miss Oakswine appeared on the brink of apoplexy, until suddenly, a cunning look came into her eyes. "My lord, perhaps you could take the animal home with you. I am certain a gentleman of your rank commands a large staff that could easily care for one cat."

To Daphne's irritation, Lord Ravenswood paused and considered this statement. Once again he turned toward the cat, who immediately replied, "Grraow," in seeming agreement to the plan.

The earl's gaze returned to Daphne. She felt what could only be called a magnetic pull when he looked directly into her eyes. She managed to refrain from tapping her foot as he surveyed every aspect of her appearance, although she could not prevent the color from rising in her cheeks.

Miss Oakswine drove the final nail into the coffin. "I need not remind you, my lord, that it would be most improper, and would, indeed, set tongues wagging if it got about that Miss Kendall, as an unmarried lady, accepted a gift from you. Especially such an expensive one."

Daphne drew in a quick breath at her companion's audacity.

Lord Ravenswood's expression was grim. "Yes. The only thing is for the cat to return to Upper Brook Street with me."

Before Daphne could voice any protest, his lordship raised a well-groomed hand. A strange-looking man promptly appeared at his side. Daphne realized he must have been standing close by, waiting for just such a signal.

He was not tall, but his height was enhanced by a large white turban that sat imperiously atop his head. In the center of the front of the turban was an enameled pin portraying a vibrant likeness of an eye.

The servant's skin was nut-brown in contrast to his flowing white garments. He wore flat, gold-colored shoes from which red tassels dangled.

The look he bestowed on Miss Oakswine was nothing short of malevolent. However, he quietly produced the required sum of money and paid Mr. Cuddlipp for the cat.

"Eugene," Lord Ravenswood directed his servant. "Remove the cat from that cage and let us be on our way."

Eugene, whom Daphne guessed was a native of India, or perhaps Egypt, and nearing his sixtieth birthday, moved silently to obey the order.

Daphne watched as the cat was gently extracted from the cage, and Eugene spoke to it soothingly in a tongue she could not understand. The animal lay calm, like a sleeping infant, in the cradle of the older man's arms.

Miss Oakswine twitched her long nose in satisfaction.

Mr. Cuddlipp took his money and began walking away with a jaunty step. He turned for a moment to call back, "The tiger's name is Mihos."

Eugene's silver eyes widened, and a faraway expression came into them. He clutched the cat to his chest.

Daphne looked regretfully at Mihos, who, she decided, really did look like a miniature tiger. Even his eyes were a golden amber color.

As if sensing her distress, Lord Ravenswood turned to address her. "Miss Kendall, after the animal is recovered, may I call on you? I shall bring Mihos with me, of course."

"Yes, my lord, you are most kind." Daphne looked into his dark brown eyes once more and felt the stirring of attraction. She curtsied to him, and he bowed, then moved away with Eugene a few steps behind.

It would not do, she told herself. Like all the others, he would find her Fatal Flaw. The one she herself did not know the exact nature of, but which eventually put off even the most ardent of her suitors.

After two Seasons full of admirers, who consistently balked at the point when they might have been expected to make a declaration, Daphne had lost hope of forming with any gentleman the kind of attachment her parents had enjoyed. Fortunately she had not had her heart broken, for her affections had not yet been engaged by any of the gentlemen. And, she reminded herself, she had long ago determined to marry only for love.

She was brought out of these depressing musings by the sight of a man in a brightly colored costume, who was leading an elephant out of the ring and toward the exit where Daphne and Miss Oakswine were standing.

Lord Ravenswood passed through the exit. Following the earl, Eugene held a sleeping Mihos. The servant paused at the portal, turned around, and stared at the elephant.

Daphne experienced an odd feeling that Eugene was somehow communicating with the elephant. She chided herself for being fanciful, but turned nevertheless to look at the large beast.

Miss Oakswine stood facing the opposite direction and did not see the elephant approaching. Daphne opened her mouth to voice a warning, but Miss Oakswine was full of her triumph in the matter with the cat and was saying, "In the future you will be guided by me, Daphne. . . ."

In the next second the elephant came abreast of Miss Oakswine, raised its trunk high in the air, and bellowed a deafening cry.

Miss Oakswine's eyes popped in her head. She clutched her chest, and with a strangled cry, fell to the ground.

Eugene had hastened after Lord Ravenswood and did not see what happened. Daphne could only stand in shock as a crowd gathered around.

A man stepped forward and leaned briefly over Miss Oakswine's motionless body, pressing his fingers to her throat. Drawing back, he shook his head sadly. "Dead. She is quite dead."

A light sandalwood fragrance perfumed the air in Anthony, the Earl of Ravenswood's, elegant London town house. It pleased him that his staff had so quickly come to know his tastes. After seven years on foreign soil, he had arrived home from Egypt a mere fortnight ago.

Home.

Home was not really this rented town house. It was his

beloved estate in Surrey, Raven's Hall. There he had grown from a boy into a young man who lived in constant conflict with his father's shrewd and extravagant young bride, Isabella.

That reckless matron spent her time lavishly entertaining friends from London with extended house parties. Of course, costly clothes and jewels must be purchased to impress the numerous guests whom she indulged with all manner of luxuries.

Rather than watch Isabella destroy the estate, Anthony had finally made the decision to leave his home after yet another pointless argument with his father over Isabella's spending. Her pretty tears always won the day with the old earl. He could deny her nothing and refused to see what was right in front of his eyes.

Anthony had left for London that bitter day. In less than two years, Isabella brought the estate to its knees. When there was nothing more to be gained, she abandoned her husband. The old earl had gone on a mad, drunken binge, which had cost him his life.

When Anthony had received word that he was the new earl, he began the long and difficult process of trying to maintain the estate in some order while deciding on how best to replenish its coffers. All the while, the question of what would have happened had he not left when he did plagued him. Would he eventually have been able to force his father to see the truth? Would he have been able to put a stop to Isabella's selfishness? Would his father still be alive?

The new Lord Ravenswood was riddled with guilt and determined never to let any woman influence *him* beyond common sense.

It had taken seven years to build his fortune, but Anthony was a skilled and resourceful dealer in Egyptian artifacts. He had been successful beyond his expectations.

Anthony could not take all the credit, though. He had been fortunate to have Lord Munro as his partner to teach and guide him. The wizened old man had been his best friend as well as his business partner, and Lord Munro had seen Anthony through the pain of losing his father.

Of course, Lord Munro had also saddled him with Eugene. "Ah, Eugene, is the cat settled, then?"

The servant entered the hall and answered in a low tone. "He is warm and safe in the kitchens with a bellyful of chicken. We are lucky to have Mrs. Ware as cook. She will treat Mihos well."

The earl flipped through numerous invitations and missives on the hall table. "Good. See that the animal is kept out of my way. You know how I feel about cats."

The Egyptian servant stood deferentially with his hands clasped behind him. "In Egypt cats have been revered for centuries. When a feline member of the family died, everyone shaved off their eyebrows as a mark of respect."

Lord Ravenswood paused over one of the notes in the rack. "Shaved off their eyebrows, eh? Deuced unattractive if you ask me."

Eugene studied the earl carefully. "What was the name of your stepmother's cat?"

Lord Ravenswood glanced up sharply and faced the servant. "Do you read minds, then, Eugene? Perhaps those cards with the pictures on them you are always fiddling with tell you things."

Eugene shrugged enigmatically.

"Very well, yes, Isabella did have a cat. He was a large black cat called Brutus. Aptly named, I might add. Devilish sharp teeth and even sharper claws. Spent his life plotting ways to ambush me."

Eugene slowly nodded his turbaned head. "Had your stepmother been a wise woman, she would have also kept a white cat, for balance. Then the black cat would have been content."

The earl's features hardened. "I shall not have that woman referred to once we return to Raven's Hall. As for the level of Isabella's intellect, I should say it was unusually high. My father was no fool, but she managed to dupe him nonetheless. His mistake was in letting a pretty face blind him to the fact that intelligence is not a trait to be desired in a woman."

Eugene leaned forward and listened to this speech intently. "Why is it not a desirable trait?"

"Because clever women are dangerous," the earl stated flatly.

"Yes, master," Eugene replied, looking thoughtful.

Lord Ravenswood scowled. "I never liked you referring to me as 'master' while we were still in Egypt, and here in England it is even more bothersome. Lord Munro asked me on his deathbed to see to your future. You are an excellent man-servant, but I do not own you."

Eugene's face was a passive blank.

Having made his pronouncement, Lord Ravenswood turned back to the table. On the surface a large Chinese bowl sat in stately distinction. The earl put the correspondence aside and carefully raised the bowl to eye level. There, across the front, was a perfect likeness of Raven's Hall. He had had the bowl commissioned while he was still in Egypt. It had served as a reminder of what he was working for.

The earl's face softened as he studied the image of his beloved home. "My steward has sent word, the repairs to Raven's Hall are running ahead of schedule. Before the Season is over, we shall be able to return home, and I shall personally oversee the estate."

"Excellent news," Eugene said quietly. "Now all that is needed to ensure the future of Raven's Hall is an heir. Is that not so?"

His lordship's mouth tightened. While in Egypt, he had often proclaimed he would never marry. Now, back in England, the need for the heir Eugene spoke of demanded his consideration.

"Indeed," he replied absently as a picture sprang into his mind of a pair of almond-shaped, light green eyes. Of masses of hair in the richest shade of red imaginable. Of a small nose and full, pink lips. A body that belonged to a courtesan.

And, if her behavior earlier in the evening was any indication, a bright and alert personality that bespoke an astute mind.

No, regardless of how lovely she was, Miss Daphne Kendall could not be a candidate for his countess. He wondered at his own actions regarding her and the cat. He could not understand what had made him intervene on her behalf with Mr. Cuddlipp.

One minute, he recalled, he had been instructing Eugene as to the seating he desired at Astley's, his gaze snagging momentarily on the odd pin ornamenting the folds of his manservant's turban. The next minute, or so it seemed, he was ordering a ridiculous amount of blunt to be handed over for a scrawny feline. All for the sake of satisfying an extremely attractive lady he did not even know.

The earl's grasp on the bowl tightened. Gammon! Was it possible that he could become as soft in the head for a female as his father?

Absolutely not. He would never allow that to happen.

Then he reasoned that being back on English soil had brought out the gentleman in him, whereas in Egypt he had been too busy with business affairs to entertain thoughts of any woman other than the occasional lightskirt. He had been born and bred an English gentleman who would no sooner turn his back on a lady in need than he would kick his own horse. Yes, that was it.

Well, he was obliged to call on Miss Kendall, and to bring Mihos, since he had said he would, and to be polite during the Season's social functions, where he might encounter her, but that would be the end of any responsibility. Once done with his duty, he could be shot of her.

Neither Miss Kendall nor Mihos would pose a problem.

With this happy thought, his lordship dismissed lady and cat from his mind. He put the bowl down and reached for a particular letter. "I have a note here from Mr. William Bullock. Says he will be showing some of my Egyptian artifacts at his new Egyptian Hall over the next few weeks. I shall have to attend."

"Yes, master. In the meantime you must call on Miss Kendall."

"That necessity had already occurred to me, Eugene." Lord Ravenswood pursed his lips briefly, but directed his attention to the note in his hand. He was surprised by the last few lines. "Good God! Bullock says the Egyptian officials are quite upset about a highly prized statue of Bastet that is missing. Seems they have been around to question him regarding his contacts

14

with dealers. Ugly business. Wonder who could be behind the theft."

Eugene was silent as the grave.

The earl gathered the note and a few others, and took himself off to his library. "I shall ring for you when I am ready to retire, Eugene. Make sure instructions are left with Mrs. Ware that the cat remain with her or in the garden."

"Yes, master," Eugene whispered through dry lips.

Late that night, after making sure Lord Ravenswood would not have further need of him, Eugene closed the door to his own room and bolted it shut.

He put a candle down on the bedside table and opened a serviceable wardrobe containing more of the same type of clothing he had on. Bending down to the bottom of the armoire, he retrieved an article wrapped heavily in burgundy-colored velvet.

He carried it gingerly across the room, unrolled the velvet, and carefully lifted the object and placed it next to the candle on the table. A pair of eyes made out of golden citrine gemstones winked at him in the light from the flame.

The statue was a woman's body with a cat's head. It was made of ebony with fine turquoise lines depicting many concentric necklaces.

"Bastet," Eugene murmured to the statue. "You have given a great sign today by sending your son, Mihos, to me. I am ever grateful for your benevolence. Your humble slave will do whatever is necessary to see to the cat's comfort."

He bowed his head and uttered a string of prayers designed to please the cat goddess, Bastet. When he was finished, he reverently held the statue in his hands for a moment. "The cards told me to bring you to this country, and now I see why.

"Lord Munro thought to foil me by giving me to a man he thought would not marry, just as he never did. Old curmudgeon! 'A slave is a slave, a servant a servant, and so it is with you, Eugene' he always said. But he underestimated Lord Ravenswood's dedication to his home and family name. The earl *will* marry for the sake of Raven's Hall, and then I shall have my freedom at last.

"And it would not have been possible if I had not brought you to England, my goddess, so you might guide us all. Yes, I am thankful for the sign you bestowed on me. You sent Mihos to direct his lordship to the woman he is destined to wed.

"Never fear, Bastet, I shall do your bidding in this as in all things." He, and the eye-pin nestled in his turban, gazed into the cat's unblinking golden eyes. "Lord Ravenswood will marry Miss Daphne Kendall."

Chapter Two

Daphne walked into the office of Miss Oakswine's solicitor, Mr. Yarlett, with her lady's maid, Biggs. Daphne assumed she had been asked to call on him in order to pay Miss Oakswine's wages, current to the date of her death.

She managed a smile at the clerk behind the counter. "I am Miss Kendall, and I have an appointment to see Mr. Yarlett."

"Yes, miss. I'll let him know you're here," the young man said, and scrambled away.

Daphne seated herself on a bench and smoothed the folds of her black gown. She had decided two weeks of wearing mourning clothes out of respect for Miss Oakswine would be proper. A nagging guilt that she should have been kinder to the old lady had disturbed her since that fateful night at Astley's.

She was brought out of these reflections when an elderly man of rotund proportions appeared before her and extended his hand. "Miss Kendall, I am Phineas Yarlett. Thank you for coming."

"You are most welcome, Mr. Yarlett. I am happy to perform any final duties necessary as Miss Oakswine's last employer," Daphne assured him.

Mr. Yarlett was past the age of retirement, and wore the air of one who could no longer be surprised by the actions of his fellow humans. He led her courteously into his office and motioned to a comfortable-looking chair across from his desk.

Daphne declined his offer of tea and noticed a strongbox sat on the desk between them. After Miss Oakswine's demise, Daphne had been loath to go through her companion's belongings, a task she had found terribly painful after her parents' deaths, and so instead had instructed one of the maids to perform the chore. She hoped all of Miss Oakswine's things were in order.

Mr. Yarlett sat back in his chair and steepled his fingers in front of him. He eyed her over his spectacles. "Miss Kendall, the matter of Miss Oakswine's wages is not my uppermost concern. I have, however, prepared an accounting of the wages due," he said, and passed her some papers.

Daphne folded them and tucked them into her reticule. Her brows came together. "I am afraid I do not understand. If the matter of the wages is not why I have been summoned, then what can I do?"

Mr. Yarlett leaned forward and opened the strongbox. He began lifting items out and spreading them across the desk. Daphne's eyes widened in shock as she gazed upon the objects.

There was a small miniature of her papa she believed she had carelessly misplaced months ago. Then, a tiny, jewel-encrusted vinaigrette—her mama's favorite—followed. A silver thimble Mama had given her when, as a child, she had first learned to sew added to the collection. While the items might not hold a large monetary value, they were priceless in Daphne's heart.

"But, how . . . why . . . *did* she take these things from me?" Daphne stammered, unable to comprehend.

Mr. Yarlett heaved a weary sigh. "They were among her possessions. I was correct, then, when I judged these things belonged to you?"

Daphne nodded, totally baffled.

"Miss Kendall, you are young," Mr. Yarlett said kindly. "When you get to be my age, you will realize there are people in this world who do hurtful things out of petty spite. It appears Miss Oakswine was one of them."

"I cannot understand, Mr. Yarlett. I thought Miss Oakswine quite comfortable in her circumstances. I cannot imagine what I might have done to so deeply offend her that she would stoop to st-stealing from me . . . oh, it is incomprehensible."

Mr. Yarlett adjusted his spectacles. "People of Miss Oakswine's ilk need no reason for the things they do other than ones they have contrived in their own heads. However, I fear there is worse." From the strongbox, he removed a stack of money. "Five thousand pounds. It was found along with this diary."

Daphne could not suppress a gasp. "That is not my money, I am certain. Although where Miss Oakswine could possibly have obtained such a sum, I cannot imagine." She raised a hand to her throat as Mr. Yarlett reached into the strongbox once again and pulled out a thick, yellowed journal.

"Well, it seems Miss Oakswine took her sister's dowry, which was twenty-five hundred pounds, and added it to her own. She apparently had a vehement hatred of men, had no intention of ever marrying, and did not want her sister to marry, either. Not that Miss Oakswine was overly fond of her sister. It seems to have been more a matter of principle. It is all spelled out in her own handwriting in this diary."

Daphne's mind struggled to assimilate this startling information. She remembered that Miss Oakswine did indeed find all men dreadful. Many was the time her companion had preached the evils of men to her, and she had often discouraged her from marrying. But for Miss Oakswine to force her views on another by making it difficult, if not impossible, for her very own sister to marry was shocking.

Mr. Yarlett's face held an expression of concern. "Are you sure you do not want a cup of tea?"

"No, I thank you." Daphne felt ill from the morning's revelations and only wanted to return home to try to sort out her feelings. "Whatever happened to Miss Oakswine's sister? She never mentioned her to me."

Mr. Yarlett shook his head. "You do not want to know, Miss Kendall."

"On the contrary, sir, I need to know in order to make sense of all this." Daphne gazed at him steadily.

Mr. Yarlett seemed to take her measure and gave a brief nod. "According to an entry in the diary about five years ago, the lady took her own life after living as a poor relation in her brother's house."

Daphne felt numb. She stared at her lap in silence.

"I shall not keep you, Miss Kendall," Mr. Yarlett said at length. He wrapped the miniature, the vinaigrette, and the thimble in a cloth, and handed them to her. "I am happy to return your things to you. I have contacted a Mr. Jonas Oakswine, who is Miss Oakswine's deceased brother's son and would be her next of kin. Ironic, is it not, that the money will go to a man? I feel sure Miss Oakswine would not approve, but as she died without a will, there is no choice."

Daphne rose. "Thank you, Mr. Yarlett. I shall settle the matter of the wages tomorrow. Please let me know if there is anything else."

She walked out of the office in a daze. She managed a weak smile for the benefit of her waiting lady's maid.

"Is everything all right, Miss Kendall? You look as if you have seen a ghost," Biggs inquired.

"Well, I have not done anything so nonsensical, Biggs," Daphne said lightly. "Only let us go home. I confess I am out of frame."

"Yes, miss."

They walked out to the street, where Daphne's carriage awaited. "And, Biggs, I shall lie down for a while, and when I get up, I shall wear the apple-green muslin. You may put away my black dresses."

Biggs nodded her approval. "Very good, miss."

With Miss Oakswine safely dead, Miss Daphne Kendall was on her own.

It was a circumstance that could not last long if she wanted to be received anywhere in Society. Unmarried females simply did not live alone.

A week after her upsetting visit with Mr. Yarlett, the task of finding a new companion loomed large in Daphne's mind. She went for a walk in Hyde Park near the Serpentine River to consider her situation. It was early morning, so none of the fashionables were out of their beds yet, much less in the Park.

There was a chill in the air, but the sun shone down on the water. One of her footmen, James, limped along a little behind Daphne. His leg had been injured while he was fighting the French the previous year. He was devoted to his mistress, as she had been the only one to hire a footman with a deformed leg.

The sounds of excited barking broke the quiet of the morning. The three dogs Daphne had acquired since Miss Oakswine's death cavorted at her side. Their happiness at being loved and well fed for the first time in their young lives knew no bounds.

"Folly! Come away from the water!" Daphne cried, exasperated. The shaggy brown dog obeyed, but not before scampering through the edge of the river, slipping on a stick, and falling face first into the mud.

James covered a guffaw with a cough.

Daphne sighed. Folly was a bit clumsy, but he would outgrow it. Hopefully.

On the way home from Miss Oakswine's funeral, which no one other than Daphne had attended, she had rescued Folly from a club-wielding merchant. The man had been angered when the dog had crashed into the merchant's display of oranges, overturning the fruit into the street, much to the delight of the eager street urchins, who made off with it.

Just now Folly shook himself violently, spraying mud and water.

Far enough away to escape damage to her blue-and-white-striped morning gown, Daphne chuckled at Folly and then gazed down at the sweet-natured black dog who walked serenely at her side. No ill-considered romps for Holly! Her size—she came up to Daphne's waist when sitting—belied her calm, gentle character.

Up ahead, the third dog, Jolly, raced through the Park. Jolly was white with a few black patches, one at a crazy tilt over his right eye. He was much smaller and chubbier than the other two canines, a fact that did not dim his happy outlook on life. His long pink tongue hung out as he ran to greet an older lady who sat alone on a bench.

Daphne quickened her pace to catch up with the scamp before he frightened the woman. Her concern proved to be unwarranted.

"God-a-mercy! What a delightful doggie! Only mark the imp of mischief behind those eyes. A court jester in a former life, no doubt," the lady pronounced cheerfully. She leaned forward and stroked Jolly's head, much to his gratification.

Relieved at not receiving a scold for Jolly's lack of manners, Daphne overlooked the woman's odd remark about the dog having a former life. "Oh, Ma'am, I am glad you are not disturbed by him. Jolly can be too lively at times, I fear." Daphne noticed the way the lady's gloved fingers rubbed behind Jolly's ears just the way he liked.

"Too lively? Fudge! Why, he is full of life, as he ought to be," the lady declared.

Daphne smiled. How pleasant it was to be in the company of someone who appreciated animals as she did. She stared at the woman curiously. Her light brown hair was streaked with gray, and Daphne placed her age past fifty. Wrinkles creased the skin around her eyes, but her complexion was clear and her cheeks a delicate shade of peach. Dressed in a plain gown of a dark blue color, with a shawl that had seen better days, the lady might have been a governess or a genteel lady fallen on hard times.

The woman dropped her hand from Jolly's head, reached over and gave Holly a thorough pat, and then glanced around the Park a bit nervously.

Discerning her unease, James moved away to stand under a nearby tree.

The woman lowered her voice and confided, "I am Miss Leonie Shelby, lately governess to the Duchess of Welbourne's two brats."

Daphne was startled by the lady's sudden air of subterfuge and at hearing the answers to the very questions which were running around in her mind. "I beg your pardon?"

The woman's blue eyes twinkled, and Daphne was struck by the kindness they held, a kindness she had not seen in what suddenly seemed like years.

"I suppose I should not have called the children that. But, my dear, the pair of them were horridly dull. I know it is hard to believe that of any child, but they both suffered from an acute lack of imagination. Deplorable!"

Daphne blinked, then nodded her head in what she hoped was an understanding gesture.

Miss Shelby continued, "But I shall have to deal with them no more. The duchess's scapegrace nephew, Lord Guy, took it upon himself to steal a carved ivory figure of a cat from Her Grace's extensive ivory collection and foist the blame onto me. Why, I was dismissed without a character—"

Here Miss Shelby interrupted herself anxiously. "Heavens, I am rambling on, and you must only be wishing for a rest. Please sit down, dear child, and bear me company. What is your big black dog's name?"

Daphne's head was reeling with the intelligence imparted by Miss Shelby. How dare a peer of the realm blame this sweet lady for his transgressions, knowing she would be cast out on the street? To be turned off without a reference! How dreadful.

Daphne's tone was tender. She would go slowly and see if she might be of assistance to the lady. "Forgive me for not introducing myself and Holly, Miss Shelby," she said seating herself on the bench. "I am Miss Daphne Kendall of Clarges Street. In addition to Jolly and Holly, I have a dog named Folly, who is running about somewhere." Daphne bit her lip and hoped Folly was not getting into any more scrapes.

Miss Shelby clapped her hands with glee. "How charming! We always kept pet dogs at the vicarage when I was growing up. Animals can be such a comfort when one is alone."

"You had no brothers or sisters, then?"

Miss Shelby laughed softly. "Oh, my, yes. But you see, I was always deemed different from them, and it is human nature to distrust what is unlike one's self."

"Indeed," Daphne replied distractedly as she noticed a portmanteau was tucked under the bench at Miss Shelby's feet.

Holly and Jolly lay down nearby, tired from the morning's exertions. Folly was still not in sight.

Daphne sat back on the bench, her mind adding up the facts and coming to the conclusion that Miss Shelby was in dire need of help.

She studied Miss Shelby closely. She dismissed as ridiculous any notion that the woman was capable of stealing. There was perhaps something singular about the lady, but to her immense credit in Daphne's copybook, she appeared to love animals.

Might Miss Shelby accept a position as companion to her? What a difference she would be from Miss Oakswine, Daphne thought, and immediately chided herself for thinking ill of the dead.

On the chance she might be mistaken as to Miss Shelby's bleak prospects, Daphne posed an innocent question. "Miss Shelby, would you give me your direction? I could send word the next time the dogs and I will be in the Park, and mayhaps we might meet you here."

All Miss Shelby's composure fled, and she burst into tears. "I have nowhere to go," she sobbed. "I am fleeing the Bow Street Runners!"

Daphne felt a frisson of alarm, but calmly fished in her reticule for a handkerchief. "I am sure it cannot be as bad as that. Are you saying the duchess reported you as a thief to the authorities?" She handed the lacy scrap to Miss Shelby and watched as the lady gently dried her tears.

Miss Shelby nodded her head emphatically. "Her Grace was very angry. She summoned a man to the house—I did not hear his name, hiding as I was behind the drawing room door—but he was an official of some sort. I assure you, Miss Kendall, I am bound to hang at Newgate. Oh, the jeering crowd, the jailer marching me to the hanging post, the feel of the rough rope going around my neck—"

"Miss Shelby!" Daphne exclaimed, her heart twisting in pain at the woman's plight.

At that moment the long-absent Folly raced into view, a gentleman's beaver hat clamped in his jaws. Both dog and hat were wet and mud-stained. Behind him, two men followed on horseback.

Daphne shot to her feet. "Folly! What have you done?"

"I believe I can answer that question, Miss Kendall."

Daphne looked up to face a hatless Lord Ravenswood. He

was seated on a fine chestnut horse, and his manservant, Eugene, rode beside him.

Squeezing her eyes shut, Daphne dropped a curtsy and murmured a fruitless prayer that she had entered a dream. For some puzzling reason, she wished the Earl of Ravenswood to look upon her with favor, and this was not the situation in which she might achieve that aim. "Good morning, my lord. May I present Miss Shelby?"

The earl gave a brief nod of his head. Eugene smiled. Miss Shelby rose from the bench, returned Eugene's smile, and dropped into a deep curtsy for Lord Ravenswood.

His lordship was not appeased. "Is that *your* canine, Miss Kendall?"

Daphne glanced at Folly. The dog had the grace to duck his head and assume a shameful look. As shameful as he could manage with a mouthful of beaver hat.

"Yes, my lord," Daphne answered in a voice filled with suppressed laughter.

Lord Ravenswood eyed her sternly. "I was enjoying a refreshing ride when that animal ran across my path, startling my horse, who reared in fright. My hat fell to the ground. Before I could dismount and retrieve it, that cursed mongrel snatched it up and ran off."

"I am sorry," Daphne managed, all her efforts concentrated on maintaining a somber expression despite the picture Lord Ravenswood had painted of the morning's mishap. His lordship would not be amused if she started to laugh.

Instead she approached Folly and attempted to remove the hat from his mouth. A low growl emitted from the dog's throat. "Oh, dear."

"Here, allow me to help," Miss Shelby said, reaching a hand down to pat Folly on the head. "Young man, you have done wrong. This is no May game. This is a gentleman's hat. We must return it to him at once."

To Daphne's relief, Folly obediently dropped the hat into Miss Shelby's waiting hand. He then trotted off to join Holly and Jolly, who had been watching the proceedings with interest.

Eugene favored Miss Shelby with another smile. "Only one with a kind soul has the power to command animals with merely the tone of their voice."

The peach color in Miss Shelby's cheeks intensified.

Lord Ravenswood looked askance at his servant.

Daphne took the hat from Miss Shelby's hands and stepped toward his lordship. She ineffectively brushed it off, for it was quite ruined, and offered it to him.

His fingers touched hers as he accepted it, and Daphne felt heat rush up her arm at the contact.

Lord Ravenswood did not appear to be affected. His dark eyes fixed on hers, and he said, "I hope, Miss Kendall, that we are not destined to be embroiled in contretemps involving animals at our every meeting."

Daphne pursed her lips at this reproof, then drew a deep breath. She found she did not like having to look up at him as he sat on his horse. "How is Mihos, my lord?"

"He enjoys renewed health," the earl answered tersely.

Eugene nodded his turbaned head. "Mihos has taken a liking to my master and has refused to be confined to the kitchen. He follows him everywhere in the house—like a shadow—and cries when Lord Ravenswood goes out. Always, he is at the door waiting when we return."

Now Daphne could not stop a grin from spreading across her face. It grew even wider when the earl twisted in his saddle to bestow a glare on his servant.

Returning his gaze to Daphne, the earl said coolly, "I shall call on you, as I promised, and bring the cat. By the way, my condolences on the loss of Miss Oakswine."

"Thank you, my lord," Daphne murmured.

Eugene's fingers tightened on the reins of his horse. "A terrible accident. I have said many prayers for her soul."

Daphne noted his distress and wondered at it. "You are considerate to do so, Eugene. And, my lord, I shall look forward to seeing Mihos again. Please come one day soon."

The earl stared down at her for a moment and then nodded. He and Eugene moved away to resume their ride.

Miss Shelby eyed her new young friend with interest. "What a handsome man Lord Ravenswood is, Miss Kendall."

To her dismay, Daphne found she had been staring off into the distance where the earl and Eugene had ridden. "Yes, he helped me rescue a cat at Astley's Royal Amphitheatre earlier this week. But, come, you must call me Daphne, and with your permission, I shall call you Leonie."

At Miss Shelby's nod of agreement, Daphne continued. "You might have heard the earl's comment on the loss of Miss Oakswine. She was my companion, and I have not yet replaced her. I wonder, Miss Shel—Leonie, if you would consider coming to me."

Miss Shelby's eyes grew suspiciously moist. She looked into Daphne's light green eyes and said firmly, "I knew I was called to the Park this morning for a reason."

Before Daphne could question this odd response, Miss Shelby said, "I want you to know I have never stolen anything in my life."

"Silly. Of course I know that." Daphne reached out and touched Miss Shelby's arm. "Tell me, how can I alone possibly be expected to look after these three dogs, one of whom is quite a disgrace," she said glancing briefly at Folly, who hung his head, "without your expert help?"

Miss Shelby's expression lightened. "Thank you, my dear, I would be grateful for the position." She tugged her shawl tighter about her shoulders and reached down to pick up her portmanteau, but James was there before her.

Miss Shelby smiled her thanks at the footman and returned her attention to Daphne. "I believe Holly might have been a lady-in-waiting to a French queen in a former life, but Folly . . . hmmm, I shall have to give his other incarnations some thought."

Daphne chuckled, but was not really paying attention to Miss Shelby's nonsense about former lives. Her thoughts had strayed back to the moment when Lord Ravenswood's fingers had touched hers, and the warm feeling that touch had evoked.

And he would be calling on her. Daphne wished the time would hurry past until she saw him again.

She did not have long to wait.

Daphne and Miss Shelby spent the rest of the day getting to know one another better, while they settled Miss Shelby into a sunny room down the hall from Daphne's bedchamber.

Daphne knew her decision to bring Miss Shelby home as her companion had been impulsive but, in her opinion, justified. A more amiable female she had yet to find since Mama's death. And Miss Shelby's loving nature acted like a balm on Daphne's self-esteem, which had been wounded over the past three years by Miss Oakswine's constant criticism.

If Miss Shelby had some odd views on past lives and what she called the Spirit World, well, Daphne was willing to tolerate it. After all, some people would call her own desire to help stray animals peculiar.

In Miss Shelby's opinion, Daphne was nothing short of an angel of mercy. The girl had earned her unerring loyalty, Miss Shelby going so far as to say dramatically, "I would lay down my life for you, my dear, and be glad of it."

The next afternoon the ladies were seated comfortably in front of a fire in the drawing room when Daphne's butler, Cramble, announced the Earl of Ravenswood.

Daphne put away the piece of stitchery she had been toiling over. Miss Shelby, who judged all needlework except dressmaking a waste of time, placed the book she had been reading, *The Planets and You,* on a small satinwood table next to where she was seated on the sofa. She turned about and gazed eagerly toward the door.

The tall, elegant figure of the earl entered the room, and Daphne could only admire his masculine appearance. His indigo blue coat sat on his shoulders without a wrinkle. Buff-colored pantaloons molded his legs and disappeared into Hessian boots that were shined to look like black glass. His cravat rose in stiff folds above his white waistcoat.

He handed his hat—a new one, no doubt—and stick to Cramble, but as the elderly butler had been nearly blind when Daphne hired him, he saw only the hat, which he accepted. To

Lord Ravenswood's credit, he said nothing, retaining the stick and merely advancing with Eugene behind him.

Unfortunately, as Cramble was exiting the room, he jostled the wicker basket that Eugene carried, resulting in the company being treated to an angry, high-pitched "Grraow!"

"My deepest apologies, my lord, did I step on your toe?" the butler asked his lordship.

Daphne's hand flew to her mouth to stop a giggle from escaping. Miss Shelby and Eugene shared a smile.

" 'Twas nothing," Lord Ravenswood said, dismissing the servant's concern. He bowed low to the ladies.

"Cramble, please have one of the maids bring fresh tea," Daphne said to the servant. Then she turned to the earl. "Do be seated, my lord."

Anthony studied the inviting room. It was done in rich, dark green with cream-colored wallpaper. Pretty pieces of furniture were placed more for comfort than style, and the room was strewn with books, magazines, and bowls of flowers.

Making sure to wait until the butler had closed the double doors, Anthony sat on a green satin chair next to a matching one where Miss Kendall was seated, and motioned for Eugene to open the lid of the basket. "Here is your cat, Miss Kendall."

Mihos slowly raised his striped head from the basket and gazed at his surroundings. Upon seeing the earl, he promptly jumped out of the wicker container to the floor, and then, with a great leap, flew into Lord Ravenswood's lap.

Anthony was seized with a desire to order the cat back into the basket until he heard Miss Kendall's musical laugh ring out.

"Did you see that? He *flew* across to you! Oh, my lord, I would not say he was my cat. Indeed, he seems much attached to you."

"Grraow," agreed Mihos. He raised a paw to the earl's chin.

"I suppose you are correct, Miss Kendall," Anthony agreed grudgingly. He patted the cat's head awkwardly. Every time Mihos stretched a paw toward his face, Anthony was convinced it was to claw his nose off. As yet, though, the cat had only been affectionate. "And he is quite the acrobat. I am persuaded Mr. Cuddlipp did not understand the cat's true value by keeping him locked in a cage."

"He appears the picture of health, my lord, and does seem rather agile," Daphne said, watching with approval as Lord Ravenswood handled the cat.

"Yes, you could say that." The cursed animal had hardly awarded him a moment's peace since taking over the household. Always "flying" from place to place and wanting to be in his lap, atop his desk, or worst of all, draped about his shoulders. And while Anthony assured himself he would never change his mind regarding felines, he supposed Mihos must be tolerated.

Feeling seven kinds of a fool, he stroked the cat's striped fur, aware of Miss Kendall's scrutiny. "He would not get along well with your dogs, so I am forced to house him."

Miss Shelby said, "You should feel honored, Lord Ravenswood, that the cat has chosen you as his person. Daphne told me the story of how you rescued him at Astley's."

Anthony eyed the woman curiously. It seemed she was Miss Oakswine's replacement as Miss Kendall's companion. She appeared foolish, but harmless, which was more than could be said for her predecessor. "What can you mean, the cat chose me? I assure you, he was in no position to choose anything, being at death's door."

Eugene spoke up from his position behind the earl's chair. "Master, a cat belongs only to himself. He chooses to share his life with a human so that he may have his basic needs insured."

Miss Shelby nodded her head adamantly. "How true, Eugene. I can see what would have happened had Lord Ravenswood not saved Mihos."

At this point her eyes grew dreamy, and her voice became impassioned. "That nasty-sounding Mr. Cuddlipp would not have taken proper care of him. Mihos would have grown thinner, more feeble, and less likely to hold the attentions of the patrons of Astley's. One day, in a fit of temper, Mr. Cuddlipp would have grabbed him from his cage—"

"And thrown him out into the snow," Eugene finished for her.

"Yes! Yes!" Miss Shelby cried. "The poor little dear would trudge on—"

"His paws barely able to cut through the snow, as weak as he was." Eugene moved to sit next to Miss Shelby on the sofa. The two became quietly engrossed in their predictions of what might have been.

Anthony shook his head at the two older people and then glanced down at the purring cat in his lap. "You have no idea of the adventures you have missed," he informed him.

Daphne's eyes twinkled. "My lord, if I may be so bold, why have I not seen you about in Society, coming to the aid of other felines?"

Anthony turned to answer Miss Kendall's question. She was a vision today in a simply cut yellow silk gown with tiny puffed sleeves. A strand of pearls was about her neck, and pearl earbobs contrasted with the red of her hair.

He found himself admiring the creaminess of the white skin exposed by the gown's bodice, which was cut low. Only when a pink tint appeared on her skin did he realize he had been staring rudely at her.

"I have just returned to England after living for the past seven years in Egypt," he answered.

Her finely arched brows came together. "You do not have the complexion of one who has spent much time in the hot sun."

No one would ever accuse Miss Kendall of being a slowtop, Anthony mused. "How astute of you. I fear the last eleven months of my stay in Egypt were spent indoors, largely confined to my bed."

"How dreadful, especially for an active gentleman."

Anthony drew in a deep breath. "Yes, it was difficult. I contracted a fever that I could not seem to shake, despite every cure Eugene pressed on me. Each time I thought I had regained my health, it would return and drain my strength again. One of the consequences was that I lost all the tan color I had acquired in my skin."

A maid entered with a tea tray, and Miss Kendall poured a cup and passed it to him. Anthony noted her long, slender fingers and suddenly remembered brushing them with his the day before in the Park.

She was kind enough to prepare tea for Miss Shelby and Eugene as well, he noted. Turning her attention back to him, she asked, "What did you do in Egypt before you became ill?"

"I dealt in Egyptian antiquities."

Her green eyes widened with interest. "How fascinating. I read in *The Times* about a very important Egyptian statue having been stolen recently. The Egyptian authorities believe someone in England may have it."

"Yes, my friend, Mr. Bullock, told me of the theft," Lord Ravenswood said, thinking what a pity it was Miss Kendall possessed a keen intelligence, was well-informed on current events, and therefore an unsuitable female. She really was remarkably pretty and well mannered.

Seated next to Miss Shelby, Eugene stiffened as he heard his master discuss the theft of Bastet. Anxious to turn the subject, he said, "Some of Lord Ravenswood's artifacts are being shown at Mr. Bullock's new Egyptian Hall."

Miss Shelby gasped with pleasure. "Oh, I have always wanted to travel, but it has not been meant to be, as yet, in this lifetime. How I would enjoy seeing wonderful treasures from another country."

A delicate flush rose in Miss Kendall's cheeks at Miss Shelby's none too gentle hint to be taken to the exhibit at the Egyptian Hall.

Lord Ravenswood was not a man usually given to impulse, but he found himself saying, "I should be delighted to have you and Miss Kendall join me next Thursday evening, if you would care for it."

"My lord, you are kind but—" Miss Kendall began, until her companion interrupted her.

"Yes, too kind," Miss Shelby beamed. "And we are happy to accept your invitation. Why, I predict it will be a most enjoyable evening, would not you say so, Daphne?"

"Of course," Miss Kendall murmured, shooting the earl a rueful smile.

The fact that he was an English gentleman forced Lord

Ravenswood to reach for Miss Kendall's hand and give it a quick, reassuring squeeze to lessen her embarrassment.

At least that is what he told himself caused the action.

He noticed when he released her fingers, she clasped them tightly with her other hand, but he had no time to wonder at the movement as a loud crash came from behind the closed drawing room doors.

Daphne rose to her feet just as Cramble threw open the door, and Holly, Folly, and Jolly rushed in. "They want their bed, miss," the elderly butler explained, indicating a large sheet of flannel in the corner of the room.

Three sets of paws skidded across the floor. Three dogs halted at precisely the same time, and three noses sniffed the air and immediately detected the presence of a feline.

"Oh, dear," Miss Shelby groaned.

"I shall take care of this," Lord Ravenswood assured them.

"Come, Mihos, back in your basket," Eugene instructed.

The striped cat slipped from the earl's grasp and jumped to the back of his chair. Balanced on all four paws, Mihos glared down his whiskers at the dogs, who seemed paralyzed with shock. Looking every bit as fierce as a great tiger cat of India, Mihos hissed at them.

As one, Holly, Folly, and Jolly turned tail and ran for the flannel, where they cowered in one big, moist-eyed heap.

Mihos sailed gracefully through the air above the tea things and into the basket Eugene held, indicating the visit was over.

Very late that night, Eugene opened the door to his room and entered, followed by Mihos. Bolting the door shut behind them, Eugene placed his candle down on the bedside table and crossed the room to light a stick of incense.

Mihos sneezed delicately.

"Little tiger, do you not like the scent of jasmine?"

Mihos sneezed again in answer, then jumped on the bed and waited expectantly.

Eugene walked to the armoire and bent to retrieve the statue of Bastet. Reverently he unwrapped the figure of a cat's head with a woman's body from the velvet and placed it on the table.

He then knelt in front of it, bowed his head, and began murmuring prayers.

From his position on the bed, Mihos studied the man and reached out a tentative paw to touch his turban.

Eugene completed his prayers, opened his eyes, and addressed the statue. "We make progress, Bastet. Lord Ravenswood held Miss Kendall's hand today. It was only briefly, but I am satisfied."

Mihos roared enthusiastically.

In his mind Eugene went back in time to once before when he thought he might obtain his freedom. He had still been a young man then. But, instead, he had been given to Lord Munro and served him for thirty years.

Now he had another chance at the freedom he craved.

Mihos leaned closer to the statue and sniffed it curiously.

"If I am not mistaken, I have an ally in Miss Shelby," Eugene said thoughtfully. "She is a knowing one. Did you send her to me as well, Bastet?"

Mihos rubbed his whisker pad against one of the ears of the cat-woman statue, and it wobbled alarmingly.

Eugene grabbed it before it could topple over. The goodwill of the goddess was crucial to his plans. Respectfully he encased her in velvet, and secreted her in the armoire.

Chapter Three

Two evenings later, Daphne and Miss Shelby handed their wraps to a footman and walked into Lady Huntingdon's crowded drawing room. Both ladies enjoyed music, and had agreed with enthusiasm to attend Lady Huntingdon's musicale.

Chairs had been arranged around the candlelit room so that the company might best appreciate the tenor's efforts. Daphne and Miss Shelby made their way through the crush to find seats before the singing began.

Daphne was nodding to an acquaintance when, next to her, she heard Miss Shelby gasp. Daphne halted and turned to look at her companion.

"What is it, Leonie?" she questioned, seeing Miss Shelby's cheeks had lost their peach color and were instead a pasty white.

"Lord Guy is here. Over by the fireplace," Miss Shelby moaned. Her hands shook, and the fan she was holding fluttered to the ground. "He will see me and turn me over to the authorities!"

Daphne turned her head and gazed across the room to see the gentleman responsible for her companion's loss of employ and her subsequent fear of the hangman's noose.

The Duchess of Welbourne's nephew was a young man in his early twenties. He stood surveying the gathering with an affected air of disdain. He was foppishly dressed in a sky-blue coat, and his blond hair had been teased high on his head.

"Leonie, as I have been telling you these three days past, I am very certain that if the duchess had any proof of treachery on your part—which of course she could not, since there was none—she would have produced it by now. You are quite safe," Daphne told her. "And Lord Guy looks like he concentrates his attention on his coats."

Miss Shelby's lips trembled in what passed for a smile of thanks at a passing footman, who had bent and retrieved her fan. "I pray you are right about the duchess. As for Lord Guy, looks can be deceiving, Daphne. He is quite penniless and dependent on the Duchess of Welbourne's charity, of which she has little. I feel he took the ivory cat and sold it to pay his tailor."

"And you were the one to suffer," Daphne responded with some heat.

"Yes, my child, but as long as I am not being charged with stealing, I am happy at the way things have turned out for me," Miss Shelby told her. "Besides, the real person to pity will be the lady Lord Guy takes for a wife. 'Tis said he is hanging out for money and not just any heiress will do. Lord Guy wishes for a wife whose combination of wealth and beauty will make him the envy of his friends."

"Is that so?" Daphne inquired, a gleam of mischief flashing in her eyes. "I may not be accounted an Incomparable—"

"Daphne, never say so! You are the most beautiful lady present," Miss Shelby exclaimed vehemently.

Daphne laughed and reached over to give Miss Shelby's hand a quick squeeze. "Oh, Leonie, I suspect you will do much to keep my spirits high. I was going to say that, while I may not possess the amount of beauty Lord Guy requires, I am sure he could be influenced by the size of my dowry. Perhaps he would be impressed enough to clear the name of my companion if I asked it of him."

Miss Shelby placed a restraining hand on Daphne's arm. "No, my dear, I would strongly advise against any pretense where Lord Guy is concerned. He has a decided cruel streak."

As if sensing their scrutiny, Lord Guy minced over to where they were standing and bowed in front of Daphne. He examined every detail of her toilette: her elegant auburn curls, the expanse of creamy-white bosom, and her russet silk evening dress and matching slippers.

Lord Guy would never have even dreamed of speaking to a personage as low as Miss Shelby, especially at a social event. However, his curiosity regarding Daphne made him put aside such strictures.

"Ah, Miss Shelby," Lord Guy drawled, tearing his gaze from Daphne. "Regrettably I did not have a chance to bid you farewell before your, er, somewhat hasty departure from our house. I can see you have done well for yourself, though. May I beg an introduction to the divine lady you accompany?"

Miss Shelby obliged him with a sour note in her voice.

Daphne, however, favored him with her best smile.

Encouraged by this beginning, Lord Guy asked if he might guide her to her seat.

"That would be most welcome," Daphne responded, taking his arm. She privately felt disgusted by the fop's persistent examination of her person, now amplified by the use of his quizzing glass.

Watching them, Miss Shelby shrugged her shoulders and wandered away to the back of the room where the companions were sitting.

Determined to maintain a pleasant demeanor for Miss Shelby's sake, Daphne seated herself and gave Lord Guy her full attention, enchanting him by opening the conversation with a remark about his boots. "Why, I have often noticed the gentlemen have tassels adorning their Hessians, but never have I seen pom-poms."

Lord Guy puffed out his chest. "I believe I shall set the fashion with them, Miss Kendall. Like these, each set is dyed to match whichever coat I wear."

"Indeed?" Daphne said in an encouraging manner. She suppressed a giggle at Lord Guy's fashion invention.

"You see," he went on, moving his leg so she might have a better view of his boot, "Meyer & Miller in Pall Mall devised this loop so I might change the pom-poms at will. Anyone must admire the way they swing with each step I take."

"They are certain to be the subject of many a conversation," Daphne assured him.

Across the room at that moment, Lord Ravenswood arrived, accompanied by Eugene. Anthony's strong masculine presence drew the eyes of several of the ladies. He wore a bottle-green evening coat over black breeches. A white waistcoat served as a cool contrast to the darker colors. His only jewelry was the sapphire ring on his right hand.

Eugene left his master's side to take up a place where he would be out of the earl's way, but at the same time could keep a watchful eye on him.

Almost at once, Anthony was set upon by his hostess and Wilhelmina Blenkinsop. The Blenkinsops were wealthy members of the untitled gentry. They were resolute in their decision that their much coddled eighteen-year-old daughter, Elfleta, should marry a title.

To that aim Mrs. Blenkinsop had arrived in Town before the Season had begun to nurse the ground for eligibles. She had a list of possibilities for her "Elf," and ever since she heard of the earl's return to London, his name had been at the top.

The Elf in question resembled a ghost more than any other storybook character. Elfleta was a thin girl with dull blond hair and an equally thin chest. However, she had been dressed by the hands of an expert lady's maid. She wore a beautifully cut gown of thin white muslin, and a coronet of tiny white roses rested in her hair. To her credit she did possess rather pretty hazel eyes.

Her expression was one of perpetual contentment. This was because she rarely had thoughts of her own, finding it simpler to go along with whatever her strong-minded Mama wished. She expected to adopt whatever opinions her husband held when she married, if, indeed, she were required to have an opinion on anything at all.

Lady Huntingdon performed the introductions, and Mrs. Blenkinsop wasted no time at all in embarking on her campaign.

"My lord, I understand you are renting a house in Upper Brook Street," she began in a friendly rush of words that contained an undercurrent of steel. "We reside just around the corner in Grosvenor Square. You must dine with us one evening this week. I am sure our excellent French chef could tempt your palate. Oh, my, where are my manners? May I present my daughter, Elfleta?"

Anthony bowed over Miss Blenkinsop's gloved hand. She smiled at him in a rather vacant way, and he studied her consideringly.

The earl cast his mind over the gossip he had overheard at White's that afternoon. Blenkinsop, Blenkinsop. Of course. Plenty of money and good bloodlines, if no title. Ah, that was it. The family desired a title and believed this wisp of a thing could get it for them.

Ten minutes later, after sitting and conversing with Miss Elfleta Blenkinsop, Anthony thought they might be correct. She was obviously well brought up and conducted herself with decorum.

She claimed modestly to be proficient at the ladylike accomplishments of stitching and watercolors, which was all well and good in Anthony's opinion. But, most to his taste, not once had a single gleam of intelligence sparkled from the depths of Miss Blenkinsop's eyes.

He accepted an invitation to dine that Wednesday evening before Almack's and sat back to enjoy the musical performance.

It was then he happened to turn his head and see Miss Daphne Kendall. For a moment he was transfixed by the sight of the candlelight glowing against her glossy auburn curls and the softness of her mouth.

Then he noticed who was sitting next to her. Deuce take it! Lord Guy.

Anthony gazed scornfully at the pair. Lord Guy was a loose fish if ever there was one. Always short of the blunt and willing to try any scheme to line his pockets. The current *on dit* had it that finding a rich bride was his latest plan.

The tenor stepped to the front of the guests. Lord Ravenswood removed his gaze from the disturbing sight of Miss Kendall and Lord Guy together.

The stern set of Ravenswood's mouth had Lady Huntingdon wondering if the wine she was serving was sour.

When the tenor cleared his throat, Daphne could have kissed him, so glad was she to be interrupted from her conversation with the odious Lord Guy. His range of topics was one: himself. In addition to the long explanation of Lord Guy's brilliant design of the pom-poms for his boots, Daphne had been subjected to a boring monologue on his skill at the gaming tables, the excellence of his taste in coats, and his superior ability to select horses.

He was quite proud of his position in Society, as well, and asked if he might see her that Wednesday at Almack's, where only the cream of Society were allowed admission.

So much the better, Daphne thought, since she needed more time with Lord Guy to further her plan to clear Miss Shelby's name. "Yes, I shall attend, my lord."

Ever certain of the power of his charm over the ladies, Lord Guy preened. "I shall be sure to arrive early and secure your promise for a dance."

Daphne smiled at him and turned her head toward the front of the room. In the process of doing so, her gaze fastened on Lord Ravenswood. She had not seen him arrive and was startled by the increase in her heart rate now that she was aware of his presence.

Goodness, she thought, why was he glaring at her with the most awful frown on his handsome face? What could she have done to cause this reaction? It happened in a mere instant of time before Lord Ravenswood turned his attention to the tenor. Daphne began to doubt the earl even saw her look at him, but there was no doubting that his black look was for her.

She sat through the entertainment with less enjoyment than she would normally have had from such a gifted talent. Her mind was too busy running over events and trying to determine what she had done to earn such censure from Lord Ravenswood.

By the end of the performance, she came to the conclusion that she had behaved in no way that would have given the earl a disgust of her. Her emotions ran from bewilderment to irritation, and she was determined to know the source of his disapproval.

"Excuse me, Lord Guy, I must speak with someone," she said, rising to her feet.

"Of course, Miss Kendall. Until Wednesday night?"

"I shall look forward to seeing you," Daphne dissembled while dropping a curtsy.

Lord Guy watched her go with a speculative expression on his long face. Why was this rich beauty not wed?

Rising, he caught the sleeve of one of his gambling cronies. "I say, Chesterfield, what do you know of pretty Miss Kendall?"

Lord Chesterfield was thin to the point of emaciation. He raised a bony hand to his quizzing glass and fingered it. "Gad. Nothing wrong with her now. Someone bound to snap her up."

Lord Guy looked at his friend through narrowed eyes. "What do you mean 'nothing wrong with her *now*.' What was the problem?"

Lord Chesterfield made a moue of distaste. "Horrible companion by the name of Miss Oakswine. Face like a hedgehog. Put it about that Miss Kendall was fond of her. Wouldn't think of marrying and not taking her along. Trust me, she was more than any man could stomach."

"What happened to her?"

"Dead as mutton, by George. Heart gave out at Astley's. Fashionable place to pop off, though, for a paid companion."

Lord Guy rubbed his fingers across his chin. "Miss Kendall's a taking little thing."

"Her third Season, but, mark me, fellows will be beating a path to her door. I would myself, but I hear her cook is always three parts disguised. I like my wine as well as the next person, but I like it in a glass, not wasted down a servant's throat. The man's drinking is well-known about Town. Can't think why Miss Kendall hired him."

Lord Chesterfield wandered away, and Lord Guy noticed he was wearing false calves. He smoothed his own coat, which boasted of generously padded shoulders, and quit the room. A consultation with his valet would be necessary before his appearance at Almack's Wednesday night.

He would dazzle the beautiful Miss Kendall and her large dowry. Pity redheads were not the fashion, but he might be persuaded to overlook the fault.

Meanwhile Daphne had placed herself in a position where she might casually speak with Lord Ravenswood, this position being a few feet behind his chair. He could not fail to see her when he rose from where he was talking to a waiflike creature in white.

He turned and saw her standing there.

For a moment they simply looked at one another before he stood and bowed to her. "Miss Kendall, how are you? May I present Miss Blenkinsop?"

Daphne met his gaze and once again felt the magnetic intensity of his eyes. "I am well, my lord." She stepped closer to the pair and offered her hand to the girl. "And happy to make your acquaintance, Miss Blenkinsop."

Elfleta murmured an unintelligible greeting and looked pained when Daphne shook her hand. She spoke in a voice that was just above a whisper, as if the very effort of speaking was too much for someone of her delicate nature. "My mama is probably looking for me, Lord Ravenswood. Do not trouble yourself escorting me back to her. I do so look forward to seeing you Wednesday night."

Wednesday night, Daphne thought. Could it be his lordship would attend the ball at Almack's? Perhaps he would ask her to save him a dance. What would it be like to dance with him?

The earl bowed, and Miss Blenkinsop dropped a demure curtsy before floating away toward a fierce-looking woman wearing a large striped turban. The striped turban reminded Daphne first of Eugene, and then of Mihos's tiger-striped fur.

"Lord Ravenswood, how goes our feline friend?"

Disregarding the cat's preferred mode of travel—flying from place to place—which had resulted in chairs being knocked on their sides, papers sliding from his desk onto the floor, and the destruction of vases too numerous to count, the earl simply said, "He continues limber, I thank you. And your canines?"

Daphne chuckled. "Miss Shelby has taken upon herself the task of teaching them some manners. Holly needs little training, if any. But Jolly and Folly are another matter."

The earl's brows came together. "I see. Would Folly happen to be the one with a fondness for hats?"

A blush crept into Daphne's cheeks. "Yes. I assure you, though, Miss Shelby will dissuade him from such behavior in the future."

"Good. Perhaps now I might only have my crop chewed or my boots mangled," Lord Ravenswood said.

Daphne felt the edges of her temper rise, then realized he was teasing her. An impish light came into her eyes. "Surely not your boots. At least not while you are wearing them."

The earl's lips broke into a grin.

Daphne caught her breath. How very attractive he was when he smiled. And he did not look at all perturbed with her now. Perhaps she should just let the matter drop. But, no, she would know the basis for that earlier annoyance.

"My lord, I could not help but notice that when you glanced my way before the tenor began singing, you seemed somewhat out of sorts." She raised a question with an elegant eyebrow.

Lord Ravenswood took a moment to consider his answer, then said, "I should not presume to tell you with whom to keep company."

Daphne tilted her head at him. "You mean Lord Guy. I have only just met him this night. He is the sort who is impressed with his own consequence."

The earl's expression was serious. "His consequence is not nearly so great as his imagination."

"You are right of course," Daphne agreed. "But, you see, I intend using that to my advantage. Dear Miss Shelby has had her reputation blackened by Lord Guy. I expect his interest in me might make him amenable to helping clear her name."

Anthony stared down at her. Schemer! Had he not said time out of number that intelligent women were all full of plots and stratagems? Here was confirmation of his theory once again.

But what was this about Miss Shelby?

Before he could pose the question, Miss Kendall answered it. "You must not think me a heartless flirt, my lord. I cannot explain everything to you, as I feel to do so might betray a confidence. Suffice it to say Lord Guy has behaved dishonorably where Miss Shelby is concerned. I merely seek to repair the damage."

To her credit Anthony noticed her expression was contrite. He inclined his head and reminded himself that Miss Kendall and her problems could be of no real interest to him. He was in Town, in part, to secure a suitable countess for Raven's Hall. One that would be the complete opposite of his stepmother, Isabella.

"Naturally one must govern one's own behavior and live with one's own conscience. Please excuse me, Miss Kendall. I see Mrs. Blenkinsop signaling to me. As I am to dine with her family this Wednesday, I must attend her. Your servant," he said, and bowed.

Daphne stood still while he walked away. She felt her whole body tense at the earl's reaction to her association with Lord Guy and at the knowledge that Lord Ravenswood must be interested in Elfleta Blenkinsop.

Why this should affect her so, she could not say. She only knew that Lord Ravenswood held an attraction for her that she could not deny. She wanted his good opinion, indeed, his admiration. And, for some reason, it eluded her.

Across the room two other people had been observing the evening's events.

Miss Shelby had sat next to another companion, a starched-up older woman by the name of Mrs. Mead, whose mouth was set into a permanent angry fold. Several times during the course of their conversation, Miss Shelby had been hard-pressed not to stuff her unembroidered handkerchief in Mrs. Mead's mouth in order to stop her from prattling on about needlework.

Not only was stitchery the ladylike activity Miss Shelby

despised above all others, but also it was difficult to watch the play of expressions on dear Daphne's face when one was forced by good manners to pay attention to another.

She finally succeeded in silencing the woman by telling her that her interest in cloth and needles might stem from a former life spent as a seamstress, or perhaps a surgeon. Mrs. Mead shot her a look that clearly indicated she thought Miss Shelby mad, and hurried away.

To Miss Shelby's frustration, by the time she was free of Mrs. Mead, all that was left to see was Daphne standing alone, a hurt and bewildered expression on her pretty face.

Eugene, who had been standing by the door all evening watching his master, took a moment to come and sit in the seat recently vacated by Mrs. Mead.

"Good evening, Miss Shelby. I hope you do not mind if I join you briefly," the manservant said.

"Not at all, Eugene. I should be grateful for some sensible company," Miss Shelby assured him.

Eugene's silver eyes darkened. "I cannot like this thin blond-haired person I hear is called Elf. She is not right for my master."

A smile broke out on Miss Shelby's face. As usual their thoughts ran parallel. Eugene would not want to see Lord Ravenswood involved with Miss Blenkinsop, either.

Impulsively she reached out and clutched the white sleeve of Eugene's tunic. Quickly embarrassed by this bold action, she released it and said, "He could not like her above Daphne."

"No, it must not be," Eugene replied. "It is not *meant* to be. Miss Kendall is meant for Lord Ravenswood. This I know."

"Yes, yes," Miss Shelby agreed excitedly. "They shall marry, and he will take her to Raven's Hall. Daphne confided how she does so miss the country life."

Eugene's face had taken on the faraway expression he had had at Astley's when he learned the striped cat's name was Mihos. He remembered Bastet and the message she had sent him by way of the cat. And how he would gain his freedom when Lord Ravenswood married Miss Kendall.

"Do not fear, Miss Shelby. All will be done that can be done to bring the two together."

Miss Shelby's benign blue eyes had taken on the intensity inspired when her dramatics took over. "Nothing shall stop us. We shall be invincible. They are as good as wed. Soon we must think of names for the babe."

Eugene saw his master signal him that he was ready to leave. He rose to his feet and bowed his turbaned head low to Miss Shelby. "You are a treasure, wise lady, as sure as any treasure my master found in Egypt."

He turned and walked toward Lord Ravenswood, leaving behind a blushing, openmouthed Miss Shelby.

On Wednesday night Eugene painstakingly helped Anthony dress for the evening ahead. He had taken his time throughout the preparations, behavior that drove Anthony almost to the end of his tether.

Mihos paced the bedchamber restlessly, in the manner of a caged tiger. The striped cat could sense his favorite person was preparing to leave the house, and this disturbed him.

Having finally gotten his lordship into a dark, walnut-brown coat, Eugene glanced over at Mihos. "The cat does not want to be left alone, master."

"Good God, you hardly think I am going to be swayed by a cat's feelings, do you?" Anthony asked, making a final adjustment to his cravat. "Besides, he will not be alone in a house full of servants. You know as well as I, he has only to walk into the kitchen, and Mrs. Ware has a treat ready for him."

"She is a good woman," Eugene acknowledged. "But Mihos wishes your companionship. It is a shame you must go to this dinner at the Blenkinsops' before Almack's."

Anthony looked at the manservant incredulously. "Eugene, you go too far. It has been obvious all evening that you have tried to delay my going to the Blenkinsops'. Indeed, I must hurry now, or I shall be late."

Eugene silently handed him his hat and stick.

Lord Ravenswood took the articles impatiently. "You do not

have to accompany me, you know, if that is what is bothering you. Following me around while we were in Egypt was one thing, but here in England I am quite safe."

Eugene heaved a sigh. "I go where you go, master." Under his breath he added, "Even if it is to the nest of a drab little mouse."

The manservant only received a black look for a reply before Lord Ravenswood walked quickly from the room.

Descending the steps that led to the hall, the earl nearly tripped when Mihos raced in front of him. "Devil take that cat! Is he trying to cause me to fall and break my neck?"

The feline in question had reached the bottom of the stairs and was standing guard at the front door. Lord Ravenswood's butler, Pomfret, tried to dislodge the cat with the toe of his shoe, but received a scratch from a sharp claw that penetrated his white stockings for his trouble.

Seeing the red line on his butler's leg, the earl's temper snapped. "Now what have you done, you feline fiend! Pomfret, go belowstairs and tend your leg."

"Thank you, my lord," the butler replied, and motioned the second footman to take his place. The young man stepped carefully around the cat and prepared to open the door at any cost when his lordship indicated he was ready to leave.

"Eugene, take Mihos to the kitchen and tell Mrs. Ware she must find a way to keep him there," the earl ordered.

"Grraow!" Mihos protested loudly.

His lordship's jaw twitched.

Eugene bent and lifted the cat into his arms. "Of course, it shall be as you wish, master, but Mihos will be most unhappy and so will Mrs. Ware. Although she likes Mihos, when she tries to contain him in the kitchen, he finds ways of getting into things and making a nuisance of himself," Eugene warned. "Hard as it is to believe of such a good-natured animal."

From the cradle of Eugene's arms, Mihos stretched a paw out toward Lord Ravenswood's chin. He added a pitiful shadow of his usual "Grraow" for effect.

The earl shook his head in defeat. "Oh, very well. Put the animal down and let us take our leave."

Eugene placed Mihos on the floor and stroked his back soothingly. "Do not worry, little tiger, I shall take care of everything."

A stubborn expression remained on the cat's face despite this reassurance.

His lordship drew on his gloves and nodded to the second footman, who promptly swung open the heavy door.

Lord Ravenswood exited the house and walked down the stone steps to where another footman stood, holding open the door to his closed carriage.

Eugene followed him, and after the two entered the vehicle, the footman slammed the door shut and called to the driver to be off.

Inside the town house the second footman was closing the front door. At the last minute Mihos darted past him and ran down the steps toward the earl's coach.

Lord Ravenswood chanced to look out of the window and saw the cat coming. But it was too late. At the very moment he banged his stick on the roof and shouted for the driver to stop, the cat flung himself at the coach.

A loud thud, followed by a scraping of claws down the side of the varnished coach door, preceded an ominous silence.

The vehicle stopped and chaos reigned.

Eugene scrambled out first and saw the cat lying on the ground, bright red blood streaked across his hind leg. "No! Bastet, this cannot be! Mihos, our little tiger, what have you done?"

The manservant began cursing in his native language while he dropped to his knees next to the cat.

The driver of the coach cried out his apologies to the earl.

"Silence," Lord Ravenswood commanded while he stepped down from the coach. He turned to the gaping footman. "Fetch a bedsheet, a blanket or something, and be quick about it."

Anthony bent over Mihos, who lay on the road stunned and breathing heavily. He saw the blood on the cat's leg and silently prayed the limb was not broken. He reached out his hand and awkwardly, but gently, stroked the cat's head. "That was a very silly thing to do, Mihos. You will not be flying about for a while, I daresay."

Mihos closed his eyes, and Anthony felt his heart lurch in sudden fear. "Eugene!"

Although frightened by the cat's condition, the manservant regained his calm air. "He is alive, master. Your touch merely soothed him, and he closed his eyes to rest. See how his sides are still rising and falling?"

The footman came running with a large white bedsheet. Eugene took it from him and folded it. Together he and his lordship delicately moved the cat from the ground and laid him on the sheet.

Eugene made as if to lift Mihos, but Lord Ravenswood was there before him. He gathered the cat, wrapped in the bedsheet, into his arms and turned to Eugene. "You do know how to take care of his wound?"

Eugene's mind raced. "In truth, master, I cannot say that I do."

"What?" Lord Ravenswood demanded.

"But I am certain that Miss Shelby will know what to do. She was raised in a vicarage around many animals. Miss Kendall, I am told, also grew up in the country among cats and dogs. Between them, they are sure to be able to help Mihos." Eugene held his breath, waiting for his master's response.

Anthony's chief concern was to get the cat help immediately. There was no time to argue with Eugene or spend time wondering why the manservant had cried out the name "Bastet."

"Let us go to Clarges Street, then," he said, and gave the driver the directions.

He entered the coach once again, this time holding Mihos. As he gazed down at the cat, who appeared to be unconscious, he felt a strange tug at his heart.

If only he could be certain Miss Kendall and Miss Shelby would know what to do. Then he remembered Miss Kendall's advocacy of the cat at Astley's. He remembered the way she had taken in three dogs, even if one of them was troublesome.

He remembered her continued concern for Mihos after he had taken him home.

Suddenly he felt himself relax in the knowledge that whatever the problem with Mihos, Miss Kendall would know how to handle it.

Chapter Four

Upstairs in Clarges Street, Daphne tried on one gown after another. Her lady's maid, Biggs, wore an expression of strained patience.

Daphne was determined to look her best this evening at Almack's. She told herself this feeling sprang from a desire to charm Lord Guy into clearing Miss Shelby's name. At the same time, a vision formed in her mind of the Earl of Ravenswood's compelling brown eyes glancing appreciatively at her appearance.

"What do you think, Biggs?" Daphne asked anxiously while holding an ivory satin gown with a green velvet trim in front of her. "Will this serve?"

Although she knew very well her mistress appeared divine in the ivory dress, Biggs paused consideringly for a moment, then nodded her approval. "Yes, miss, I believe it is the very one. Only, the green velvet band around the sleeve is coming loose. Let me mend it for you quickly."

Daphne handed her the dress and threw on an old gray gown she used to wear on walks in the country. "Thank you, Biggs. How are your hands today? I wondered with the weather turning a bit warmer if the pain had lessened—"

She got no further because Miss Shelby burst into the room. The peach color in her cheeks was heightened, and her eyes were round with fear. "Daphne, you must come at once!"

"What is wrong, Leonie?"

Miss Shelby gasped for breath. "Cramble says Lord Ravenswood and Eugene are in the hall, and Mihos is bleeding to death!"

Amid groans from Biggs, Daphne rushed past Miss Shelby and hurried down the stairs. In the hall she saw the elegant figure of Lord Ravenswood clutching what looked like a bundle of bedsheets. Eugene stood apprehensively at his side.

"My lord, what happened? Cramble told Miss Shelby that Mihos is on the brink of death."

"I hope not," Lord Ravenswood replied. He briefly outlined the particulars of the accident, ending with, "Miss Kendall, I apologize for calling like this, but Mihos is badly injured, and I need your help."

"And you shall have it, of course," Daphne assured him. She stepped forward and lifted the white cotton that his lordship had used to cover the cat. Her gentle fingers felt around Mihos's head, then examined the wound on his leg. "I do not believe he is in any serious danger."

Since she was mere inches from him, Lord Ravenswood was able to study the loveliness of her creamy-white complexion, marred only by the furrow of concern between her brows. He noticed her lashes were long and dark, a pretty frame for her light green eyes.

Miss Shelby stood uncertainly, twisting her hands together in her concern. "How is he?" she asked, and peered over Daphne's shoulder. "Oh! I have never been able to bear the sight of blood."

Fortunately Eugene was standing nearby and was able to catch her when she swooned.

"Good heavens," Daphne cried, faced with both an unconscious companion and an unconscious cat. "Eugene, would you be good enough to take Miss Shelby into the morning room? I shall ring for Biggs to assist you."

Eugene lifted Miss Shelby as if she weighed nothing and carried her away.

Daphne turned back to a rueful Lord Ravenswood. He said, "I have well and truly disrupted your household, Miss Kendall."

"Nonsense. Now, I believe we might find a cozy spot for Mihos in the kitchen. Would you like me to take him?"

Lord Ravenswood shook his head. "No, I shall carry him."

Daphne led the way to the kitchens. The smell of roast beef permeated the air, and the kitchen was alive with the preparations for dinner. A big, burly man with vibrant red hair, obviously the cook, held sway, shouting orders to the maids.

A silence descended when Daphne and the earl entered the room.

"Hamish," Daphne began, "excuse the intrusion, but we have an injured cat here, and I wish for a place where I might tend his wounds."

Lord Ravenswood thought the brutish-looking cook would soon be shouting at them rather than the maids, but instead the man's expression softened at the sight of Miss Kendall.

"A kitty, is it? You just come right over here, miss, and I'll bring the whiskey. Nothing like it for cleansing cuts . . . and the soul, if I do say so meself." A boom of laughter emitted from the man's chest after this pronouncement. He ambled over to a corner of the kitchen and spread a towel on a wooden table.

Daphne and Lord Ravenswood moved across the room, and the earl carefully laid Mihos down.

Daphne hurried away to the stillroom, leaving Hamish to look his lordship up and down in a measuring way. Lord Ravenswood felt like he was being judged by a considering father and could not like the feeling.

No more than a moment or two passed, though, and Daphne reappeared with two small bottles. Hamish returned to his pots, and Daphne rolled up the sleeves of her gown and tied an apron around her waist. Ignoring the whiskey Hamish had placed on the table, she poured some of the contents of one of her bottles onto a clean cloth and gently began cleaning the wound on Mihos's leg.

Lord Ravenswood heard a small sigh escape her lips. "Is it severe? Will he lose the leg?"

Daphne turned and smiled at him. Anthony experienced a rush of emotion at that smile, but told himself it was concern for Mihos that caused the sensation.

"No, I believe the wound looks worse than it is because of the amount of blood on his fur. See, when it is cleared away, there is a nasty laceration indeed, but I am confident we can take care of that."

"Why has he not woken?"

"Well, as to that, did you not say he bumped his head when he threw himself at the coach?"

"Yes."

"There is our answer. He may have a very slight concussion. I cannot feel any lump on his head, so I believe it not to be critical. He should regain consciousness at any time." She chuckled. "One might say we are fortunate he has not yet awoken, so we may tend him without any protests."

Lord Ravenswood watched her every movement as she spread a vile-smelling liniment over the cleaned wound. "You are a capable lady, Miss Kendall. I am most grateful for your assistance, and am pleased Eugene suggested we bring Mihos to you."

Daphne felt a glow inside at the earl's compliment, but it was followed by a little pang of disappointment that he had not thought of her himself.

Still, she smiled her thanks at him. "You are aware, I think, of my fondness for animals. Mihos holds a special place in my heart."

"He is not a bad fellow," his lordship allowed.

Daphne thought the cat had worked his way into the earl's unwilling heart, but kept her opinion to herself. She called to an eager maid of about fourteen years and gave instructions on watching the cat and what to do if he woke. Another maid entered the kitchen and reported that Miss Shelby had recovered and had asked for tea.

Hearing Hamish grumbling about his roast having to be kept warm, Daphne gathered her medicines and impulsively turned to the earl. "My lord, would you care to dine with us this evening?"

Lord Ravenswood put a hand to his head. "Good God, the Blenkinsops. I was to dine with them before Almack's. I have been horribly rude, as they expected me almost an hour ago."

"Almack's," Hamish blustered. "Glad I ain't a member of

the Quality and forced to drink that weak punch I hear they serve."

Daphne ignored the cook and pinned a bright expression on her face. "You must go, then, my lord, and perhaps I shall see you later at Almack's."

Lord Ravenswood bowed. "Thank you for your invaluable assistance, Miss Kendall, and for your kind invitation to dine. As you are to attend Almack's as well, may I ask that you save a waltz for me?"

Daphne's breath caught in her throat. He was standing so close. His eyes held hers and mentally took her to that place where they were alone. "Yes, I shall save you a waltz," she whispered.

Lord Ravenswood kept his gaze on hers for a moment while he gave a last stroke to Mihos's head. Then he left the room.

Daphne stood imagining how it would feel to be held in the earl's arms for their promised dance. She remembered hoping at the Huntingdon's musicale that she might share a dance with him tonight at Almack's, and now her wish would be granted.

She absently washed her hands, then reached behind her to untie the apron about her waist, and her hands froze. Heavens! After all the trouble she had put herself and Biggs through earlier deciding on a gown to wear, here his lordship had seen her in her oldest, plainest gown!

Tarnation! Embarrassment brought color to her cheeks, and she determined she would captivate him at Almack's.

Then a stray thought flitted across her mind. Was she capable of affecting the aloof earl in matters of the heart? Or was he destined to become yet another gentleman put off by her Fatal Flaw?

If only she knew what it was.

Lord Chesterfield's observation, about how gentlemen would flock to Daphne's side now that Miss Oakswine was dead, proved accurate. Daphne herself had no idea Miss Oakswine had ever put about such a nonsensical story about living with her once she was wed. Therefore the attentions she received when she arrived at Almack's bewildered her, pleasing as they were.

Miss Shelby remained at her side before the first dance, making predictions about each gentlemen who rushed to present himself.

Of Sir Tredair, she said he fancied himself a poet and would bore her to death with his prose.

Puritan-looking Lord Edgecombe was undoubtably a monk in a former life.

Mr. Smythe-Benton's thoughts were impure in the extreme, Miss Shelby said while fanning her cheeks vigorously.

Daphne giggled through all of Miss Shelby's declarations. In truth, she found none of the gentlemen interested her, save one who had yet to make his appearance.

Her dance card was filling rapidly so she hastily scribbled Lord Ravenswood's name for the second waltz of the evening.

At present Lord Guy bowed before her. "Miss Kendall, I congratulate you on a wise choice of gowns for one with your hair color."

Daphne could not miss the implication that red hair was not the fashion. While she knew it to be the truth, it was rude of Lord Guy to remind her. She gritted her teeth. "Thank you, my lord."

His coat this evening was vibrant purple. The intricately embroidered waistcoat he wore contained threads of every shade of purple Daphne had ever seen. His quizzing glass was encrusted in amethysts.

"May I hope, Miss Kendall, that you have a dance for me?"

"The first waltz is not yet claimed," Daphne replied. She had reserved it for him, thinking it would give her an opportunity to talk with him and thereby further Miss Shelby's case.

Lord Guy was content. He had noted the number of gentlemen bestowing their attentions on pretty Miss Kendall. She was in demand. Therefore Lord Guy wished for her presence at his side to increase his own consequence.

He raised her gloved hand to his lips and kissed the air above it. "Every minute that passes until our dance will seem an hour."

And every minute spent *with him* will seem an hour, Daphne mused. She dropped a polite curtsy to Lord Guy before he moved away.

Her first partner, Lord Christopher, was an amiable gentleman who danced well and set himself to please. But Daphne's attention was soon caught by the party just entering the room. Lord Ravenswood escorted Mrs. Blenkinsop and her daughter, Elfleta.

The earl had changed his clothes since his visit to her house earlier. He now wore a very dark blue evening coat over pearl-colored breeches.

Daphne felt a rush of excitement upon seeing him. He was the most handsome gentleman in the room, she decided in that instant.

Well, she thought, tilting her head and attempting to study him objectively, perhaps if she viewed all the gentlemen in the room impartially, the earl's features to some would not be the most pleasing. It did not matter. What was significant was the effect Lord Ravenswood's company had upon her.

Seeing the direction of her gaze, Lord Christopher said, "Ravenswood is back in England after a long absence. Do you know him?"

Daphne flushed at her discourteous behavior in ignoring her partner. "Yes, I have made his acquaintance."

"I do not expect he will be in Town long."

Daphne raised an eyebrow. "Oh?"

Happy to have her attention at last, Lord Christopher warmed to his subject. "Everyone knows the earl is only in London while his country estate is made livable again. He cares for Raven's Hall much more than his father ever did. You know the old earl married a beautiful, younger woman who led him to his ruin."

"No, I did not know," Daphne replied slowly. Her gaze traveled back to where Lord Ravenswood stood in conversation with Mrs. Blenkinsop and Elfleta. They had come from their dinner together, she surmised, and the earl was continuing to award his attentions to Elfleta.

Lord Christopher nodded his head toward the couple. "Miss

Blenkinsop would never follow in those type of footsteps. Quiet little thing. Would not give Ravenswood a minute's trouble. And I imagine he would value a compliant wife."

Daphne pursed her lips. Was that what Lord Ravenswood was looking for here in Town during the Season? A compliant wife? How disappointing. How dull. It was certainly a good thing she learned this bleak truth before she became overly fond of him!

Her dance with Lord Christopher ended, and her next partner came to claim her. For an hour Daphne danced and flirted with several gentlemen, all the while a part of her mind dwelled on Lord Ravenswood and his search for a submissive wife. One fact was clear in her brain. *She* could never be thought of as docile and manageable.

It was only when Lord Guy minced over to her with a glass of lemonade that she was able to turn her thoughts to other matters.

"You must be thirsty, Miss Kendall, after being dragged about the dance floor by those clodpoles," Lord Guy asserted in his superior way.

In truth, something to drink was welcome, but Daphne feared Lord Guy's presence alone was enough to put a sour taste in her mouth, without the addition of the tart lemonade. She reminded herself of Miss Shelby's reputation, though, and thanked him warmly.

Across the room Anthony watched them with a jaundiced eye. He stood beside Mrs. Blenkinsop, who was holding a conversation with another woman. Miss Blenkinsop had been led away for the dance.

Anthony could hear Mrs. Blenkinsop boasting at the fact that her daughter's hand had been immediately solicited for a dance by no less a personage than a marquess upon their entering the ballroom. He believed the calculating woman had probably arranged it herself. He was no green one and recognized blatant attempts at matchmaking when he saw them.

The Blenkinsops had been all affability when he had tried to apologize for his tardiness earlier at dinner. But of course, they gushed sympathetically, they understood about the accident.

And how was the poor dear kitty? Why, their Elf would be positively downhearted at the thought of an animal being hurt.

This assertion had not proven correct, however, in Anthony's estimation. Upon hearing the story of Mihos's accident, Elfleta had asked quietly if the cat was dead. When assured it was not, no great relief could be detected on her pale face.

Anthony found himself puzzled at his own reaction to Miss Blenkinsop's uncaring attitude toward Mihos. What did it matter if she disliked animals? He was surely not allowing the striped cat to hold a place in his affections, he thought, forgetting how his heart had stood still when he saw the cat lying on the road unconscious.

Still, he could not help but compare Elfleta's disregard for the cat's well-being to Miss Kendall's compassionate nursing of the animal.

He gave himself a mental shake. There were enough servants at Raven's Hall to handle any injuries to the creatures in their care. It would not matter if his wife ignored the needs of animals.

Furthermore it was absurd to make the assumption that Miss Kendall's caring nature for animals would extend to humans, most particularly himself. His chances of leading a peaceful, well-ordered existence were much greater if he chose a plain, obedient girl to wed, regardless of how lukewarm her nature was.

Elfleta was returned by the marquess to her mama, who cheerfully handed her daughter over to the earl for the waltz.

On the floor Anthony marveled at the fragile girl who performed the steps of the waltz flawlessly.

"Miss Blenkinsop, I must congratulate you on your dancing."

"Thank you, my lord."

"Did you spend many hours with a dancing master?"

"Yes, my lord."

"I am not holding you too tightly, am I?"

"No, my lord."

Anthony felt smug. She was exactly what he wanted in a wife.

Then he raised a gloved hand to cover his yawn.

In the act of doing so, he spied Miss Kendall being twirled about the room in the arms of Lord Guy. Her auburn hair shone in the candlelight.

'Twas a pity Lord Guy would not appreciate her beauty, being too concerned with his own. The coxcomb did know how to dance, he would give him that. He wondered how Miss Kendall's plan to clear Miss Shelby's name was progressing.

Dancing with Lord Guy, Daphne was very much pleased with the way things were going. Even though the fop would never admit it was he who stole the ivory cat figurine from the duchess, he had been brought around to saying he did not think it all likely Miss Shelby had been the culprit.

Daphne smiled at him. "Oh, Lord Guy, I am happy to hear you say that. Dear Leonie has been so troubled by the whole affair."

"Well," Lord Guy said a bit uncomfortably, "my Aunt does have a way of taking an idea and running with it."

Daphne nodded knowingly. "I am certain the duchess would take your word if you were to express the opinion that Miss Shelby was innocent."

Lord Guy looked doubtful. "Best, perhaps, to let sleeping dogs lie, what?"

Daphne looked shocked. "If only you could! But I know someone of your honor and integrity could not let an innocent woman stand accused of a crime she did not commit. No, indeed. Why, it would totally go against your nature."

Lord Guy puffed out his chest. "Alas, what we gentlemen suffer—gladly, mind you—in the name of honor. Yes, I shall speak to my Aunt, Miss Kendall, never fear."

Daphne felt a twinge of conscience as Lord Guy strolled away. She really had turned him up sweet for her own motives. But these motives were of the purest, she reminded herself, which was more than she could say for Lord Guy's purposes.

Her hand was claimed for every dance. She had no time to converse with Miss Shelby, who she thought appeared bored to death, sitting with the other chaperons. Daphne decided Leonie was missing Eugene's company. The manservant must have decided to wait outside for the earl.

At last Lord Ravenswood bowed over her hand. "Miss Shelby told me you saved the second waltz for me."

Daphne found herself trembling at the touch of his gloved hand and chided herself for behaving like a young miss in her first Season. "Yes, my lord."

The music began, and he swept her into his arms.

If she felt shaky before, it was nothing compared to the rush of feelings coursing through her now. The pressure of the earl's hand at her waist was light, yet her body responded as if he was using all his strength to pull her against him. She was shocked down to her soul to find herself wanting to close the distance between them.

None of this inner struggle showed on her face, however. "You will want to know that Mihos awakened before I left home. He took a little water and went back to sleep."

"I am relieved to hear it. He will not be too much of a burden for you, will he?" Lord Ravenswood asked, straining to keep his gaze well above the green velvet band that framed the low cut of her dress.

"Not at all," Daphne assured him. It was difficult to keep her breathing steady with his face so close to hers. She noticed his eyelashes were black and heavy. "I am looking forward to seeing some of the artifacts you brought back from Egypt, my lord."

"I hope you will not be disappointed, Miss Kendall." God, but her skin looked smooth. He longed to rip off his glove and touch her shoulder with his bare fingertip to see if it could possibly feel as soft as it looked.

And the way she smelled reminded him of the flowers that grew in spring at Raven's Hall. "I received a message from my friend, William Bullock, informing me the exhibits have been quite popular since the opening of his Egyptian Hall."

"I know I shall enjoy it," Daphne assured him. She also knew they must be floating over Almack's, as the feeling she was experiencing could not be of this earth.

Anthony looked down at the pink curve of her lips. He had

a sudden urge to know their taste. He stiffened his shoulders. This would not do. He had already determined Miss Kendall was not a candidate for his countess. "How goes your plot with Lord Guy?"

The smile faded from Daphne's lips. There was a definite note of censure in the earl's voice. She raised her chin. "My lord, I get the impression I do not have your approval in my efforts to help my companion."

The earl affected an air of boredom. "On the contrary, Miss Kendall, I neither approve nor disapprove of your actions where Lord Guy is concerned, since they do not pertain to me."

Daphne felt her cheeks grow hot. "How true. I do not seek your approval anyway," she lied. "But just so you know, Lord Guy is going to clear Miss Shelby's name of a crime she did not commit."

Lord Ravenswood raised a brow. "A crime? Are you and Lord Guy taking on a task best left to the Bow Street Runners?"

"You would have me allow Miss Shelby to be subjected to the questioning of those rough men?" Daphne asked, her voice tight.

Ignoring the question, Anthony asked one of his own. "Just what is this misdeed Miss Shelby is accused of?"

Daphne was rattled by his cool demeanor. "It would not be proper of me to discuss it with you. I assure you, though, I am intelligent enough to handle the situation without any help at all."

"Of that, Miss Kendall, I am more than confident," the earl stated dryly.

Daphne frowned. What did he mean by that cryptic remark? But she had no time to explore the meaning as the music died away and the earl bowed before her.

"Ah, here is your next partner. Beyond a doubt, you have been in demand this evening, Miss Kendall. But then, with your beauty it could be no other way."

Daphne stared at him. One moment it seemed he had thrown her a veiled insult, then he was complimenting her.

His gaze held hers for an intense moment.

Sir Tredair grew impatient. "I say, Miss Kendall, the reel is about to begin . . ." He held out his arm to her expectantly.

Daphne accepted the poet's arm. "Good evening, Lord Ravenswood," she said dismissively.

"Until tomorrow. I shall call for you at three of the clock."

The earl returned to Miss Blenkinsop's side and claimed her hand for a second dance. Fans raised, and whispering about the couple pervaded the room. Could it be that mouse-like Miss Blenkinsop had stolen a march on all the other hopefuls?

Daphne mechanically performed the steps of the reel. Her spirits were low, and she was angry at herself for allowing the earl to affect her this way.

His behavior was a mystery to her. But then, the gentlemen often puzzled her with their long, appraising looks and pretty speeches, which never amounted to anything more.

What was no mystery, she reflected grimly, was that Lord Ravenswood was making his preference for Miss Blenkinsop clear to all.

Chapter Five

"Grraow!" Mihos growled angrily.

"James," Daphne said, a touch of exasperation in her voice, "Perhaps it might be best to move the dogs' bed to the kitchen."

James chuckled and limped across the drawing room to obey his mistress. "Yes, miss. I never seen no cat what got along with dogs in my life. Don't reckon that striped devil will be any different."

Daphne rested a restraining hand on Mihos, who lay on his side on the sofa. He had been awake and grumpy since early that morning. He was really too weak to try to stand on his own and took severe exception to the bulky bandage wrapped around his hind leg, reaching back to bite at it angrily every few minutes.

Matters had worsened when Daphne moved the cat from her bedchamber, where he had slept the night before, to the drawing room. Mihos had raised his nose at once and smelled the sheet of flannel in the corner. He had not been pleased at the canine fragrance exuding from the cloth.

Now James folded the material and took it out of the room while Daphne spoke soothingly to Mihos.

The cat began to relax under the gentle massage of Daphne's fingers, but then suddenly lifted his head and looked expectantly toward the drawing room door.

"Miss," Cramble said from the doorway, "Lord Ravenswood."

"Grraow," Mihos cried joyfully.

Daphne immediately tightened her grip on the cat, fearful he would try to run to the earl and end up on the floor with a reopened wound.

Attired in a beautifully cut burgundy-colored coat and dove-gray pantaloons, Lord Ravenswood crossed the threshold of the room and stopped at the picture presented by Miss Kendall seated on the sofa next to Mihos.

Her gown of pale blue muslin with deeper blue dots fell about her gracefully. A pretty long-sleeved spencer in the same shade of blue as the gown's dots flattered her figure. Her eyes sparkled a welcome, and her dark auburn hair gleamed under a fashionable bonnet of dark blue.

He bowed to her. "Miss Kendall, you enchant me. Few are the ladies of my acquaintance who do me the honor of being ready to leave upon the designated hour."

"Thank you, my lord," Daphne responded, pleased. "But how tiresome for you that you only know females so sadly lacking in manners."

Lord Ravenswood's dark eyes twinkled in appreciation of this sally. "I daresay you are correct. I hope you may care for roses," he said, referring to the dewy-blossomed bouquet he held. Often gentlemen gifted their dancing partners from the evening before with floral tributes. For some reason he had taken special pleasure in selecting this offering for Mihos's lovely caretaker.

"I do indeed, and yellow roses are my favorite." Daphne smiled at him, then felt the cat under her hand strain toward his lordship. "No, Mihos, you must stay where you are."

To the earl she said, "Mihos spent a restful night and is refreshed enough to have become a difficult patient."

Lord Ravenswood removed his gaze from Miss Kendall with a seeming effort. He saw that the cat looked ready to spring from his place, and at that moment the animal stretched a paw out to him.

The earl placed the flowers on a side table. He closed the few steps between himself and the sofa, and bent to stroke the cat, who purred contentedly. "I am grateful for your efforts on Mihos's behalf, Miss Kendall. But I must say, we are in a coil now."

Daphne raised a questioning eyebrow at him. She felt her pulse quicken at his nearness, and when he turned to look at her, she felt more drawn to him than ever. "What is that, my Lord?" she inquired softly.

Anthony experienced an urge to transfer his hand from the feline to trace a line along Miss Kendall's jaw. He did no such thing, however, but said in a low voice, "Now that I am here, I wonder how I can leave."

As she looked into his dark eyes, Daphne told herself Lord Ravenswood surely meant it was because Mihos would likely cause a commotion at his departure. But perhaps he was implying something else—

A cough sounded from the direction of the doorway.

"Yes, James," Daphne said, feeling an unexplainable wave of frustration at the footman's presence.

Lord Ravenswood straightened and moved away.

"Excuse me, miss," James said, coloring up at what Daphne knew must appear to be an intimate scene. "I wanted to tell you Hamish wouldn't hold with having the dogs' bed in the kitchen. I took it upon myself to move it to the library."

Daphne felt her cheeks grow hot. Here was James looking uncomfortable at having interrupted her and the earl. And most embarrassing, for a moment, she had believed Lord Ravenswood was forming a *tendre* for her. She must have taken leave of her senses.

She pulled herself out of these ruminations, realizing the footman was waiting for her response. "An excellent scheme, James. Thank you."

But her troubles were not over. Miss Shelby could be heard fretting to herself in the hallway. "Oh, dear, and I did think perhaps with the full moon coming tomorrow night, something romantic might happen, and the two of them were indeed smelling of April and May."

The older woman swept into the room as James departed, though, and acted as if nothing had happened, totally ignoring the mortified expression on Daphne's face.

Thankfully Miss Shelby's unfortunate musings must not have reached Lord Ravenswood's ears. He exchanged greetings with Miss Shelby without discomfort, answering that yes, Eugene had accompanied him and was waiting outside.

All the while he was busy mentally reading himself a lecture on the senselessness of dwelling on Miss Kendall's charms and where such stupidity might lead.

"My lord," Miss Shelby prattled, "I am so anxious to visit the museum. And to have you along to explain how you acquired the items will be so educational. I am not one of those females, you know, who believes all a lady should know is how to paint watercolors and sew a neat seam. Deplorable!"

The picture sprang into Daphne's mind of Lord Ravenswood dancing with Elfleta Blenkinsop. "Go carefully, dear Leonie, for I fear that is exactly the sort of female his lordship admires."

Miss Shelby started at this singularly tart remark from Daphne. She then looked to the earl, whose countenance reflected only composure. She stared hard at him for a moment and then shook her head, saying, "I do not see that about his lordship. When is your birthday, my lord?"

"The twentieth day of March," Lord Ravenswood responded indulgently, deciding to be amused.

"Just as I thought," Miss Shelby declared, seemingly self-satisfied with his answer.

Daphne felt baffled by the turn of the conversation. She glanced down at the cat beside her, and saw that the earl's ministrations had relaxed Mihos into a sleep. Rising from the sofa, she let her eyes meet Lord Ravenswood's. "There seems to be no impediment to our departure now. Shall we go?"

Having already observed the feline in repose, Lord Ravenswood returned Daphne's scrutiny. He knew full well she was thinking of his earlier remark and its implications. Some imp prompted him to reply, "Yes. While we can. For next time, who knows what fate may hold in store for us?"

He disregarded the startled look on Miss Kendall's face and allowed himself to be drawn into a conversation with Miss Shelby regarding the stars and how they revealed a person's fate. As this was one of Miss Shelby's favorite topics, it lasted quite the entire journey to the Egyptian Hall, Piccadilly, enlivened by supporting remarks from Eugene.

This left the earl free to stare out the window of his coach in bemused silence at his behavior, which he judged no better than that of the veriest moonling.

Inside the Egyptian Hall, Mr. Bullock had strived to create a mysterious atmosphere he felt would add to the appeal of the ancient artifacts.

The lighting was low, with a minimal use of candles. An aroma of foreign spices infused the museum. Tables where items were displayed were draped in heavy black velvet and roped off from inquisitive hands. Other pieces were enclosed in glass cases.

Perhaps because of the Haute Ton's recent affinity for decorating their rooms in the Egyptian mode, interest in the museum was high. It had become quite the fashion to visit the Egyptian Hall.

Lord Ravenswood proved an excellent guide and teacher. Both Daphne and Miss Shelby listened intently as he spoke of the rare objects he had acquired, as well as ones his friend, William Bullock, had collected. The earl's knowledge was impressive, and Daphne could not help but admire it.

Eugene followed the party with a distracted air. The museum brought about a longing for Egypt in him. While he did not find England in any way distasteful, it was not his home, and he wished to return to his distant land. After he had done what was necessary to gain his freedom, of course.

To add to his discontent, Miss Shelby was not being as attentive to him as he suddenly realized he had come to expect. She and Miss Kendall were engrossed in the displays.

Daphne was particularly entranced by the masks and was conversing with Lord Ravenswood regarding a ceremonial mask, when the Duchess of Welbourne and her nephew appeared.

Miss Shelby uttered a soft cry when she saw the duchess.

"Do not worry, Leonie," Daphne whispered discreetly. She raised her chin, and faced Lord Guy and the duchess.

Lord Guy bowed to Daphne and introductions were made all around.

The Duchess of Welbourne eyed Lord Ravenswood. "Knew your father. Made a fool of himself over some frivolous young gel. Heard you went off to make a fortune to rebuild the estates."

Anthony bit back an angry retort at the insult, however well-deserved, to his father. Instead he said stiffly, "The repairs to Raven's Hall are nearing completion."

"Hmpf," the duchess sniffed. She turned and gave Daphne two fingers to shake.

Daphne saw at once the lady was awful. She had a forbidding air about her massive person and peered out at the world with two of the smallest eyes Daphne had ever seen.

Her Grace noticed Miss Shelby and directed a scowl at Daphne.

"Miss Kendall, are you aware that Miss Shelby was formerly in my employ?" The duchess spoke as if Miss Shelby were not standing a mere few feet away.

"Why, yes, Your Grace. Miss Shelby told me all about her circumstances before coming to me," Daphne answered with a confident air. She looked at Lord Guy, who was nervously fingering his quizzing glass, and gave him a blinding smile.

Lord Ravenswood felt his temper rise again at the sight of that smile.

The duchess was undeterred. "Is that so? I cannot believe she told you *all* of the situation. Did she perhaps leave out the fact that I have a rare collection of old ivory carvings, and one of my favorites, a cat, is missing? Never have I been the victim of thievery until Miss Shelby took up residence in my house."

Her Grace fixed her beady gaze past Daphne onto Miss Shelby, who looked ready to sink.

Lord Ravenswood's mind was working rapidly, putting pieces together of the puzzle. So this was the crime of which Miss Kendall had been trying to clear Miss Shelby's name. He could not view Miss Shelby as a thief. Although he had initially judged the older woman foolish, he had since realized his error. He dismissed the thought of any guilt on Miss Shelby's part.

His thoughts settled on Lord Guy, who he knew had only recently come to live with the duchess. The mincing fop must have been responsible, probably selling the piece to pay gaming debts or his tailor.

So why was Miss Kendall bestowing her attentions on him? Was she relying on him to clear Miss Shelby's name? Surely he would not at his own cost.

The earl's question was answered in the next moment.

Daphne turned a charming face to the duchess. "Lord Guy and I were just sharing our opinions on the matter last night at Almack's."

All eyes turned to the young man, today dressed all in mustard-yellow, including, of course, the matching mustard-yellow pom-poms on his boots. "Yes, that is to say, I seem to recall something of that nature . . ."

Daphne's mood veered sharply to anger. Why, it was obvious Lord Guy had not spoken to the duchess as he had indicated he would! Furthermore the milksop was not taking the opportunity now to come to Miss Shelby's defense.

"Lord Guy," Daphne said firmly, "is of the same opinion as I. Miss Shelby could not have taken your carved ivory figure, Your Grace."

The duchess glared awfully at her nephew, who was staring at the floor. "You have never expressed this conviction in my presence, Guy. As I recall, you were quick to point the finger of guilt at Miss Shelby the very day the carving was discovered missing. If you do not believe she took it, then who did? All of my servants have been with me this age, and I trust them completely."

Eugene had moved close to Miss Shelby to give her courage. "Lord Guy is responsible," she proclaimed at last. "I saw him."

"That is not possible," Lord Guy protested hotly.

"Are you saying, among these witnesses, Miss Shelby, that *you saw* my nephew, a peer of the realm, steal something from his own aunt?" the duchess demanded.

"Yes," Miss Shelby stated matter-of-factly. "After the butler told me the carved ivory figure was missing, I concentrated on the problem. Soon a vision came to me of Lord Guy creeping into the muniment room in the middle of the night. He knew he could not take any of the family relics to sell, but the carvings housed in their case tempted him. His hand hovered over the bird, but then he smiled evilly and took the cat instead."

Lord Guy's face was white. But when he found his voice, it dripped with contempt. "A *vision* you say. Come, Aunt, the woman is mad."

Eugene could no longer remain silent. "That is what one of your character must say when faced with the truth."

"Who are you?" Lord Guy asked with snapping sarcasm, raising his quizzing glass to study Eugene's turban.

"This is hardly the place for such a discussion," Lord Ravenswood interrupted in the voice of authority. "Naturally Your Grace would want the culprit brought to justice. But since you have no evidence Miss Shelby took the carving, you might be better served by ordering your footmen to make inquiries at pawnshops that could result in the return of your property."

The duchess looked like she would dig in her heels, then thought better of it. " 'Twas only a trifle, after all. You have the right of it, Ravenswood. But, mind, I shan't have you, Miss Shelby, gabbing about visions of my nephew as a thief!"

Miss Shelby opened her mouth to contradict the duchess regarding her vision, but Lord Ravenswood spoke before her. "I feel positive Miss Shelby wishes an end to the matter just as you do, Your Grace."

Lord Guy was all too happy to endorse this plan. "Yes, Aunt, let the matter drop. Recollect the children told you Miss Shelby had the queerest ways? They are happier now with Miss Dumfrey."

The Duchess of Welbourne gave the party a stately dip of her head, which was marred by her air of pinched disapproval. She turned away with a rustle of silk.

Eugene spoke quietly to a flustered Miss Shelby.

Lord Guy lingered for a moment to address Daphne. "Miss

Kendall, will you be attending the Pelhams' ball tomorrow evening?"

"Yes," Daphne answered.

Lord Guy smiled. "Then, may I reserve the first waltz?"

Daphne eyed the fop coldly. "I feel sure I shall twist my ankle between now and that moment."

"Red hair does bespeak a bad temper, then," Lord Guy sneered. "And to think I was willing to overlook your most unfashionable shade."

"Oh, do go away, you popinjay," Daphne said in a bored way.

"Yes, go away," Lord Ravenswood echoed with a note of steel in his voice. "Do not trouble Miss Kendall again, or you shall answer to me."

Lord Guy cast them both a malevolent look before turning on his heel and following the duchess.

Daphne looked after him in disgust. She then took a step away from where Eugene and Miss Shelby were standing deep in conversation, in order to have a private word with Lord Ravenswood. As private as possible when surrounded by the well-dressed throngs of exhibit viewers.

When his lordship took his cue and joined her, she addressed him. "My lord, I own I know not what to think of Miss Shelby's assertions about a vision, and confess I do not care. What I do know is that I am grateful to you for your assistance. I cannot think how I came to be so corkbrained as to believe Lord Guy would help me. I can only say that it was beyond bearing that Miss Shelby should be served such a turn, and I sought to right the wrong."

"Certainly, the duchess rushed to a conclusion, and her actions were not at all what Miss Shelby deserved," Lord Ravenswood stated.

Daphne smiled at him.

"As far as your behavior is concerned, Miss Kendall, I wonder that you ever believed your plan with Lord Guy would serve."

The smile faded from Daphne's face. "Did I not just say I had been mistaken in my hopes?"

Ignoring this question, the earl said, "I find it fatiguing when a lady is clever and invariably uses her intelligence to plot and scheme—no matter the purity of her motives."

Just then, Elfleta Blenkinsop entered the room, trailing behind her mother.

"Well, here is Miss Blenkinstop to refresh you, my lord," Daphne told him in a low voice, bristling with indignation.

She abruptly moved away to study a case of ancient jewelry. The sparkling gems in a necklace blurred in front of her tear-filled eyes.

How could he behave toward her with such a want of understanding? It seemed Lord Ravenswood had no tolerance for a lady with a mind of her own.

Would his attitude have been different had Lord Guy denounced the duchess's accusations regarding Miss Shelby as he had agreed to do last night at Almack's?

No, Daphne decided in that moment, it would not matter to the earl what the outcome of her efforts had been. As Lord Christopher had informed her during their dance, Lord Ravenswood wished for a bride who would not give him a moment's trouble. No doubt this meant a brainless female who would follow his dictates and never put a thought of her own forward!

But stay a moment. A frown creased Daphne's brow. Earlier, had not Miss Shelby expressed the opinion that his lordship would not care for that sort of lady? 'Twas a puzzling contradiction, Daphne reflected. Perhaps Lord Ravenswood did not know his own mind, or maybe Miss Shelby was mistaken.

"The necklace is too barbaric for a delicate lady such as you," Daphne heard a male voice say from behind her.

She swung around to see a tall gentleman dressed in a fine coat of darkest blue superfine. His hair was a medium shade of brown, heavily streaked with blond. His skin was the bronze color of a man who spent much time in the sun, and the shade enhanced the brilliant blue of his eyes. He appeared to be just past his thirtieth birthday.

"Sir, we have not been introduced," Daphne told him curtly.

"It is too bad that I have given myself away. You will know that although I was born to an English daughter of a baron, my father was Egyptian, and I have not been raised to follow the conventions of Society," he said with disarming candor.

Daphne detected an accent to his otherwise flawless English. He was attractive, and was gazing at her in obvious admiration, but without being rude or over-warm in his attention.

She glanced around and saw Eugene and Miss Shelby were not far away. Then she saw Lord Ravenswood bending his head in conversation with Miss Blenkinsop.

She pursed her lips and turned back to the stranger. "Do you own some of the items on display, sir?"

He laughed shortly. "I wish I did. But, please, my name is Vincent Phillips. May I know yours?"

"I am Miss Daphne Kendall. Do you live in England now, Mr. Phillips?"

"I am considering it, Miss Kendall. My parents are both dead and recently my grandfather, the baron—of whom I was quite fond and even took his name as a mark of respect—died. His estate in Suffolk was left to me, but I have been too busy with business affairs in Egypt to come to England before now."

Daphne chatted with Mr. Phillips for several minutes about the jewelry she had been studying. He was as knowledgeable as the earl, and his manners, except for a certain boldness in addressing unknown young ladies, were impeccable.

All at once, however, his attention seemed to be caught by someone or something down the room, for he abruptly said, "Miss Kendall, you must excuse me. I had already completed a tour of the museum when I was fortunate enough to meet you. I am afraid I must excuse myself now."

He bowed over her hand before walking away. Daphne stood wondering if she would ever understand gentlemen.

Seeing Miss Shelby and Eugene absorbed in contemplation of a sundial, Daphne wandered a little farther into the museum.

Meanwhile, across the room, Lord Ravenswood had experienced a maddening desire to follow Miss Kendall. Their unsatisfactory conversation gave him the urge to shake some sense into her, but he quickly got himself in hand and continued his conversation with the Blenkinsops.

Here, all was light and cordial. Mrs. Blenkinsop was full of compliments on Lord Ravenswood's artifacts. Elfleta looked about her with a bewildered expression on her pale face.

Lord Ravenswood admired the excellence of her pink gown and the air of serenity about her. "Miss Blenkinsop, is there anything in particular you are interested in seeing here at the museum?"

Elfleta turned to her mother as if to gain an answer to the question. However, that lady was standing a little away from her daughter, busily exchanging the latest gossip with one of her friends, Lady Armbruster.

Elfleta looked at the earl. "Yes, I am interested in Egyptian things. It is the fashion now to decorate one's rooms in the Egyptian mode."

Lord Ravenswood considered this answer. "Quite so. What types of Egyptian things do you like?"

To his horror, Miss Blenkinsop looked ready to burst into tears at the effort of responding to these inquiries. She regained her composure almost at once, though, and fluttered a thin white hand. "I have always had a fondness for far-eastern things."

His lordship rubbed a hand across his forehead and decided not to correct Miss Blenkinsop's knowledge of geography.

"Well, Ravenswood, come to be certain none of your artifacts are stolen?"

Lord Ravenswood grinned when he saw his friend, William Bullock. The two men shook hands, and after Anthony introduced Miss Blenkinsop, she made a pretty excuse and escaped back to her mother's side.

"Seriously, Bullock, what news is there of the missing Bastet statue?" Lord Ravenswood asked.

Mr. Bullock shook his head. "Nothing, really. The Egyptian officials are gnashing their teeth over the whole situation. Leads are nonexistent, everyone is tight-lipped."

"Who are they questioning?"

"Wyndham, Sanderson, Grantley, all the well-known dealers. But they'll catch cold at that. None of those fellows will trade his reputation for what he would profit from the sale of one statue."

Lord Ravenswood nodded. "The statue would fetch quite a price, though, from an unscrupulous collector. I should think the officials would be concentrating their efforts on dubious exporters."

"They are covering all angles of this case, of that I am certain. The Egyptian government would not take the theft of one of its treasures kindly." Mr. Bullock shrugged. "Who knows, Ravenswood, could be Bastet was stolen by someone touched in their upper works. Someone who thinks the statue will bring him luck, or should be worshiped, or some such muttonheaded idea."

Lord Ravenswood clapped his friend on the back. "If that is true, the fellow will have the devil to pay once he is apprehended."

"That he will. Well, Ravenswood, let me know if everything here is not just to your liking. The exhibit is doing far better than I hoped."

Mr. Bullock walked away leaving Anthony to contemplate his words alone for a moment. But it was not long before he realized he had been sadly remiss in his duties as host. Some ten minutes had passed since Miss Kendall had abandoned him.

Looking around, Anthony saw Eugene and Miss Shelby standing before a display, looking close as inkle-weavers. He strode down the museum hall in search of Miss Kendall.

Over at a glass case, Eugene and Miss Shelby discussed the crude cooking utensils used by the ancient Egyptians. After a few minutes, Eugene said, "Come, Miss Shelby, my master has walked away, and I must find him."

"Oh, dear," Miss Shelby moaned. "Maybe I should wait here. I have no wish to see the Duchess of Welbourne again. She does cast my spirits down so."

Eugene looked at Miss Shelby fondly. "Your employer was a self-important, foolish woman. Think no more of her, wise lady."

"I wish you would call me Leonie," Miss Shelby told him shyly. "After all, I call you by your first name. Indeed," she said with a laugh, "I do not even know your proper name."

Eugene smiled placidly. "Leonie. I approve of the way it sounds. It is right for you. The name sounds gentle, yet knowing, like you."

The peach color in Miss Shelby's cheeks intensified, and she drew her paisley shawl closer. "You are kind, Eugene."

"You are the kind one, Leonie. You are taking care of the cat, are you not?"

"Oh, yes, Eugene, the best possible care," Miss Shelby assured him.

"You see. I knew the cat would be safe with you. You are caring, wise, sympathetic—"

"Stop!" Miss Shelby begged with a smile.

"Now, what could the Duchess of Welbourne possibly say to disturb a lady of so many virtues? There is no more to be said. Let us enjoy the rest of the exhibit."

Boldly taking her hand and drawing it through his arm to rest on the sleeve of his white tunic, Eugene began leading Miss Shelby in the direction Lord Ravenswood had recently gone.

Suddenly the manservant stopped and turned around. He reached up and touched the eye-pin in his turban, his face wrinkled in concentration.

"What is it, Eugene?" Miss Shelby asked in concern.

Letting his hand drop to his side, Eugene once more took Miss Shelby's arm. "Nothing. It was nothing." His features relaxed. "A mere feeling, but it has passed. We can continue on our way."

A few steps away from where they had been conversing, and hidden from view by a sixteen-foot-high stuffed giraffe, Vincent Phillips watched them go, his heart pounding with excitement in his chest.

Earlier, when he had been talking with the beautiful red-haired woman, Vincent had been unable to believe his luck when he spied Eugene across the museum.

Good fortune, it seemed, had finally found him. It had certainly not been with him three and a half weeks ago at the museum in Baluk.

Vincent was quite an accomplished thief. His career had

begun over ten years ago when he was a mere youth. The story he had told Daphne was a crafty blend of fact and fiction.

Brought up in Egypt, he was left to his own devices when his parents had been killed by bandits. He received only a small sum after his family's debts were paid off, and had written to appeal for help to his grandfather in England.

The gentleman was a baron, but of little consequence or wealth. His reply to his grandson was brief. The young man was welcome to make his home in Suffolk, where he might enter the clergy or apply for a post as a secretary, but the baron had not the financial means to support him in Egypt.

Having a very high opinion of himself, Vincent had been angry at this response. He was loath to leave the country where he had lived all his life to eke out an existence in a land he did not know. Indeed, his intention was to become rich at any cost.

Good looks and quick ways soon provided a living on the wrong side of the law. He had confined the first part of his career to jewelry theft. But, in the last three years, he had branched out to the art world.

When a collector in Philadelphia let it be known how much he was willing to pay for a particular statue of Bastet, Vincent became determined to be the one to lay the statue at his doorstep and receive his reward.

The plan to steal the treasured Bastet statue had been carefully conceived. Dressed in black and heavily masked, on the night he was to carry out the theft, Vincent had entered the Baluk Museum, only to see another man reaching into the case and removing the statue.

Vincent had been struck dumb. How had the man gotten in? Vincent himself had overcome three guards. In addition, there had been a powerful lock—still intact—on the door to the room where the statue was housed, which had taken even one with Vincent's talents several minutes to pick. Then there was the matter of the lock on the case where Bastet stood.

During the moments when Vincent stood in shock, the other man turned around, and their eyes met. That was all Vincent remembered. The next thing he knew, he was waking up on the floor. The man and the statue were gone.

Fortunately only a short time had passed, and no hue and cry had been raised. Vincent was able to make his escape.

Over the next two weeks, he had questioned what seemed like every person in Egypt, trying to find out the identity of the man in the museum. Vincent took it as a personal insult to have had the Bastet statue stolen out from under his nose.

When at last he learned the man was a mere manservant to Lord Ravenswood, his fury knew no bounds. Upon gaining the knowledge the two had left for England, he made plans and followed suit.

Vincent had only arrived in London two days before. After checking into the Clarendon Hotel, he had picked up a copy of *The Times* and seen the notice of artifacts on display at the Egyptian Hall.

Here, his luck had turned. First, in finding Eugene so easily. Second, in just now overhearing his conversation with this Miss Shelby. It seemed Eugene had given her the cat, as they called the Bastet statue, for safekeeping.

Vincent smiled. Eugene was even kind enough to reveal where Miss Shelby was employed. It should be no trouble at all to find the direction of the Duchess of Welbourne. And then, Vincent reasoned, he could steal back the statue he should have had in the first place.

He hurried out of the Egyptian Hall to make plans. Yes, his luck had definitely turned for the better.

Chapter Six

The next morning in Clarges Street, Miss Shelby was just coming down the steps leading to the hall when the knocker sounded.

Cramble shuffled over to open the door. To Miss Shelby's delight, Eugene stood framed in the doorway, his white tunic rippling in the early morning breeze.

The elderly butler squinted and said, "I see his lordship coming up the steps behind you. You must wait for him to enter the house first. What kind of manservant are you?"

Eugene swung around and looked at the empty air behind him, then turned back to the butler with an expression of strained patience on his face. "I am alone this morning. You are mistaken—"

Miss Shelby hurried to the doorway, the skirts of her chocolate-colored gown swirling about her. She placed a gentle hand on Cramble's shoulder. "I shall take care of our guest, Cramble. Hamish has prepared a large batch of scones. Why do you not retire to the kitchen and enjoy one or two?"

The old man turned reluctantly from the doorway and allowed Eugene to pass through. "A good idea, Miss Shelby. But I have no doubt that Scottish devil has contaminated the scones with some of his whiskey. Thinks I don't see, but I've got eyes in my head."

Cramble continued to mumble to himself as he turned toward the kitchen. Miss Shelby closed the front door behind Eugene. "The poor man. He is nearly blind, you know, and has become cantankerous. Daphne keeps him out of kindness."

Eugene stood with his hands clasped behind his back. "Miss

Kendall is good. That is one of the reasons I have come to you this morning, Leonie. I hoped we might speak privately."

Miss Shelby's face brightened. "I should like that, Eugene. Would you mind accompanying me to the Park? I was going to exercise the dogs. Daphne and Biggs are occupied with working on her gown for the Pelhams' ball this evening."

Eugene nodded in agreement. "The Park will be invigorating, wise lady. My master is spending the morning at Gentleman Jackson's, so my time is my own."

A short while later Miss Shelby and Eugene strolled comfortably along the Serpentine River near the place where she had first met Daphne.

"How is Mihos this morning, Leonie?"

"He cannot be made to be still. Would you believe the valiant fellow is hobbling about on three legs?"

Miss Shelby went on to describe how Mihos managed to stalk around with his injured paw held off the ground, and how pathetic he was when he found he could not jump up onto the furniture and had to be lifted.

Outside in the sunshine, Holly, Folly, and Jolly were ready for larks. Miss Shelby had been working diligently on their manners, though, and did not expect any mischief from them this morning.

Holly, of course, was the picture of canine stateliness as she pranced obediently beside Miss Shelby.

Jolly, who had acquired a few more pounds to his already stout body, squirmed and rolled on his back in the grass, an expression of bliss on his doggie face.

Then there was Folly. Ah, well, Folly. He had not turned out to be one of Miss Shelby's triumphs thus far. Not that she despaired of him, since she was the sort of lady who appreciated high spirits in people and animals.

Still, the shaggy brown dog needed minding.

Just now, Folly watched Miss Shelby out of the corner of his eye as he crept quickly toward the water. A frolic along the shallow edge was all the more enticing as it was forbidden territory.

Unfortunately, since his gaze was on Miss Shelby rather

than where he was going, he ran headlong into a small boy of about five years old.

A scream emitted from the boy's governess.

"Folly!" Miss Shelby cried, taking in the scene.

The little boy fell to the ground, but only laughed in delight. Reaching into his pocket, he produced a red ball, which he threw across the grass with a mighty heave. Folly raced after it, excited at this new game. The boy scrambled to his feet and followed, much to the consternation of his governess.

"Thomas! Come back here at once!"

"Yes, Miss Greystone," the boy shouted. "After I gets my ball."

The severe lady turned a furious face to Miss Shelby. "That dog is dangerous!"

"Dangerous? Folly?" Miss Shelby chuckled. "Oh, no. But his behavior certainly does deserve a reprimand, I grant you."

Miss Greystone was not convinced. "I want Master Thomas returned to me at once."

At Miss Shelby's side, Eugene stared intently at Folly's retreating form. All his concentration appeared focused on the dog.

Abruptly Folly stopped in his tracks and cocked his head at an angle, the red ball clamped in his jaw. He turned around and began trotting back to where Eugene, Miss Shelby, and the governess were standing.

The boy grinned and trailed after the dog.

Upon reaching the adults, Folly dropped the ball in Eugene's outstretched hand. "Good dog!" Eugene said, and returned the ball to its small owner.

Reunited with her charge, Miss Greystone marched him away in a huff, leaving no doubt in anyone's mind what her opinion was of Folly and his keeper.

Miss Shelby looked bemusedly at Folly. "I imagine, young man, trying to tell you of your imprudence would be a waste of time."

Folly put on his best contrite expression.

"Oh, would you look at that, Eugene," Miss Shelby said. "Where can that dog have learned his scapegrace ways? I have pondered the question of who he might have been in a former life and cannot bring any satisfactory answer to mind."

"I would not waste precious mental energy on such a matter, Leonie."

Miss Shelby sighed. "You are right, Eugene. Was that not a darling little boy? I do hope Daphne might have many children one day who can run and play with the dogs on a large estate in the country. Preferably Lord Ravenswood's estate."

Eugene drew Miss Shelby's arm through his, and they began retracing their steps through the Park, the canines following.

"That is my wish also, as you know, Leonie. Because of it, I admit I am disturbed by the continued attention my master is paying to Elfleta Blenkinsop."

Miss Shelby nodded in enthusiastic agreement. "Such a lifeless girl! Lord Ravenswood cannot think she would be able to hold his interest year after year."

"I do not believe my master is thinking judiciously. Instead he is letting past events distort his judgment."

A furrow appeared between Miss Shelby's brows. "Past events?"

Eugene drew a deep breath. "I understand that when my master was but a boy, his mother died in childbirth. The babe, too, was lost. Anthony adored his mother, as she was a sweet woman, even if she was not very bright."

"How dreadful for a child to lose his mother at a tender age," Miss Shelby said, thinking perhaps this explained Lord Ravenswood's stiff, cool manner. Most members of the aristocracy were haughty, in Miss Shelby's view, but Lord Ravenswood seemed to hold himself even more aloof.

"It was just he and his father for years, and then the old earl remarried. His new wife, Isabella, was much younger and quite beautiful, I hear. She was also willful and shrewd. Anthony could not tolerate her, and eventually, he left home. Isabella's reckless ways destroyed Raven's Hall, and my master came to Egypt to earn enough money to restore it."

Miss Shelby shook her head sadly. "What became of Isabella and the earl?"

"Once the woman had gone through the old earl's money, she left him to drink himself to death."

"How horrible!"

"Yes. My master is bitter. It is understandable, perhaps, but such long-held anger can only do a person harm. In my master's case, I fear it will lead him to make a poor marriage."

Comprehension dawned on Miss Shelby's face. "Oh, dear. That is why Miss Blenkinsop is receiving his attentions, is it not? Because she is rather plain and lacking in her upper works. Although I fear, Eugene, you will think me unkind for saying so."

"Nothing could make me think you unkind, Leonie," Eugene said. He admired the heightened peach color his words called forth in Miss Shelby's cheeks. "And your assessment of Miss Blenkinsop's appeal is correct. My master thinks he wants a wife who is not too intelligent and therefore will not cause him any problems."

Miss Shelby bridled. "What nonsense!"

"Yes. We must make him see the error of his ways. I ask you, though, not to repeat what I have told you, even to Miss Kendall."

"Since you ask it of me, of course I will not. But what can we do?" Miss Shelby asked with a hint of despair in her voice.

Eugene led her out of the Park and toward Clarges Street. "Tonight at the Pelhams' ball I would like to keep Lord Ravenswood and Miss Blenkinsop apart, but alas, I am not allowed to mingle with the distinguished guests. However, I have learned that on Monday a fair will be held just beyond Richmond, in the village of High Jones."

"A fair? Oh, that sounds like an adventure," Miss Shelby exclaimed.

Eugene patted her hand, bringing a smile to her lips. Then he said, "We must convince Lord Ravenswood and Miss Kendall to attend. They can come to know one another better and enjoy each other's company. With luck, Miss Blenkinsop will not be there. I hear it is to be a small fair, nothing grand enough for Mrs. Blenkinsop to consider taking her daughter to visit."

They had reached the back of Daphne's town house, and

Miss Shelby shooed the tired dogs toward the kitchen door. " 'Twill be the very thing, Eugene. How clever of you to think of it."

Eugene gazed into Miss Shelby's light blue eyes, and a warm feeling overtook him. It was a feeling he thought he saw returned in her expression. "Until this evening, wise lady," he said, and gave a slight bow of his turbaned head.

Disconcerted at the intensity of his regard, Miss Shelby ushered the dogs into the house, with only a fleeting glance back at Eugene.

The manservant remained where he was after the door closed quietly behind Miss Shelby.

Eugene's mind was uneasy. He reflected that he had allowed himself to form an attachment for Leonie Shelby. Involvement with women was something he had avoided assiduously over the years, fearing none would ever be able to understand or accept him.

But Leonie was different. She possessed an uncommon knowledge combined with a sensitivity rarely found. If only he had his freedom so he might further their relationship!

He turned and walked north toward Bond Street and Gentleman Jackson's, his mind hard at work. Bastet had been clear in her choice of bride for Lord Ravenswood when she had sent Mihos to guide them to Miss Kendall. Now he must concentrate his efforts on bringing the two together. If he was successful, he could gain his freedom and also please the cat goddess.

He must meditate on the matter.

Another subject had been teasing the edges of his brain since the visit to the Egyptian Hall yesterday. He reached up and touched the eye-pin nestled in his turban and recalled the unusual sensation he had experienced as he was escorting Leonie back to Miss Kendall. He felt as if they had been watched. His intuition had indicated a sense of danger.

And Eugene was not one to ignore his intuition.

Daphne prepared for the Pelhams' ball with a fast-beating heart. Late that afternoon she had been arranging flowers in a bowl in the drawing room, when a messenger arrived from Lord Ravenswood. Daphne had put aside the roses and opened the missive with suddenly nerveless fingers.

His lordship apologized for the lateness of the request, but would she accept his escort to the ball this evening? He had heard there would be a crush, and he could not like her and Miss Shelby arriving without male protection.

Daphne normally prided herself on her hard-won independence but, oh, what a delicious feeling it was to think Lord Ravenswood was concerned for her safety. She had promptly returned a grateful agreement to his offer and found herself humming the rest of the day.

Now she sat rather impatiently under Biggs's ministrations. She noticed the lines of strain on the abigail's face and guessed the older woman's hands ached abominably.

Biggs finally stepped back and surveyed her mistress with an air of satisfaction. "You'll do, miss."

Daphne's gown was made of taffeta in an unusual shade of sea-green that shimmered with blue lights when she moved. The dress had a very high waist and a daringly low bodice. A sea-green band of velvet tied directly under the bosom and was clasped with a spray of small flowers made of the gown's material.

The dress was elegant in its simplicity, designed not to detract from the wearer's beauty, but instead to enhance it. A delicate gold and diamond necklet and matching earbobs were her only jewelry.

Biggs had painstakingly fashioned a coronet of tiny flowers made of the same material as the dress to place on Daphne's shining dark red locks. Her hair had been swept high on her head with curls falling over one ivory shoulder.

As Daphne smoothed on her long white gloves, a maid scratched at the door. "Ooooh, miss, you do look a treat tonight," the girl gasped, wide-eyed.

"Thank you, Betsy."

" 'Is lordship is downstairs in the hall. That strange servant 'e's got is outside by the coach. Miss Shelby 'as gone outside with 'im." Betsy curtsied and left.

"Well, I had best hurry, then," Daphne said, picking up a fan and smiling her thanks at her lady's maid. "Biggs, do not wait up for me. No, I shall not argue with you. It has been a busy day, and you have worked hard so I could look my best. You deserve a rest."

Biggs nodded wearily. "Thank you, miss. I hope you enjoy the ball."

Daphne's eyes sparkled. "I confess, I am very excited."

She tried not to admit to herself how much Lord Ravenswood's offer to escort her had added to her anticipation of the evening.

It was hard not to acknowledge this feeling, though, when she walked down the stairs and saw him standing alone in the black-and-white tiled hall, waiting for her in all the glory of his evening finery.

He was an elegant figure. The white sculpture of his cravat rose above the trim line of a beautifully cut white silk waistcoat. His evening coat of charcoal gray, above paper-white knee breeches, fit to perfection. His muscular calves were shown to advantage in fine white stockings that fitted finally into thin black pumps.

Daphne stopped at the bottom of the stairs and met his eyes. She once again felt the spellbinding intensity of his gaze. A silent promise of intimacy in their dark depths sent a warm shiver running through her.

His lordship bowed, his eyes never leaving hers, then raised one white-gloved hand to the pin in his cravat. It held a large, bright peridot, the stone known as "evening emerald" for the wondrous green glow it produced by candle flame. "I wore this in an effort to see if the stone's color duplicated your unusual eyes, but I see now no mere jewel could replicate their loveliness."

Daphne felt heat infuse her cheeks. His lordship was not one, in her estimation, to give Spanish coin to a lady. Thus, the compliment affected her deeply. Indeed, now that he had given it, Lord Ravenswood looked decidedly uncomfortable at his own words.

Daphne curtsied and strove to lessen the tension that had

suddenly sprung between them. "My lord, lest you are careful with such flattery, I shall become as full of myself as Lord Guy," she said lightly.

"Impossible," he replied, his voice tight. His countenance brightened, though, as he walked toward the door. Opening it, he observed their coach waiting on the street, but he noticed there was another thing amiss. He said, "Your Cramble seems to have deserted his post."

"Oh, no, my lord," Daphne corrected him as she glided out the door and stood in waiting on the top of the stone step. " 'Tis much too late for him to still be awake. On my orders he retires every evening by eight."

Lord Ravenswood shook his head and began pulling the door closed. "Miss Kendall, you are too softhearted—"

"Grraow!"

"Good God, is that Mihos?" Anthony stopped and bent to pick up the striped cat who had nudged his head through the opening. Mihos nestled himself against his lordship's bosom and commenced a loud purring in pleasure.

Oblivious to the cat hairs gathering on his evening coat, Lord Ravenswood said, "I am sorry, my feline friend, I should have inquired after you. I see your leg is still bound with that bandage. Troublesome for you, I wager."

Mihos lifted his head and raised a paw to Lord Ravenswood's chin.

Daphne tried hard not to let a chuckle escape her lips. Here was the impeccably dressed, reserved earl with Mihos cradled in his arms only a minute after declaring that *she* was softhearted.

She watched his gloved hand stroke and caress the purring animal, who gazed at him with adoration. Every time she saw Lord Ravenswood treat the cat tenderly, it touched her heart.

All at once, Daphne's skin seemed to ache for his lordship's touch. She imagined what it would feel like if he were to run his fingers across her face, down her neck, along her shoulder.

As if sensing her thoughts, Lord Ravenswood transferred his gaze to her, and they stood, framed in the doorway, looking into one another's eyes. He stood so close to her, Daphne could feel the heat from his body in the cool of the evening. The light from a full moon gleamed on his dark hair. She felt a sudden yearning to run her fingers through the shiny locks. To do to him what she had been envisioning him doing to her a few seconds before. Touch his face, his lips . . .

"I say! Is that Ravenswood fawning over a demmed cat?" The voice, barely discernable, came from a passing coach but was loud enough to reach Anthony's ears. Loud enough to break the spell.

Daphne was glad of the darkness, which hid the flush she knew stained her cheeks.

"Oh, here you are, dears," Miss Shelby called from his lordship's coach, where she and Eugene had been deep in conversation.

Eugene had been telling Miss Shelby how he had convinced Lord Ravenswood to offer his escort to Miss Kendall this evening. He had simply contrived a rumor about a gang of footpads planning to prey on the Pelhams' guests this evening.

Miss Shelby clapped her hands in delight at this imaginative ploy. Eugene thought her the sweetest woman he had ever known, and in the best of looks tonight in a pretty coral-colored dress.

At the top of the stone steps, Lord Ravenswood struggled to convince Mihos to remain at Daphne's house. The cat obviously wished to come with his owner, prompting Daphne to say, "My lord, Mihos misses you. You must take him home soon."

"I should not wish to do so before he is completely recovered, Miss Kendall, unless it is an inconvenience to you."

"No, indeed. I am happy to have him with me. Here, let me unhook that claw from your coat."

Lord Ravenswood watched her gloved fingers gently detach the cat from his coat. Together they managed to get Mihos inside and close the door, ignoring his outraged roar at such Turkish treatment.

As they walked down the steps to the coach, Anthony decided he would secure a waltz again tonight with Miss Kendall. How enchanting she looked in that gown.

He grimaced as he remembered that she had reduced him to spouting off that drivel about the peridot stone in his cravat. He had had no intention of telling her what prompted his choice in pins. But the words seemed to come out of his mouth of their own volition when he saw how beautiful she appeared coming down the stairs to the hall.

Thank God he had stopped short of telling her how the peridot had caught his attention in the window of Rundell and Bridge's jewelry shop earlier in the day. Upon seeing the stone, he had impulsively decided to purchase it and wear it this evening. Mentally he shook his head at his foolishness.

Waving aside a footman, Anthony held out his hand to Miss Kendall and helped her into the coach. Her hand was so small and delicate in his, the mere touch of it caused an almost unbearable desire in him.

He could smell her light flower perfume and the effect on his senses, combined with his earlier reactions to the sight of her, was enough to make him wonder if he was mad as a March hare.

The ensuing drive to the Pelhams' was short, but the press of carriages in the street necessitated almost three quarters of an hour's wait outside the town house.

Daphne fought hard to push aside the feelings that threatened to overwhelm her regarding his lordship. She was successful enough in this endeavor that conversation inside the comfortable coach was lively. A wide range of topics was covered, including Mihos's recovery and the exhibits at the Egyptian Hall.

While they were discussing a stuffed cobra they had seen on display at the museum, Eugene saw an opportunity to further his plans.

"With all due respect to Mr. Bullock," Miss Shelby remarked, "I cannot see why anyone would admire a cobra, even stuffed as it was."

Eugene addressed her smoothly. "Leonie, I understand your aversion to snakes. However, I am certain that you would perceive their value if you could but see them from a different perspective."

Miss Shelby caught the conspiratorial look Eugene gave her, and she inserted a challenging note. "I do not see any way that would be possible."

Daphne agreed with a shudder. "In my view, the creatures have no redeeming qualities."

Lord Ravenswood's mouth stretched in a half smile. "You surprise me, Miss Kendall. I would think someone with your loving nature toward animals would find good in all."

"I do not consider vipers to be animals. They are reptiles," Daphne said, and squirmed in her seat. "Oh, by the way you are smiling, my lord, I see you must be funning."

"Have you ever seen a live snake, Miss Kendall?" Eugene inquired.

"Well, no," Daphne confessed. "Only that horrid stuffed cobra. I have read about them in books, though. Nasty creatures!"

"I know of a place where one might see serpents dancing on silk ropes to the sound of music," Eugene entered casually.

Miss Shelby gasped. "How intriguing."

All eyes were on Eugene.

"I saw an announcement of a fair to be held in a village called High Jones, just outside of Richmond. In addition to the dancing serpents, it said there will be men who can run knives through their hands without producing blood, tumbling performances, and many other diversions."

Daphne smiled wistfully. "I have not been to a fair since, well, the last time Mama and Papa took me."

"Gracious, I cannot remember when I have enjoyed the simple pleasures of a village fair," Miss Shelby mourned.

"Is Richmond far from Town, master?" Eugene asked innocently.

"No. It is only about seven or eight miles from Mayfair," his lordship estimated. "I have passed through High Jones many times on my way to Raven's Hall. It is just beyond Richmond."

Now all eyes were on Lord Ravenswood.

Even in the dim light of the carriage, Anthony could see the look of anticipation on Miss Kendall's face. He knew at that moment he would not, nay, *could not* do anything to displease this auburn-haired beauty. He sighed. "When is the fair, Eugene?"

Eugene allowed himself a slight smile. "Monday, master."

"Would you and Miss Shelby honor me by being my guests, Miss Kendall?" Lord Ravenswood asked, knowing the answer, yet wondering how on earth he would live through a tedious day at a country fair.

Daphne's eyes shone. The look of excitement in her eyes made Anthony glad of his offer. "I should like it above all things, my lord."

"Lord Ravenswood, you are the most amiable of gentlemen," Miss Shelby said, and then beamed.

For a brief second Anthony thought he saw her wink at Eugene. But that could not be.

Amiable, Miss Shelby had said? No, his lordship reflected. He was mad. Quite mad.

Chapter Seven

Inside the Pelhams' town house, there was indeed a crush of people. Lady Pelham had two marriageable daughters, Lady Rachel and Lady Stephanie. She was determined that the ball be a triumph to impress the eligible gentlemen in attendance and had, therefore, ordered the best of everything.

Lord and Lady Pelham had already joined their guests by the time Lord Ravenswood's party arrived, so they made their way directly into the ballroom.

Daphne entered the massive room and blinked. In her two Seasons she had never seen quite the level of opulence created here.

Crystal chandeliers filled with candles sparkled a rainbow of colors overhead. Hundreds of hothouse flowers perfumed the air from pots placed around the room. Liveried footmen carried gleaming silver trays containing glasses of champagne for the guests' pleasure. In the musician's gallery, an orchestra began the strains of a Scotch reel.

It seemed all of the beau monde were in attendance. They themselves heightened the lavishness of the spectacle with their flashing jewels and rich satins and silks. Feathered heads nodded, and painted mouths whispered the latest *on dits* behind opened fans.

Upon her arrival in the ballroom with the earl, several gentlemen approached Daphne and secured dances with her. One of these admirers, a young baron named Lord Clifton, wished her to join him in the Scotch reel just beginning.

Flushed from all the unexpected attention, Daphne placed

her hand on his arm and turned to Miss Shelby. "Enjoy yourself, Leonie."

"Heavens, Daphne, all the world and his wife is here. I shall sit with the chaperons," Miss Shelby said, indicating the rows of gilt chairs set up on one side of the ballroom.

"I shall stand at your side," Eugene said. They walked off together, leaving Daphne with an eager Lord Clifton and a glaring Lord Ravenswood.

Anthony did not know why he thought Miss Kendall would remain at his side once they arrived. It was a crackbrained notion and would hardly be proper. Had he lost his common sense? "A moment, please, before you whisk the lady away, Clifton. Miss Kendall, may I have the honor of the first waltz?"

"I am sorry, my lord, but it has already been claimed," Daphne said, trying to keep the tone of her voice from revealing the extent of the regret she was feeling.

"The second, then?"

Daphne smiled up at him. "I should be pleased."

Lord Ravenswood bowed and went to greet his hostess.

For the next hour, Daphne danced and conversed with various partners, none of whom interested her more than casually.

Breathless after a vigorous country-dance, she left the floor and stood fanning herself. She could hardly credit her ears when a low voice said, "I see nothing has changed in my absence from London, Miss Kendall. You are still a Toast."

Daphne whirled about to face Lord Quinton. This exquisite, languid sophisticate had been one of her most ardent suitors last year during the Season.

He had claimed her for two dances at every ball and party they attended. He had invariably followed this marked attention with a call the following day, always bringing her the loveliest of flowers or the most extravagant boxes of sweetmeats.

She had not been indifferent to him and had hoped their feelings for one another might deepen and result in a proposal of marriage. Alas his attentions had abruptly cooled. She had been overwrought with anxiety when he proved to be yet another gentleman put off by what she had by then, in her own mind, dubbed her Fatal Flaw.

Staring into his familiar blue eyes, Daphne felt a sting of the pain she had endured when his attentions had ceased and his engagement and subsequent marriage to Lady Cecily had been announced. "My lord," she said, and dropped a brief curtsy. "I never had an opportunity to congratulate you on your marriage."

Lord Quinton gave a slight nod of his golden head. "Thank you, Miss Kendall. Lady Cecily has proven to be a satisfactory wife. My heir should make his arrival into the world this autumn."

A sense of inadequacy swept over Daphne. She could be awaiting the birth of her first child if not for . . . if not for . . . If not for what? she wondered. She must know.

She raised her chin and looked directly at Lord Quinton. "My lord, I know it is not at all the thing, but I must beg a favor. Would you tell me if there was something I did during the time we, ah, knew each other that gave you an inalterable disgust of me?"

Lord Quinton appeared discomfited for a moment at this forthright request, but gazing into Daphne's earnest countenance, he yielded to the plea in her eyes. His voice was tender. "You do yourself a disservice, Miss Kendall. It was, er, your companion that caused me to have second thoughts about a more permanent relationship with you."

Daphne was all at sea. "Do you mean Miss Oakswine?" At his answering nod she asked, "What did she say about me?"

"Only that you were extremely fond of one another and could not be parted. Any man that offered for you would be getting the old horror in the bargain. The woman made sure this fact was quite clear and well-known among the gentlemen of the ton."

Daphne could only gape at him, her eyes nearly starting from her head.

Lord Quinton reached out a gloved hand to chuck her under the chin. "Goose. What could *you* have done, sweet lady, to put off any gentleman? The very idea is ludicrous."

Shock was giving way to indignation. Daphne's eyes flashed. "I never once discussed with Miss Oakswine her remaining with me should I marry. Indeed, I cannot think that under any circumstances I led her to believe such a farrago of nonsense."

Lord Quinton looked grave. "Lud, you have been the victim of duplicity, my dear. Heard the old frump had been laid in the dust recently, but one cannot too much deplore such a loss. We all thought the Odious Oakswine—that is what fellows called her—probably had another ten years left on her plate to bedevil us all. More than any man could take, don't you know? Gentlemen will be beating a path to your door now that Odious Oakswine is gone."

It was true. Never had her popularity been greater. Daphne stiffened her spine. She felt some of her long-dead confidence in herself return. "Well, I *did not* know, but I am more grateful than I can say for this enlightening conversation, my lord."

"Obliged enough to favor an old acquaintance with a dance?"

They smiled at each other, much in charity. Daphne nodded her agreement and placed her hand on his arm. Lord Quinton flirted outrageously while gracefully leading her through the steps of the dance.

Daphne felt lighthearted. The world seemed a more friendly place. Naturally any gentleman would have been daunted by the prospect of living with Miss Oakswine, she reflected, while holding up her end of the conversation and chuckling over Lord Quinton's witty remarks about some of the assembled guests.

Although if a gentleman truly loved her, she mused, would he allow such an obstacle to come between them? Daphne eyed her fair-haired partner and deliberated whether Lord Quinton had loved her, or was, in fact, capable of strong emotions.

She recalled his comment about his wife. *Lady Cecily has proven to be a satisfactory wife.* No, this was not the sort of marriage her parents had enjoyed and not what she envisioned for herself. She found it in her heart to be a tiny bit sorry for Lord Quinton.

Perhaps it had worked out for the best that Miss Oakswine's trumped-up story had driven him away along with the others.

Perhaps, as Leonie would say, fate had played a hand in the matter, and the stars had another plan for her.

Her gaze sought Lord Ravenswood. He was standing alone, watching the dancing. At precisely that moment, his lordship happened to glance her way, and their eyes met. Daphne felt heat flood her cheeks, and she quickly turned back to Lord Quinton. "Will you be in Town long?"

Lord Quinton observed the exchange between Miss Kendall and Lord Ravenswood with a knowing eye, but kept his comments to pleasantries.

At the other side of the room, Lord Ravenswood just managed to restrain the scowl that threatened to darken his face. Devil take it! The minx was flirting with Quinton. George always was a bit of a rattle. Their friendship went back to Eton days. He had heard marriage to Lady Cecily had settled him, but from the way George was ogling the bodice of Miss Kendall's dress, Anthony could only surmise the leopard had not changed its spots.

The dance ended, and Anthony was toying with the idea of taking himself off to the card room until his promised dance with Miss Kendall, no other lady having caught his interest, when Mrs. Blenkinsop and Elfleta wormed their way into his path.

"My lord," Mrs. Blenkinsop cried with the air of one relieved to see a savior. "This ball is a positive crush. My Elf is dying for some lemonade. Champagne is not for one of her delicate constitution."

Eyes cast down, Elfleta dropped a curtsy and murmured a greeting. She wore a shiny satin gown that's very brightness seemed to drain what little color Elfleta had.

Anthony bowed to the ladies. "I should consider it an honor to procure a glass of lemonade for Miss Blenkinsop."

Mrs. Blenkinsop's lips spread in a wide grin. "I knew I could rely upon you, my lord," she gushed, and instantly disappeared into the crowd.

Anthony held out his arm to Elfleta and led her away into the adjoining refreshment room. Here a long table had been set up with an assortment of fruits, cheeses, and nuts along with punches and lemonade. A full supper would be served around midnight, but many of the guests were partaking of a little food now to lessen the effects of all the champagne they consumed.

Anthony handed Elfleta a glass of lemonade. "Are you enjoying the ball, Miss Blenkinsop?"

"Yes, my lord."

"Do you prefer the gaiety of Town life with its parties and soirees to the country?"

Elfleta knew all about his lordship's love for his country estate. Mrs. Blenkinsop had made it her business to find out everything she could about Lord Ravenswood and had then drilled the information into her daughter's head. Even though Elfleta thought she would die of boredom inside of a week in the country, all her interests being confined to the fashions and the fashionable, she replied, "I adore the country."

Anthony promptly began a long monologue—it turned out to be that way because Elfleta had not the knowledge nor the inclination to ask questions and partake of the conversation in depth—regarding Raven's Hall.

Elfleta confined herself to a look of fascination, long practiced in her mirror, at Lord Ravenswood's words. An expression of absorption when a gentleman spoke was guaranteed to impress him, her mama had often told her.

The ploy apparently succeeded as Lord Ravenswood eventually led her from the refreshment room and into the dance, feeling again the satisfaction of having singled out a very possible candidate for his countess.

Oddly enough, though, Anthony reflected, he felt no real need to keep Miss Blenkinsop at his side and gladly turned her over to her next partner, an aging dandy with a protruding stomach.

He stood watching the two dance with none of the unpleasant sensations coursing through him he had experienced when watching Miss Kendall with another partner.

"Anthony! I have not seen you this age. Heard you had buried yourself in some tomb in Egypt."

Anthony turned to see Lord Quinton at his side. He held out his hand. "George. Good to see you. And I was not burying myself in Egyptian tombs but digging myself out of my father's debts."

"You were successful, I am sure. Always managed to obtain anything you set your mind to," Lord Quinton said amiably.

"I did well enough. But who would have thought, George, that I would be standing here today congratulating you on an excellent match? Thought you would avoid the parson's mousetrap as long as possible. Not that I can blame you for snapping up a suitable bride like Lady Cecily."

Lord Quinton's face took on an expression of boredom. "Yes. Very proper Cecily is. Handsomely dowered, good bloodlines, already breeding. I expect to hold my heir cradled in my arms by the time the leaves turn color."

Lord Ravenswood smiled on his childhood friend. "You must be the happiest of men, George."

A shadow crossed Lord Quinton's face. "Cecily is all that is pliant and agreeable. 'Tis one of the reasons I married her. But, depend upon it, Anthony, a man needs a woman with vitality and a certain zest for living."

Anthony noticed his friend's gaze was following Miss Kendall as she danced with Sir Tredair. If he was not seriously mistaken, George's face was pained with regret.

He had heard George's Cecily was a bit wooden and found himself at a loss for words.

Lord Quinton suddenly clasped his friend by the shoulder and looked directly into his eyes. "Rumor has it you are often with Miss Blenkinsop. Do not make the same mistake as I, Anthony." He dropped his hand. His expression became bland once more, and he walked away before Anthony could respond.

The dance ended, and the musicians began the strains of a waltz. It was the second of the evening, and therefore the dance was promised to Miss Kendall.

He located her promenading about the room with Sir Tredair and bowed low before her.

"Tredair, I fear I must take the lady from you. She is promised to me for the waltz."

"You wrest this enchanting goddess from me above my

protest, Ravenswood," Sir Tredair grumbled good-naturedly. "Miss Kendall, you must allow me the next country-dance, else I shall die of a broken heart on the spot."

"Good heavens," Daphne declared lightly, although her color heightened. "I suppose I must agree, Sir Tredair, if only to prevent a scandal for Lady Pelham."

Anthony barely noticed the peer move away. His gaze was focused on Miss Kendall. He felt a particular excitement every time he saw her face that he had never experienced with any other lady.

The feeling discomforted him. He judged it perilous and did not wish for it to continue. Despite his friend's warning, Anthony held firm in his conviction that beautiful and intelligent women were nothing but trouble. His stepmother, Isabella, had taught him this lesson, and he had learned it well.

Daphne saw the frown on his face. The high spirits enjoyed since Lord Quinton's revelations regarding Miss Oakswine—her Fatal Flaw!—lowered.

She determined she must put up a guard against the tender feelings for Lord Ravenswood his person evoked in her, but this foolhardy notion flew out the tall windows of the room the instant he placed his strong, white-gloved hand at her waist.

For his part Anthony swung her easily into the steps of the waltz. She was so feminine, so delicate. His heartbeat quickened when he smelled her light, flowery perfume.

Daphne noticed he watched her intently, and his interest did strange things to her breathing.

She missed a step.

Without delay, his arm tightened around her.

Daphne chided herself for her clumsiness; all the while her heart jolted and her pulse pounded at the intimacy of the way he held her. "Do forgive me, my lord," she whispered.

Anthony bent his head to catch her words, bringing them even closer together. He had a mad desire to crush her to him. Good God, why must the chit have this effect on him? He felt like tearing his hair out. "It is of no consequence, Miss Kendall. You have danced every dance, have you not? I imagine you are growing weary."

"No, I am not," Daphne said. What was he about? Why did he look at her in that captivated manner, then speak to her with a harsh edge to his voice?

"I have seen you dance twice with that spotty-faced young puppy, Piers Fitzwilliam." Anthony knew he was acting peevish and could not for the life of him understand why he could not bring himself under control.

There was a short silence between them that grew tight with tension.

Then Daphne said, "Mr. Fitzwilliam was a charming partner, ever conscious of my pleasure in our dances. I judged myself honored by his company, especially his lively sense of humor. If his pursuit of partners this evening has not flourished because of the unfortunate condition of his complexion, then the ladies in question are the ones to suffer a loss."

This speech, which Anthony deemed overly noble, had the irrational effect of setting up his back even more. "Fitzwilliam has found a champion indeed."

"Is kindness so very foreign to you, then, my lord?" Daphne snapped, out of reason cross.

His straight glance seemed to accuse her coldly. "There is a line where once crossed, kindness becomes gullibility."

She could not know he was thinking of his father's naive response to Isabella.

"I like to believe compassion and benevolence are things we want for ourselves and should therefore give to others," Daphne said.

Lord Ravenswood turned a jaded eye on her. "Tsk, tsk, Miss Kendall. A limping footman, a companion who had been accused of thievery, a nearly blind butler, a drunken cook. What else? A deaf lady's maid?"

"No, she suffers from aching joints and a stiffness, mainly in her hands," Daphne said guiltily.

"You are a pigeon ready for plucking. It will not serve you well in this world."

Daphne drew in a quick breath. "Perhaps not, my lord. But surely it is better than closing oneself off to deeper feelings."

The barb struck home. Ever since that last bitter argument

with his father over Isabella, Anthony had not permitted himself to become close to anyone.

Daphne's perception of this fact caused him to quickly reach the end of his tether. He glared down at her haughtily. "I have always regarded as horrendous the thought of becoming attached to a female with a sharp tongue."

Daphne, who had noticed Lord Ravenswood's disappearance into the refreshment room earlier with Miss Blenkinsop, looked pointedly at where Elfleta stood with her mama. "Well, my lord, you may be easy. You are certainly in no danger whatsoever."

That silenced him.

Across the room by the chaperons, two eager observers to the scene were standing together and becoming increasingly anxious.

"Eugene," Miss Shelby whispered apprehensively. "We must do something. They are cross as crabs with one another."

The manservant's normally serene countenance crinkled with concern. Just as his master and Daphne waged war with each other, a war was waging inside him. He had learned at a young age that his powers could be a blessing or a curse. Eugene used them sparingly and only when he had ascertained they would cause positive results.

He rarely made an error in judgment, the last time being with that elephant at Astley's. He had meant only to give a fright to that loathsome woman and instead—but he would not think of it now.

Miss Shelby twisted a fold in her coral-colored gown. "Eugene, please."

He slowly turned and looked deep into her eyes. What if she turned away from him in aversion or fear? "Leonie, mayhaps you should leave the room for a moment."

"You underestimate me, Eugene," Miss Shelby informed him. She returned his gaze unwaveringly.

Eugene studied her carefully and then his face relaxed. "Very well." He turned and looked at Daphne, one hand reaching up to touch the eye-pin nestled in his turban. He concentrated hard.

Waltzing with Lord Ravenswood, Daphne was not enjoying her victory. Neither she nor his lordship had spoken a word since her tart comment regarding Miss Blenkinsop. Why, she asked herself, had it come to this?

Her annoyance at the situation increased when she found her hands were shaking. Surely he could feel her hand trembling in his. Tiresome man!

The dance ended, and Daphne was grateful. A wave of treacherous heat was invading her body. She had heard older ladies confide about sudden feelings of being hot, but surely she was too young for such maladies.

A second later she believed she might have to rethink this idea. Her head spun, and she felt disoriented. If only she were not so very warm. She raised a hand to her brow.

"What is it, Miss Kendall?" Lord Ravenswood asked, seeing her distress.

" 'Tis nothing, my lord," she lied, then swayed a little. "Perhaps the heat of the room . . ."

"By the Lord, you are ill. Come with me." Lord Ravenswood drew her hand firmly through his arm. He adroitly guided her through the ladies and gentlemen changing partners for the next set. Leaving the ballroom, they proceeded through the refreshment room and out into the hall.

Back by the chaperons, Miss Shelby craned her neck, watching them go. "Dear me, as Daphne's companion I really should not let her go off with a gentleman unchaperoned."

She turned to Eugene, and her lips spread in a mischievous grin. Eugene's wrinkled, tanned face mirrored the action.

Out in the hall, Lord Ravenswood found an open door a few steps away. They walked into a deserted anteroom, and he closed the door firmly behind them.

The anteroom was dark except for the light coming in the tall windows from the full moon. Daphne leaned heavily on Lord Ravenswood's arm. She felt like she was suffocating from heat.

"Here, Miss Kendall, can you sit down on this settee for a moment while I fetch some punch?"

"Yes. Thank you," Daphne said weakly, and carefully seated

herself. "I do not know what has come over me. Nothing like this has ever happened to me before."

"Do not worry," Lord Ravenswood assured her, although his brow was creased with concern. He chastised himself for his boorish behavior, which, in his view, may very well have brought on Miss Kendall's sudden disorder. "You shall be put to rights after partaking of something cool to drink."

Daphne favored him with a tremulous smile, and he walked quickly out into the hall. She fanned herself, but the heat would not go away.

In seconds he returned and offered her a glass. She accepted it after a murmured thanks and sipped gratefully. It was an arrack punch, and quite potent, but Daphne did not care.

He waited until she finished the drink and then said, "Are you better? I fear I should have summoned Miss Shelby for the sake of propriety."

Daphne raised a forestalling hand. "I do not wish to alarm her. Certainly I was only too warm and shall recover presently."

Lord Ravenswood crossed the room to the tall windows. He opened the latch, and the window swung open. He returned to Daphne's side and offered her his hand. "Come, the night air is cool."

"How resourceful you are, my lord," she said, and rose. She reached the window and inhaled a deep breath.

"Is the air helping?" Lord Ravenswood inquired.

The gentle breeze coming in the window was indeed restorative. Daphne felt the heat begin to seep from her body in gradual degrees. "Yes, thank you."

He stood close to her in front of the open window, and the light of the moon showed Daphne the worry on his face. She could see his feelings toward her were sympathetic, and his behavior had been most charitable.

The combination of the strong punch and the night air had brought about a rejuvenation of her spirits. Adding to this was her pleasure in his care.

"I am feeling much more the thing, thanks to you, my lord," Daphne told him. The moonlight shone on his dark hair. She was suddenly acutely aware that they were alone.

"There is no need to thank me," he said quietly. "I fear it was my churlish behavior during our dance that caused you to become ill."

Impulsively Daphne reached out and placed a hand on his shoulder. "Nonsense."

Anthony felt as if her hand touched his bare skin through his coat, so powerful was the effect she had on him. "I must beg your pardon for the things I said to you. I do not know what came over me."

Daphne gave a little shake of her head. "I do not wish ever to quarrel with you, my lord."

Anthony was so touched by this sentiment, he placed his fingers on the side of her cheek in the barest of caresses.

That was when he lost control.

Daphne stood transfixed by the magnetic pull of his dark eyes. She saw his mouth lower to hers in a kind of dream. She knew immediately she craved his kiss. Had been craving it.

His lips pressed against hers, then gently covered her mouth. Daphne felt the warm firmness of his mouth in every fiber of her being. Her hands came up and wound around his neck. She returned his kiss with a hunger that belied her outward calm.

Anthony's head reeled. As he roused her passion, his own grew stronger. His hands went around her back to hold her against him. Abruptly he stripped off the glove from his hand, enabling him to reach up and feel her hair with his bare fingers. It was as soft as kitten fur. He moved to stroke the smooth skin of her face, all the while smothering her lips with demanding proficiency.

A loud burst of laughter from down the hall brought him reluctantly to his senses.

He raised his head and placed a quick kiss on her forehead. "We must go back to the ballroom before we are missed," he told her. His voice was very low and hoarse.

They looked into one another's eyes, and Daphne gloried in the shared moment. She felt wrapped in a silken cocoon of happiness. This was the feeling she knew her parents had shared. The feeling she had been waiting for.

She was in love with Lord Ravenswood.

The earl moved a little away from her so he could deftly put his white glove back on. Neither of them spoke. Daphne felt neither of them wished to break the enchantment of that first long kiss.

He offered her his arm, and they walked down the hall to the entrance of the ballroom. A couple stood just inside the doorway, apparently new arrivals.

The gentleman looked near seventy years of age. The lady seemed much younger, not yet past her fortieth birthday, and was tall and expensively gowned in a rich Turkey red silk. Diamonds shone around her neck, her wrists, and at her ears. Bright gold hair curled about her face in the latest fashion.

Daphne felt Anthony tense at her side. She looked up at him questioningly, but his gaze was fastened on the lady. At that moment the blonde turned and saw him. Her face hardened. "Anthony."

Lord Ravenswood's voice was curt. "Hello, Isabella."

Chapter Eight

A thin chill hung in the air.

Anthony suddenly felt himself back at Raven's Hall. His father was alive, and they were engaged in a hell of a row about Isabella's bills. She sat languidly on a chair, one dainty foot swinging off to the side, while she tried to stifle a yawn.

As usual, he could not convince his father of any wrong-doing on the young countess's part, and only succeeded in widening the gulf between them.

It could have been any one of a number of such occasions. He experienced all the old feelings of frustration, fear . . .

"Anthony, have your wits gone begging?" Isabella scolded, bringing him back to the present. "I have just introduced my new husband, the Marquess of Lamberton."

Civility forced Anthony to incline his dark head briefly in his stepmother's direction and to bow to Lord Lamberton. From the marquess's nervous looks toward the doorway, Anthony surmised he knew something of the nature of his wife's relationship with her deceased husband's son and wished to be no part of their encounter.

Before Anthony could present Miss Kendall, Isabella spoke again in a tone of voice he knew well from the past.

"Lamb, darling, do run off to the card room," she positively cooed to the marquess. "I know how these parties weary you so."

The relief on Lord Lamberton's face was comical. "Zooks! You have the right of it, Bella. There's my good girl."

"I hope to goodness I know what my Lamb needs!" Isabella crooned, and blew him a kiss.

Lord Lamberton scuttled away muttering, "Buy you another bauble with my winnings."

Isabella turned hard eyes back to Daphne and Anthony. "And who have we here, Anthony?"

Stiffly he performed the introductions, all the while wishing Isabella would disappear, and that he never again had to lay eyes on the woman responsible for driving his father into an early grave. But she was here. And now she was a marchioness. He gave her credit for success in her ambitions, if nothing else.

He glanced at Miss Kendall as she exchanged pleasantries with Isabella, and thought he detected a hint of curiosity about her expression. What must she think of this strange meeting? And what had he been about earlier, kissing her with a passion he had not realized he felt for her? He brutally pushed the memory from his mind. He could not think of it now.

"We met at Astley's Royal Amphitheatre," Daphne was saying, answering Isabella's query as to where they had been introduced. "Lord Ravenswood helped me rescue a cat."

Isabella's thin eyebrows rose. "Did I hear you correctly, Miss Kendall? Anthony assisted you to the benefit of a feline?"

Daphne nodded. "Had it not been for Lord Ravenswood's kindness, Mihos might now be dead. He was being used most abominably by a man who wanted to make money by claiming Mihos was the world's smallest tiger. Lord Ravenswood purchased him and took him home."

"You amaze me, Miss Kendall. I have always believed Anthony despised cats."

Lord Ravenswood looked pointedly at Isabella. "Only a select few."

Isabella correctly interpreted, but chose to ignore, the deeper meaning of this wry statement. She turned a mocking face to Anthony. "My poor dear Brutus never did earn your favor."

"No, neither of you did," Anthony said quietly.

Anthony heard Daphne's intake of breath, and felt a qualm for subjecting her to this purposeful display of bad manners.

Isabella's beautiful eyes narrowed. There was a short

silence, during which the polite mask slipped from Isabella's face, and the animosity she felt for Anthony was plain to see.

Within a minute, though, she had herself under control. She waved her fan languidly. "La, 'tis a pity I shall not be in Town longer. Lamberton and I are only passing through on our way to Lamberton Castle. You cannot conceive of the many improvements I must make before my first house party at the end of the Season. I daresay I shall not have a minute's peace. Heavens, I see Lady Jersey signaling to me."

She closed her fan with a snap and walked away.

Nothing had changed, Anthony thought. He could quite clearly imagine the costly refurbishing Isabella would wish to make to Lamberton Castle. An older man and his money had once again fallen victim to Isabella's charms. Lamberton was extremely wealthy, however, and Anthony doubted even Isabella could go through all his blunt. He told himself it was nothing to do with him.

"My lord," Daphne said, placing a hand on his arm. Her gentle touch made him realize how tense every muscle in his body was. "Should you like to go into the refreshment room? We could have something to drink and perhaps talk."

Anthony looked down at the concern in her light green eyes. The compassion he saw there overwhelmed him. Though she knew nothing of the situation, Miss Kendall, he was sure, was ready to stand his friend, offer her sympathy, and listen to him pour out his regrets and his pain into her willing ears. He could not bear it.

"I must return you to Miss Shelby." He took Daphne's arm and escorted her through the room to the area where the chaperons sat. Eugene stood near by, but Anthony looked past him. He bowed briefly to Miss Shelby, who smiled a welcome at him, which he knew invited a conversation. But he murmured an excuse, turned on his heel, and strode away.

"Goodness, Lord Ravenswood looked to be in a taking. Whatever is amiss?" Miss Shelby asked. Eugene stared after his master for a moment, then drew closer to hear the answer.

Daphne hesitated before she responded, torn by conflicting emotions. Her brain was in a tumult. Hardly had she caught her breath after that soul-shaking kiss when propriety had demanded Lord Ravenswood take her back to the ballroom. Then there had been that confrontation—she could not put another name to it—between his lordship and the woman who had once been his stepmother. Daphne's thoughts scampered around in her head, and she found it difficult to focus on any particular one. She was more upset than she cared to admit in front of Miss Shelby and Eugene.

"Lord Ravenswood introduced me to the woman who used to be married to his father, Isabella, the Marchioness of Lamberton. Apparently the lady and her husband have been traveling and are on their way home to Lamberton Castle. The earl and Lady Lamberton did not seem, well, happy to see one another." Daphne spoke this last rather reluctantly.

Miss Shelby gasped. "Oh, dear."

Eugene became instantly alert. "Where? Where is this female?"

Daphne looked around until she spied Lady Lamberton in conversation with Lord Quinton. He did not look pleased to be in her company either, Daphne noted. "She is the tall, blond lady dressed in red, Eugene."

Both the Egyptian manservant and Miss Shelby studied Isabella. Eugene said, "She is what I expected. It is very bad for my master that she has returned at this time."

"What makes you say so?" Daphne asked him, puzzled.

But she had no time to hear a reply as Sir Tredair chose this moment to bow before her. "You assured me of a second dance, Miss Kendall, and I will not let you break your promise."

Daphne forced a smile to her face and took his arm. Sir Tredair did not deserve to be treated shabbily merely because her heart felt as if it had been tossed into a churning sea.

After watching the two join the dancers on the floor, Miss Shelby turned anxiously to Eugene. "How terrible for Isabella to have returned."

Eugene shook his head. "I should have known. Last night the cards showed the Queen of Swords reversed. A sly and deceitful woman."

"What effect do you think her reappearance will have on dear Lord Ravenswood?"

Eugene's face was grim. "Isabella's return is a bad omen. It will bring everything back to my master's mind, I am afraid. He may resolve not to marry or to marry where he should not. We must hope that Isabella will leave Town before they have a chance to meet again and more damage is done." He paused. "It seems likely she will do so from what Miss Kendall said."

Miss Shelby pursed her lips. "I wonder what transpired earlier when the earl took her away from the ballroom?"

"Perhaps you can find out later, wise lady."

Miss Shelby twisted her hands together in her lap. "I shall try. Oh, Eugene, I am uneasy. I am having the most dreadful premonition that Lord Ravenswood will do something hasty. The moon is full tonight, and under its effect people can succumb to the queerest starts, you know."

Eugene stood motionless and watched his master walk alone through the ballroom and out the door that led to the balcony. "You are correct regarding the moon, but let us hope your feeling about Lord Ravenswood is wrong. He is meant for Miss Kendall and must marry her. Everything depends upon it."

"Yes," Miss Shelby said sadly, as if to herself. "I believe it does."

Outside on the balcony, Anthony closed the door to the ballroom behind him and inhaled the night air. The night's darkness was lit by the glow of a full moon.

He gripped the balcony railing tightly and stared down at his gloved hands. How he would like to wrap them around Isabella's white throat!

He released his grip on the railing abruptly, only to slam a fist on the iron. Damn! The woman probably had not spared a thought to the havoc she had left in her wake when she abandoned his father. She had never bothered to look back, certainly had never expressed her condolences or her sorrow at his death. She was a user of people, beneath his notice, and worthy only of his contempt.

He should not even have acknowledged her. He should have cut her right there in the Pelhams' ballroom, right in front of the cream of Society. She deserved no less. But he had not wanted to subject Miss Kendall to such a scene. She had seen enough as it was.

Anthony passed a hand across his eyes and groaned. Miss Kendall. Good God, he should not have permitted himself to kiss her. There was a capital blunder. It was not the act of a gentleman. A true gentleman did not kiss a lady of good breeding the way he had kissed Miss Kendall in the moonlit anteroom, not unless he was prepared to marry her.

He closed his eyes and let the memory of the kiss wash over him. He had kissed her mouth like he would devour it, and her. He had stripped off his glove and with his bare hand had caressed her hair, her face. She had responded so passionately, had felt so warm, and had tasted so very sweet. It had seemed right and natural holding her in his arms. He had not wanted to ever let her go.

When had his feelings for her escalated to these proportions? When had she eased her way into his heart? Devil take it! Was he unable to control himself where she was concerned?

Anthony's eyes snapped open. Hell and damnation! He had vowed never to make himself vulnerable to a pretty face, especially when underneath the beauty lay an intelligent mind. And had he not committed this very transgression? Made himself vulnerable to Miss Kendall?

Raven's Hall needed a mistress to produce heirs for its safekeeping. He needed a compliant countess, one who could be trusted to obey his wishes and not interfere with the running of the estate. He could not, and would not, be distracted from his purpose by romantic notions.

In the grip of strong emotions, he straightened and turned around to face the ballroom windows. As if drawn by some evil force, his gaze immediately found Isabella. Carefree and flirtatious, she conversed with old friends.

Then Elfleta Blenkinsop danced by the windows in front of the earl on the arm of Lord Guy.

Anthony strode purposefully toward the door to the ballroom. He entered, closed the door behind him, and followed Miss Blenkinsop to where Lord Guy was returning her to her mother. That Tulip, tonight all in leaf-green, must have sensed his presence was no longer required as he bowed before the ladies and sauntered away with only a quick look of censure at the plainness of Lord Ravenswood's coat. Anthony ignored him.

"My lord," Mrs. Blenkinsop exclaimed, her face wreathed in smiles. "We began to despair of seeing you again this night."

Anthony nodded to Mrs. Blenkinsop and raised Elfleta's gloved hand to his lips. He barely brushed the cloth, but the action was enough to cause Elfleta to titter and a predatory gleam to enter Mrs. Blenkinsop's sharp eyes.

"May I have the honor of this dance, Miss Blenkinsop?"

Elfleta looked doubtful, but Mrs. Blenkinsop glared down a young calvary officer on his way to claim his promised dance.

Anthony led Elfleta to the floor, his mind working. He recalled that earlier Miss Blenkinsop had declared a preference for country life. She had seemed enthralled when he spoke of Raven's Hall. Miss Blenkinsop was quiet, agreeable, modest, and well-bred. If she possessed only the barest degree of intelligence, well, that was exactly what he required in a bride.

Was it not further proof of her suitability that with the dance nearing an end, and although he had not spoken a word to her, not one protest had issued from her lips?

His gaze traveled to her lips. They were rather thin. The treacherous thought occurred to him that he might not enjoy kissing Miss Blenkinsop as much as he had Miss Daphne Kendall. He dismissed this unwanted conjecture.

Thoroughly convinced that Miss Elfleta Blenkinsop should be the next Countess of Ravenswood, there was only one thing left for him to do. While escorting her back to her mama, he turned his head and looked down at her. "I shall call on your father tomorrow, Miss Blenkinsop."

"Yes, my lord," Elfleta breathed.

They reached her mama, and Lord Ravenswood bowed once again over Miss Blenkinsop's hand. An urgent desire for strong drink led him away in search of the refreshment room.

At the other side of the room, Daphne's dance with Sir Tredair ended, and she congratulated herself on successfully covering her topsy-turvy emotions. She saw the earl enter the adjoining room and nervously bit her lip. A mental battle ensued within her, but then she threw caution to the winds and followed him.

A footman held a silver tray containing a glass of brandy for his lordship. Daphne watched the earl accept the glass, before making her presence known. She admired the strength and width of Lord Ravenswood's shoulders, shown to advantage in his beautifully cut gray coat. His dark hair gleamed in the candlelight. It looked tousled, though, like he had been running his hands through it.

Daphne approached him, the skirts of her sea-green gown rustling. "My lord," she said advancing to stand at his side.

He turned to her. She was caught off guard by the coldness in his dark eyes. Where was the magnetic intensity that usually made her feel intimately drawn to him?

Daphne swallowed hard. She hoped he would not think her presumptuous, but surely after that kiss it would be all right to express her concern. "I can sense you are dismayed by Lady Lamberton's—"

"Dismayed?" He interrupted her and took a swallow of brandy. "Miss Kendall, I am out of patience with myself. My behavior this evening has been uncouth; indeed it has bordered on the unforgivable."

When Daphne would have protested, he raised a forestalling hand. "Please. Allow me to extend to you my most heartfelt apologies."

"Apologies?" Her voice rose in surprise, and she began to shake. Desperately she tried to ward off what she feared he was about to say. "There is no need. We all have things in our past we had rather not have brought to our attention. Obviously the relationship between you and Lady Lamberton—"

Again he stopped her flow of words. "I have no relationship with Isabella any longer, thank God." His voice dripped ice. "I am sorry you were witness to our first meeting since my return to England from Egypt. I can only explain my ungentlemanly behavior by saying it was somewhat of a shock to see the woman I hold responsible for the destruction of my family and my estate."

Daphne watched with acute and loving anxiety as the coldness left his eyes for a moment to be replaced by pain.

Lord Ravenswood drained his glass and placed it on a nearby table. When he turned to her, she saw the wintry look had come back and apprehension coursed through her. She fixed her gaze on the floor, unable to meet his eyes.

"Miss Kendall, the regret I feel at your being a party to the unpleasant spectacle with Isabella cannot compare with the self-disgust I am experiencing for taking advantage of your earlier illness to press my attentions on you. The only excuse I have for embracing you is hardly credible. I found myself alone with a charming woman in the moonlight. It was a mistake. I most sincerely beg your pardon."

It was a mistake. Thunderstruck and mortified to the greatest degree, the four words seemed to ring in Daphne's ears. She felt as if she had been dealt a physical blow.

Daphne fought hard against tears she refused to let flow. Pride came to her rescue. She resolved not to let him see how he had hurt her. Instead she let her pain turn into anger. She would show him she did not care a snap of her fingers for his kisses!

She raised her chin. Her heart pounding, but her voice steady, she said, "Let us forget the matter, my lord. Neither of us has conceived a partiality for the other, so we can chalk up our imprudence to moon madness."

Daphne could have sworn she saw him flinch before he bowed low over her hand. "May I escort you back to the ballroom, Miss Kendall?"

Searching for an escape, a place where she might compose herself, Daphne said, "No, I thank you. I shall retire to the ladies' withdrawing room to repair my hair."

Lord Ravenswood looked skeptically at her perfect coiffure, but, as he was relieved to have his apology over and done with, let her pass without further comment.

His conscience nagged him, and he sought to silence it by signaling to a footman for another glass of brandy. He told himself Miss Kendall had accepted his justification and apology gracefully. He ignored the voice in his brain that asked what he had expected her to do when spurned.

An unexpected weariness overcame Anthony, and he concluded he was past tired of dealing with females. He had made up his mind to marry Elfleta Blenkinsop, and it was a wise choice. Accepting a second glass of brandy from the footman, Lord Ravenswood took himself off to the card room.

He would have been appalled had he returned to the ballroom and observed his soon-to-be fiancée's behavior.

Elfleta Blenkinsop had triumphantly told her mother of Lord Ravenswood's stated intention to call on her father. The girl was doubly happy to impart the news to her parent as Mrs. Blenkinsop had lately chided her daughter about the slow progress she was making in bringing the handsome, wealthy earl up to scratch.

To say Wilhelmina Blenkinsop had been enthusiastic at what was tantamount to a proposal of marriage for her daughter would indeed be an understatement. She just barely managed to refrain from broadcasting the news throughout the ballroom. Only the certainty that her socially powerful hostess, Lady Pelham, would surely take exception to having Lady Rachel and Lady Stephanie's ball overshadowed by such a juicy bit of gossip kept her silent.

Elfleta experienced the heady feeling of superiority. With the earl's few words, she convinced herself of what she secretly had believed all along. She was a Toast. One of the Season's belles. How could it be otherwise when the Earl of Ravenswood intended on making her his countess?

She swept onto the dance floor with her partners, nothing short of giddy. She flirted as she had never dared in the past, secure in the knowledge she was soon to be the envy of every other girl of the beau monde. Never a thought was spared that Lord Ravenswood, had he witnessed it, would scarcely appreciate such behavior.

It did not take Lord Guy long to notice Elfleta's heightened color and shrill laughter. He begged a second dance with her and under his carefully sensitive questioning, she confided the news to him. Lord Guy wished her happy with every appearance of ease, promised to keep her secret, and told her the earl was the luckiest of men.

After he returned Elfleta to her mother, Lord Guy leaned moodily against a pillar and artfully took a pinch of snuff. Ravenswood had stolen a march on him, he decided. Miss Blenkinsop had been dangling after *him*, he was certain. Had she not particularly remarked on the fineness of his coat?

During their dance earlier in the evening, they had gone on quite comfortably about the latest fashions and scandals. Why, Miss Blenkinsop was a taking little thing and had enough sense to recognize he was setting a new fashion with his pom-poms and to compliment him on his savvy.

Lord Guy felt ill-used. The ball was flat. He pushed himself away from the pillar and wandered outside. A game of cards for higher stakes than what were being offered in the Pelhams' card room was what he needed. There was a special deck of cards he found exceptionally lucky. He would stop at home and pick them up, then proceed to one of the gaming hells where he was not known.

Still in a sulk when he reached the Duchess of Welbourne's town house, Lord Guy meandered up the stairs and threw open the door to his bedchamber. The sight that met his eyes checked him on the threshold.

Like a rainbow of spring flowers blown across a meadow, Lord Guy's precious wardrobe of colorful coats lay strewn about the room. The drawers of his desk, bed table, and chest of drawers were pulled open, their contents spilling drunkenly out. A high-back chair by the fireplace was overturned. The open window swung to and fro in the night's gentle breeze.

"My coats," Lord Guy uttered faintly.

"Umh, umh" came a muffled voice.

Lord Guy walked to the other side of his bed, carefully avoiding stepping on any of his coats. He saw his valet laying upon his stomach on the floor, his hands and feet bound tightly with cravats.

"What the devil—" Lord Guy began, outraged almost beyond words at the mistreatment of his wardrobe.

Strong hands grabbed him from behind, and he found himself flung up against the wall. The breath knocked out of him, Lord Guy gasped for air and stared in horror at the masked intruder who was inches from his face. He did not dare struggle. The man twisted one of Lord Guy's arms painfully behind his back. So great was the man's hold around his collar, Lord Guy choked on his cravat.

"Where is the cat?" the housebreaker growled.

"C-cat? What cat?" Lord Guy stammered, terrified for his life.

The intruder tightened his grip. "I want the cat statue, and I want it now."

Lord Guy's mind raced. The ivory cat figurine he had stolen from the duchess? Is that what this was about? Had the duchess put this ruffian up to this? No. 'Twas impossible. He was dealing with a madman. Someone who had heard about the theft—

The intruder knocked Lord Guy's head sharply once against the wall. "You have had enough time to think. The cat. Where is the cat!"

"I p-pawned it," Lord Guy babbled, his head throbbing.

"What?" the housebreaker demanded. "You *pawned* it?"

"Y-yes. Needed the ready. You know how it is. A fellow finds himself in dun territory—" His head flopped on his neck as the thief shook him.

"What pawnshop did you take it to?" the man interrupted, his voice furious.

Lord Guy could not believe the burglar was going to all this trouble for one little cat carving. But who cared what motivated the man? He simply wanted out of this nightmare with his skin whole. He gave the direction of the pawnshop and said feebly, "I did not get that much for it. Only enough to keep my tailor at bay."

A savage blow to the head met this statement, and Lord Guy crumpled unconscious to the floor. The valet moaned in fear.

Ignoring him, Vincent Phillips climbed out of the window from which he had entered the house and deftly descended the outside wall to the ground.

He had remained undetected long enough to search all the servants' quarters in the attics. He had started there, believing that, as a servant, the attics were where Miss Shelby was housed. His efforts in finding the Bastet statue had nonetheless been fruitless.

Desperate, he had expanded his search to Lord Guy's room, where he was discovered by the valet coming into his employer's room with a stack of newly laundered cravats.

Now Vincent ripped off his mask. His nostrils flared with rage. He could not believe a priceless statue had been sold for a fraction of its worth by some stupid fop, and it now lay in a pawnshop. He neither knew, nor cared, how the idiot had come upon the statue.

Disgusted, he made his way back to the Clarendon to wait for the opening of the shop on the morrow. He would pay whatever ridiculous price the shopowner required, take the Bastet statue, and book passage on the first ship headed for America. He hoped the Philadelphia collector appreciated all his efforts.

In Upper Brook Street safe in his room that night, Eugene stared into the Bastet statue's glowing citrine eyes.

"My goddess, we have suffered a setback tonight. I am fearful my master will not take the action necessary to secure Miss Kendall's hand in marriage."

To Eugene, Bastet's golden eyes reflected scorn. His turbaned head dropped into his hands. "Matters are slipping out of control. And what is worse, I desire my freedom now more than at any time during my life, Bastet. I must be free for my wise lady, Leonie. I want to take care of her and show her the world."

He raised his head and gazed into the cat goddess's eyes once again. "Help me, Bastet."

Eugene prayed long into the night. Before he finally retired, he vowed he would stay by his master's side at every moment to prevent him from doing anything careless.

Monday was the fair. Perhaps there a way would be revealed to him on how to bring the two together. For all their sakes.

* * *

In Clarges Street, Daphne, too, remained awake long into the night.

The ride home from the ball in Lord Ravenswood's coach progressed in a silence broken only by the earl's brief outline of his plans to escort them to the fair.

At his distant, aloof manner, Daphne had been hard-pressed not to cry off from the outing. But she could not be so cruel to Miss Shelby, whom she knew was looking forward to the venture.

Pleading fatigue once they were home, Daphne excused herself from an inquisitive Leonie and retreated to her room. She removed her beautiful sea-green gown, washed her face and hands, and slipped into a warm night rail.

Dark red hair tumbled down her back when Daphne removed the pins holding it. She seated herself in a chair by the fire to brush it before going to bed.

Her thoughts immediately returned to Lord Ravenswood. Her heart danced with excitement as a picture of his handsome face sprang into her mind's eye. Her brush strokes quickened.

But, almost at once, the joy turned to foreboding as she recalled his cold words. *It was a mistake.* The mingling of their lips, their breath, the shared intimacy. It had all been a mistake in his lordship's opinion. She shivered in spite of the fire.

He had removed his glove to touch her hair with his bare hand, sending a rush of warmth through her body. How she would relish the feel of his hair against her fingers.

She would never have such an opportunity. Like the other gentlemen Daphne had known, Lord Ravenswood did not really want her. He had made his feelings clear. And this time, Miss Oakswine was not to blame.

Even more difficult was recognizing that, while it had not truly mattered with the others, it mattered with Lord Ravenswood. She loved him.

Daphne's anguish peaked to shatter the last of her control. Her brush fell to the carpet with a soft thud, and she wept.

Several minutes passed before a low roar from the other side of the bedchamber door alerted her to Mihos's presence. She rose, wiping the tears from her cheeks with one swift motion.

She opened the door, and Mihos entered with a majestic tilt to his head. Ever since the accident, the cat had developed a swagger. Seeing it now brought a reluctant smile to Daphne's lips. "Come, Mihos, I am for bed."

"Grraow," the striped cat said in apparent agreement.

As she pulled the coverlet back and climbed into the four-poster, Daphne wondered how she would be able to part from the tigerlike cat. Surely at some point she would have to return Mihos to the earl.

The feline in question showed no signs of wishing to go anywhere that night. He curled up contentedly on top of the coverlet, directly between Daphne's calves, and promptly fell asleep.

Without any such good fortune, Daphne stared up at the canopy, telling herself nothing would change between her and Lord Ravenswood by the time of the fair on Monday. Hoping, all the while, everything would.

Chapter Nine

By breakfast the following morning, a cross Lord Ravenswood decided his old business partner, Lord Munro, must have held a secret grudge against him. Otherwise, he would not have cursed him with Eugene.

Since the earl had woken, Eugene had driven him near the brink of madness. The manservant had hovered over him, fussing like a mother hen, taking forever with the selection of the day's attire and the grooming of his master. By the time Eugene shaved him and helped him dress, Anthony felt smothered.

In the small dining room, the earl tried to use *The Times* as a shield against further contretemps with the manservant. A footman poured him some coffee and moved to an array of hot dishes on the sideboard, but before he could inquire what his lordship desired, Eugene dismissed him with a flick of his fingers.

"Master, Mrs. Ware has cooked the eggs to perfection this morning. May I bring you some?"

"Very good," Anthony replied vaguely.

Spooning the eggs onto a plate, Eugene asked, "And a rasher of bacon would be tasty as well, would it not, master?"

Anthony felt his temper rise. He snapped the newspaper. "Yes, Eugene. Add a muffin and some kippers, and that will be all," he told him dismissively.

"Yes, master." Eugene placed the heavy plate in front of Lord Ravenswood. "What are your plans for today?"

Anthony knew at once he did not want Eugene shadowing him while he went to ask Mr. Blenkinsop for his daughter's hand in marriage. The manservant knew nothing of his decision to offer for her, and Anthony preferred to keep it that way. "I am going to Hoby's to order a new pair of Hessians. I shall not require your presence."

"As you wish, master."

Drinking coffee, while Eugene stood guard from his position by the sideboard, Anthony considered his proposed meeting with Mr. Blenkinsop. The family would be pleased to accept his suit, of that there was no doubt.

Indeed, he reflected cynically, Mrs. Blenkinsop would lord his capture over the other matchmaking names. The ton in general would view the couple with approval.

A picture of a pair of light green eyes sprang into his mind. What would Miss Kendall think of his betrothal?

Anthony placed his cup back in its saucer. The brew tasted bitter. Rather than dwelling on a lady he had decided would not suit him, he set his mind to the difficult chore of disentangling himself from Eugene. He wished to offer for Miss Blenkinsop free of interference and have the matter over and done.

It proved no easy task. Anthony ordered Eugene to remain at home while he went to Hoby's. Upon reaching the boot maker's shop, though, he sighed when he spotted Eugene getting out of a hackney a short way down the street. The Egyptian man's white garments stood out in the bustling crowd. The earl threw the reins to his tiger and told him to wait twenty minutes, then take the phaeton home.

Anthony ordered a new pair of boots, then resorted to the old ploy of slipping out the back way of the shop, all the while cursing the circumstances that had brought him to such a pass. He could not fathom what Eugene's motivations were for staying with him like a sticking plaster.

He wryly congratulated himself, however, when he arrived at the Blenkinsops' house in Grosvenor Square without Eugene being the wiser.

He asked for Mr. Blenkinsop, confident he would not have long to wait. In this, he was wrong. He cooled his heels in the Blue Saloon a good thirty minutes. During this time, he heard a scream followed by a loud crash coming from the floor above him.

Beginning to wonder what the deuce was going on, Lord Ravenswood was further puzzled by the entrance of Mrs. Blenkinsop and her daughter instead of Mr. Blenkinsop.

He rose and bowed to the ladies. They seated themselves on a sofa, and he sat opposite them, observing that Miss Blenkinsop was even paler than usual. She wore a white muslin gown with a lace fichu tucked in the neck of the dress. Her manner, though, seemed a bit more animated to the earl.

In sharp contrast to her daughter, Mrs. Blenkinsop's color was high. She wore a gown of purple silk and an air of fury.

But the tone of her voice when she spoke to the earl was mollifying. "My lord, it is most provoking. I have just learned that Mr. Blenkinsop has taken the buffleheaded notion into his brainbox that he must race off to Surrey chasing after some musty old book."

"Father collects antique volumes, my lord," Elfleta explained.

Mrs. Blenkinsop eyed her repressively. "It is too bad of him and aggravating beyond words that he should choose to indulge himself at this time. He left at the crack of dawn this morning, quite without my permission, and is not expected back until midday Monday."

For some unexplainable reason, Anthony felt his shoulders relax and tension drain from his chest. "I shall call on him Tuesday, then."

"Pish!" Mrs. Blenkinsop exclaimed. "There is no need to wait that long. Mr. Blenkinsop will be happy to receive you Monday afternoon. You young people should not be forced to postpone announcing your, er, happy news." Mrs. Blenkinsop winked awfully.

Repressing a shudder, Lord Ravenswood said, "I am afraid I cannot call on Monday. I am promised to friends for a country fair in High Jones."

Elfleta tilted her head at him. She despised the country, but now that she and the earl were all but betrothed, he belonged to her. By rights, if he were going to a fair, he should be escorting her. "A country fair. How diverting, my lord."

This broad hint for an invitation caused Lord Ravenswood a moment of unease. He had no desire to increase the party by including his intended and her mother. This would be the only occasion where he would meet Miss Kendall before she learned of his engagement. For some perplexing reason, it was important he share this last day with her.

"A prior commitment requires me to attend. I fear it will be dull work, Miss Blenkinsop." He rose. "I shall do myself the honor of calling on Mr. Blenkinsop on Tuesday. Pray excuse me, ladies." He bowed, and raising an eyebrow at her unexpected boldness, he accepted Miss Blenkinsop's proffered hand and kissed her knuckles.

"We shall look forward to it, my lord," Mrs. Blenkinsop trilled.

Lord Ravenswood took his leave, bent on spending the rest of the day at his club, White's, where he would be certain not to encounter any females.

As soon as he quit the room, Elfleta slouched back on the sofa and pouted. "I want to go to that fair."

"But, Elf, you know you detest the country," Mrs. Blenkinsop said in some surprise.

"It makes no difference. Lord Ravenswood should have invited me."

"Well, you shall soon be engaged and appear on his arm at all the events that matter. Surely a country fair cannot be important." Mrs. Blenkinsop stood and walked to the door. "No need for a fit of the sullens, Elf. All will be well. Except, of course, for your father. All will not be well for him when he returns. I shall see to that! The vexing man."

Left alone, Elfleta picked listlessly at her gown. Her lips pressed firmly together, she wondered who his lordship planned to attend at the fair.

Coming to a sudden decision, she rang for a servant. "Fetch me a pen and paper," she instructed the footman who appeared.

The man ran to do her bidding. Elfleta smiled to herself. She would ask Lord Guy to call on her. He seemed smitten. Perhaps he could be persuaded to take her to the fair.

In St. James Street, Lord Guy had a number of the gentlemen in his set gathered around him outside White's club. He gave them a highly altered tale of the previous evening's events.

"Weary from dancing with all the beauties at the Pelhams', I returned home to find my bedchamber in shambles."

"What do you suppose they were looking for, Guy?" a voice asked. "The secret of how your hair stays up high like that?"

A round of good-natured ribbing followed this question. Lord Guy laughed and remained unperturbed. He knew he looked his best today in a coat of tawny orange and pantaloons of a paler orange shade. His waistcoat, also pale orange, had yellow birds frozen in flight embroidered across it.

His pride and joy, the pom-poms on his boots, were a tawny orange to match his coat. He observed with no small measure of satisfaction that young Lord Trimmer had emulated the style. The peer's boots sported pom-poms of a bright blue shade to coordinate with his coat. This validation of his ability to set a fashion pleased Lord Guy no end.

Lord Guy noted Lord Ravenswood approaching the club and made as if to hail him. Having his friends see he was on intimate terms with the earl could only increase his standing. But Ravenswood's black expression challenged anyone to greet him as he walked by the group with an all-encompassing nod. Lord Guy's mouth formed a moue of distaste after the earl passed into the club.

He continued his story. "As I was saying, my poor valet lay bound and gagged on the floor. I swung around and saw the intruder was a huge man with a chest like a barrel. The blackguard towered above me and had the wild look of a bedlamite, but I was not deterred. I delivered a right-handed blow and the fellow went down."

At this juncture, the company's attention was distracted by the arrival of a sedan chair. This elegant vehicle was lined with white satin, and on its floor lay a white fur rug.

A hush fell over the group as the vehicle's occupant alighted, obviously intending on going into White's. Lord Guy felt his pulse gallop. Here was no less a personage than Mr. Brummell himself to see him surrounded by friends in his moment of glory!

Lord Guy aligned one booted foot so that Brummell, the unchallenged leader of fashion, could not fail to observe his pom-poms.

Beau Brummell paused. His fingers found his quizzing glass. He slowly raised it to his eye and leveled it at Lord Guy's boots. Silence reigned.

"Did Hoby make those boots?" the Beau inquired mildly.

Lord Guy puffed out his chest with pride. " 'Twas my invention, but Meyer & Miller made them."

Brummell dropped his quizzing glass. "Ah, that is welcome news. For a moment I thought I would be forced to take my custom elsewhere."

As one, Lord Guy's friends followed Brummell into the club. Lord Trimmer dropped behind for a moment to rip the offending pom-poms from his boots and toss them into the street.

Lord Guy, crimson with anger and humiliation, stood alone.

"My lord, my lord!"

Lord Guy swung around and recognized one of the Duchess of Welbourne's footmen. "What is it?"

"Message for you, sir."

"Give it to me and be gone," Lord Guy said curtly. Opening the missive he scanned the contents, and his eyes narrowed. Miss Blenkinsop requested him to call on her at his earliest convenience. He would most certainly go. He wondered what service he might perform for Lord Ravenswood's soon-to-be fiancée.

Minutes later he bowed low over Elfleta's hand. "Lovely lady, I came at once."

The new Elfleta did not demur at the compliment. She knew it was only her due. Her charms would shortly be held incomparable by all once the announcement of her engagement reached the ears of the ton.

"Lord Guy, I knew I could count on your assistance."

"Indeed, your trust was not misplaced, Miss Blenkinsop. Why, only last night I fought off a vicious housebreaker."

At Elfleta's gasp Lord Guy recounted the fictionalized tale. Some of his pride was restored by the girl's fascination with the account and her murmured admiration for his bravery.

Lord Guy concluded by asking what service he might perform for her.

Elfleta pouted. "Oh, it is only that Lord Ravenswood has refused to escort me to the fair in High Jones this Monday. It is too bad of him as I hear a group of very fashionable people plan to attend." She had heard no such thing, of course, but was determined to attend the fair and knew the inducement of other members of the ton might sway Lord Guy.

"I say," he said with a frown. "Never heard of it myself. High Jones?"

"Yes," Elfleta assured him. Her hazel eyes gazed at him hopefully.

Lord Guy took the bait. Why not? Here might be an opportunity to put the superior Earl of Ravenswood out of curl. "I shall consider it an honor to escort you, Miss Blenkinsop. Would noon suit you?"

Elfleta smiled. "Oh, yes. I never stray from my room before then."

Sensible girl, Lord Guy thought, walking down the front step of the town house. A large dowry, he would wager, and what was equally important, she knew how to dress. Her pretty distress at his story of the housebreaker could only serve to further endear her to him. All in all, Miss Blenkinsop was unexceptionable.

What a shame Ravenswood had been before him. Still, nothing was official. Miss Blenkinsop said her papa was away from Town and not expected to return until Monday. The earl had not had an opportunity to speak with him.

Lord Guy remembered Ravenswood's high-handed treatment of him at the Egyptian Hall and his subsequent coolness. It would afford Lord Guy a great deal of pleasure to come between the haughty Ravenswood and his intended. And how his friends would stare if he stole the prize out from under Ravenswood's nose!

Lord Guy whistled a jaunty tune and mentally planned the ensemble he would wear to the fair Monday.

In Clarges Street, meanwhile, Miss Shelby entered the drawing room and stopped short. Daphne sat on the dark green settee with an open book in her hand. Her attention was not on the pages, however. Instead her gaze focused somewhere beyond the tall window.

Air dreaming, Miss Shelby thought and sighed. *Something* of significance had occurred last night at the Pelhams' ball, of that she was certain. Miss Shelby's intuition told her it was more than just Isabella's disturbing arrival. But it was clear her young friend was not yet ready to talk about whatever was troubling her.

"Daphne, my dear, how are you this morning?"

Daphne wrenched her thoughts back to the present. She had once again been in that deserted anteroom with the earl. Grateful to Miss Shelby for the interruption of these pointless contemplations, she smiled and patted the seat next to her. "Good morning, Leonie. Did you sleep well?"

"Oh, indeed, yes," Miss Shelby dissembled.

She had, in fact, tossed and turned upon her bed for the majority of the night. Her thoughts had centered on Eugene and her deepening feelings for him. She believed he returned her sentiments, and this view caused her great joy. But the manservant was not free to declare himself. Miss Shelby was at a loss as to know how, or even if, this would happen.

But Daphne did not need to be burdened with anyone else's problems. She sat on the settee next to her.

Daphne reached over and squeezed her hand affectionately. "I am glad you rested well, Leonie. Mihos kept me company last night. His leg has healed nicely."

"Thanks to your tender nursing," Miss Shelby reminded her.

Daphne smiled. "I am very fond of him, you know. Soon we must return him to Lord Ravenswood, and I shall be sad to do so."

Miss Shelby's sharp gaze recognized the wistful expression on Daphne's face. While Mihos was an adorable feline, she would wager the young woman's forlorn countenance was caused by the cat's owner.

Miss Shelby lifted a hand and delicately smoothed Daphne's hair. "Mihos is a love. One must get past his ferocious, growling meow to know the true gentleness of his character."

"He does sometimes behave like a tiger, roaring and acting fierce."

Miss Shelby nodded and gave a little laugh. "So like the gentlemen, would you not say? They often present one face, even say certain things, when what lies in their hearts is something altogether different."

"Perhaps you are right," Daphne replied absently. She swallowed hard, and her gaze strayed back to the window.

Miss Shelby dropped her hand, content that she had planted a seed. "Does it not appear to be a lovely day? I wonder, dear, if you might wish to do some shopping. I confess I have allowed Folly access to my bedchamber, and the lamentable result is I need a new bonnet for our trip to the fair."

Daphne turned her head back to her companion, her eyes twinkling. "Never say that ramshackle fellow has chewed your bonnet. He has quite the penchant for headgear."

Miss Shelby chuckled. "I am afraid so. I believe it might be beaver that attracts him. Recollect that Lord Ravenswood's hat was made of beaver, and my bonnet was trimmed in beaver."

"You may have the right of it," Daphne replied. "I remember when Folly mangled his lordship's hat."

"Shall we spend the day shopping, then?"

"Yes. I am sure to find several things I will not know I need until I see them," Daphne said.

If the cheerful note Daphne injected into her voice was a trifle forced, Miss Shelby was encouraged by it nonetheless. Besides, what lady's spirits were not raised by shopping?

Later Miss Shelby's prediction that the excursion would do her young friend good proved accurate. Daphne's face glowed with pleasure as the ladies examined one fashionable trinket after another.

James limped along beside them until Daphne noticed the strain on the footman's face. She promptly sent him to the carriage with their packages. The two ladies entered a millinery shop, prepared not to leave without the perfect new bonnet for Miss Shelby.

A few blocks away down an alley, Vincent Phillips stood outside in front of the pawnshop where Lord Guy had told him he had sold the cat statue. The thief huddled in his greatcoat, the English climate harsh to one used to the warmth of Egypt.

He waited until another customer left the shop, then entered. He nodded to the burly proprietor and quickly ran his gaze over the goods displayed. There was no sign of the Bastet statue.

"Lookin' for somethin' in particular?" the man behind the counter asked.

Vincent took the man's measure. Despite his large size, his face was weak. In this part of Town he would be used to dealing with members of the Quality rather than rough commoners. "Yes. I hope you can help me. I am truly in the suds with my sister," he said, lies tripping easily from his tongue.

"Heh. Females. You don't needs to tell Joe Simmons they're nothing but trouble."

Vincent smiled cordially. "Well, Mr. Simmons, I have been playing rather deep and pledged a cat statue that is a favorite of my sister. Unfortunately I lost and have had the devil's own time of it with Prunella ever since."

His expression turned rueful. "Abominable of me, I daresay, gambling away my sister's adored trinket, but there it is. All I can do now is try to get it back. Fellow that won the cursed cat from me said he sold it here."

Mr. Simmons winked. "Don't you worry, sir. I believe I haves it."

Vincent's eyes glittered. "Excellent. I did not see it on display and despaired that you still possessed it."

The shopkeeper moved away to a cabinet behind the counter. "The gent that brought it in had a nervous way about him. Put me in mind of thinkin' it might be stolen. I've been keepin' it aside for a whiles."

"Was he a slim gentleman with blond hair worn high on his head?" Vincent asked. He paused and remembered the dandy's colorful coats. "Probably dressed in a garish color."

Mr. Simmons nodded. "That be him. And here is your Miss Prunella's cat. Although I would call it more a figure than a statue."

Vincent stared at the ivory cat figurine in the proprietor's hand. His fists clenched at his sides. What kind of trick—but the instant the thought formed, he recalled the terror on the face of the fop at the Duchess of Welbourne's house. The man would fear retribution too much to lie.

The tinkling of a bell heralded the arrival of another customer, a finely dressed gentleman.

Having no desire to call attention to himself, Vincent paid for the figurine with every evidence of relief when in fact he was seething. So close. He had thought himself so close to having the Bastet statue at last.

He thrust the ivory cat into his greatcoat pocket and went out into the street. Walking rapidly, he tried to think. Somehow he would have to find Eugene and beat the truth out of him.

Fury made him almost blind. He would have walked right past Miss Shelby and Daphne had the younger lady not hailed him. "Mr. Phillips? I thought it was you."

Vincent froze in his tracks. His gaze rested on Miss Shelby, and he could have laughed out loud in glee. Here was Eugene's ladylove dropped like a ripe plum into his hands!

He bowed over Daphne's hand. "Miss Kendall. How delightful to see you again. And looking so fresh and lovely in that azure pelisse."

"You are kind, sir. May I present my companion, Miss Shelby," Daphne said.

Vincent nodded at the older woman. Miss Shelby gave a brief nod in return. Her brow furrowed as she listened to Daphne and Mr. Phillips exchange pleasantries.

"We were shopping for a new bonnet for Miss Shelby. She had to have one today, for Monday we are to enjoy a rare treat, a country fair."

"I hope you may enjoy yourselves."

"Thank you, sir. I thought we might see you last evening at the Pelhams'. But then I realized, had you received an invitation, you must have felt you could not attend out of respect for your grandfather," Daphne said sympathetically.

Having completely forgotten about telling Miss Kendall that the baron was dead, Vincent stood silent for a moment. Then, recalling the lie, he said, "In truth, Miss Kendall, I do not feel it proper to attend spirited functions as yet."

"I can understand, Mr. Phillips."

"Perhaps you would allow me to call on you, Miss Kendall. I shall wait until Tuesday as you say you will, er, be away from home all Monday, is that correct?"

Daphne blushed a little but answered positively and gave her direction for lack of an excuse not to. She could not be interested in any gentleman other than Lord Ravenswood, but that did not make her unable to pass the time in a morning call with Mr. Phillips.

Her sunny demeanor must have had a beneficial effect on the Egyptian gentleman, Daphne thought, because he walked away with a wide smile on his face which had not been there at the beginning of their conversation.

"How do you know Mr. Phillips, Daphne?" Miss Shelby asked as they made their way to their coach.

"I met him at the Egyptian Hall, Leonie. He has come to England from Egypt. His grandfather, who was a baron in Suffolk, died recently."

"I see," Miss Shelby said slowly. "There is a sinister aura around him, dear. I cannot think well of him."

"Really? I thought him quite companionable."

"Appearances can be deceiving. Do be careful, Daphne."

Daphne linked her arm with her companion's. She could only love dear Leonie all the more for her sweet concern. "Come, let us go home and admire your new bonnet. Do not fret about Mr. Phillips. What harm could he possibly cause me?"

ball expected Lord Ravenswood to cancel their outing in spite of the inclement weather. He had been very insistent when he had asked her to drive out with him this morning. He had seemed eager to put the argument behind them, and she only hoped his high spirits would last throughout the day. Her thoughts returned to the present. She picked up a book from the table beside her and pretended to read. Should she tell Miss Shelby what was in her heart? No, perhaps it would be better to wait.

Chapter Ten

Not one to stay in her bed until noon, Daphne sat with Miss Shelby in the drawing room a few minutes before ten of the clock Monday morning.

She gazed at her companion, and her thoughts turned to her good fortune in meeting Miss Shelby the first time in Hyde Park. Since then, the older woman had won a permanent place in her heart.

She was not blind to her companion's growing attachment to Eugene, either. The situation both gladdened and concerned her, as she would not have Miss Shelby hurt. Daphne sighed. If she were not careful, her views on men would soon become as dubious as Miss Oakswine's had been. There was every indication Eugene returned Miss Shelby's regard.

"Leonie, the blue ribbons on your new bonnet match your eyes. The effect with your blue gown is most becoming."

"Thank you, dear," Miss Shelby said. Her thoughts, too, were on Eugene, and she privately hoped he would be as impressed with her toilette.

A movement across the room caught her eye. "Daphne, would you look at Mihos? He is pacing in front of the window like a caged tiger."

The cat with the apricot fur, striped with brown, walked back and forth, his tail swishing from side to side, his expression fierce.

Daphne chuckled. "I think he knows Lord Ravenswood will be here soon and wishes he would hurry."

She glanced nervously at the clock on the mantel. She had

half expected Lord Ravenswood to cancel the outing, but surely he would not do so at this late date.

How would she feel seeing him again after that kiss at the Pelhams' ball? Hardly five minutes had passed since that momentous event without Daphne reliving every move the earl had made and every sensation he had called forth in her.

Her stomach clenched tight when the clock struck the hour. Cramble appeared in the doorway and addressed the fireplace. "The Earl of Ravenswood, miss."

Daphne lifted her chin and focused her gaze on the doorway.

Lord Ravenswood strode into the room with Eugene behind him. Daphne's heart jumped painfully in her chest. He looked even more handsome than she remembered in a fawn-colored coat and leather breeches. She wanted to fling herself into his arms and hold him until he retracted the hurtful words he had spoken about their kiss. *It was a mistake.*

She did no such thing, of course. Instead she rose and shook out the skirts of her muslin gown. The dress looked like springtime, being lilac muslin with a light green sprig.

Anthony nodded at Miss Shelby, then bowed before Daphne. "Miss Kendall, you continue to amaze me with your ability to be ready at the appointed hour."

" 'Tis nothing, my lord," she replied, and curtsied. "Good morning, Eugene. How are you?"

The manservant, who had been smiling at Miss Shelby, bowed. "I am well *today*, thank you, Miss Kendall." He shot his master an accusing glance.

On Saturday morning, upon finding his master was not in Hoby's as he thought, Eugene had been frantic. He had relentlessly hunted the earl down and waited for him outside White's, scowling and looking ready to go into strong convulsions.

When Anthony had finally emerged from the club very late in the evening, he had endured a jaw-me-dead from Eugene worthy of a strict Methodist parent. The earl had not been able to attend to the lecture properly, though, being drunk as a wheelbarrow.

Sunday morning, Eugene had satisfied himself by speaking only when spoken to by his master—a punishment not as great as the manservant would like to think—and making sure that in performing every one of his morning duties, he made enough noise to cause certain distress to his master's aching head.

These actions had eventually resulted in Lord Ravenswood spending the day in bed, the door to his bedchamber bolted against his servant.

"Grraow," Mihos said, appearing at his feet and demanding the earl's attention. Anthony bent immediately and picked up the purring animal.

"Feeling better, my friend?" he inquired. "No more pesky bandage?" His lips spread into a smile when the cat raised his paw to touch his chin. Anthony remembered when he used to fear the cat's gesture would lead to his nose being ripped by a sharp claw. Only after several favorable occurrences had he realized the cat's purpose was one of affection.

"Oh, my lord, Mihos is so beautiful. And he quite dotes on you," Miss Shelby said fondly.

Eugene nodded his turbaned head in agreement. "Miss Shelby is right. He is beautiful, and beauty is more than fur deep. Mihos has a beautiful soul. And little tiger knows his destiny is with Lord Ravenswood."

The cat in question, never one to hide his light under a bushel, said, "Grraow," and looked up at the earl as if for confirmation of Eugene's theory.

"That reminds me, my lord," Daphne said. "You must take Mihos home with you whenever you wish. H-his leg is healed, and he is himself again."

Anthony noticed the tremble in Miss Kendall's voice when she made his pronouncement. She was not eager to part with the striped cat. "Could we not share him, Miss Kendall? Surely he belongs to both of us."

Daphne gave a little shake of her head. "I do not see how that would be practical."

No, Anthony thought with gloomy regret. She was correct. After his betrothal was settled, he would be free to return to Raven's Hall. At that time the cat would either have to come with him, or remain in London with Miss Kendall. Both choices seemed unacceptable.

A sudden feeling that Miss Blenkinsop might not appreciate Mihos the way Miss Kendall did added to his unease.

Anthony stroked the cat's head. "We need not think of it now. 'Tis a beautiful spring day, and I have brought an open carriage."

Miss Shelby let out an exclamation of delight. Daphne's expression brightened. "How thoughtful of you, my lord."

Anthony felt a surge of contentment at having pleased her. "The day is unusually warm. You need only bring a shawl, Miss Kendall. I promise to have you home before the sun sets."

Daphne nodded her approval. "Let me just leave instructions with James to be sure the dogs have a good airing, and then I shall be with you."

Bowling about the countryside a short while later, the four put their troubles aside in order to enjoy the fine day and the promised delights of the fair.

Lord Ravenswood could not help noticing how a few of Miss Kendall's dark red curls escaped from under her chipstraw bonnet to dance across her face in the warm breeze. When she laughed at something Eugene said, he admired the glow in her green eyes. Her cheeks, warmed by the sun, were pinker than usual. Some gentleman would be fortunate one day to call her his own.

Anthony abruptly felt restless and irritable. He brushed aside a noisy insect and frowned at a cow in a field.

At last they reached the village of High Jones. The annual fair must have been one of the main events in the local people's lives. The village green was crowded with adults and children of all ages. They heard music played by strolling musicians and smelled the spicy aroma of fresh gingerbread wafting from one of the booths selling food.

Anthony held out his hand to assist Daphne from the carriage. Accepting it with thanks, she said, "Do you think we could find the performing tumblers? Their skill always used to fascinate me as a small child. For hours after Mama and Papa would take me to the fair, I would roll in the grass trying to duplicate their feats."

"What?" Anthony exclaimed feigning surprise. "I thought it

was your heart's desire to see the snakes dancing on ropes, Miss Kendall," he said with a mischievous smile. He paid the small amount necessary for admission, and the four entered the fair.

"Not I," Daphne retorted. " 'Twas Leonie's wish to see the vipers."

Miss Shelby stood a few feet away, but heard this playful comment. "Eugene will take me to see the snakes, Daphne. You and Lord Ravenswood can find the tumblers."

"An excellent suggestion," Eugene hastened to add. "Shall we meet back here in two hours' time?"

Anthony looked at Daphne, but she appeared interested in a notice announcing a contest for Hot Hasty-Pudding Eaters. "Very well, Eugene. Enjoy yourselves."

Eugene and Miss Shelby hurried away like two children released from their governess.

The earl came to stand next to Daphne. Although the breeze carried a cornucopia of smells from the fair, Anthony could detect her light flower perfume. "Does the idea of watching grown men 'Contend for superiority by swallowing the greatest quantity of hot hasty-pudding in the shortest period of time' appeal to you?"

Daphne wrinkled her nose in distaste. "No, sir. I am for the tumblers."

He extended his arm, and she placed her hand on it. Happiness filled him at the simple gesture.

This would not do, he chided himself, as he led her through the crowd. He was as good as promised to another. He should not be having these tender feelings for Miss Kendall.

But the general air of gaiety infected him. He told himself again that he had this one last day with her before his formal proposal to Miss Blenkinsop. He must be content with that.

They watched a family of tumblers, and Daphne clapped and laughed at the antics of a precocious boy of about four years. Anthony caught himself imagining her playing with their young son. She had the loving qualities it took to be a good mother.

Did Miss Blenkinsop? Or was she the sort to turn over the

raising of children to a nurse and only have the young ones trotted out for her inspection occasionally?

He reminded himself that he had made a wise choice in Miss Blenkinsop.

It was an assertion he found he needed to silently repeat all through their hours together as they laughed at a silly puppet show, stood entranced by the conjurer, and enjoyed warm gingerbread washed down with lemonade.

Anthony did not know when he had last had so much fun. Certainly he appreciated the culture and amusements Town life had to offer, but he loved the country. He believed Miss Kendall shared this view, and her presence played a large part in his pleasure.

For Daphne's part, she was blissfully happy. Being in the country again made her feel more alive. She loved nature and all it had to offer. The amusements of this simple country fair reigned supreme over the most elegant of Society affairs in her judgment.

And she loved Lord Ravenswood.

Presently they stood in a large stall set up with all manner of trifling goods to tempt the purses of fair-goers. Daphne gazed at the earl from under her lashes, thinking over his lively sense of the ridiculous, displayed when they watched a man who claimed to be swallowing a fork. The earl's ready sense of humor was a side of him she had not really seen before.

In addition, he was conscious of her comfort at all times, guiding her around puddles, adjusting her shawl about her shoulders, anticipating when she might be thirsty.

And she admired his intelligence. He clearly was a man comfortable in any setting, and knowledgeable on many subjects.

"Woolgathering, Miss Kendall?" Lord Ravenswood asked with a raised brow.

Daphne straightened. She found she had been smoothing a length of ribbon with her fingers while staring into the distance. "No, my lord. Merely admiring this color."

The ribbon was a pretty shade of green with flowers embroidered on it. "I shall buy it for you," he said, motioning to the merchant.

Daphne tried to protest, but was ignored. A minute later he handed her the small package, tied with a string. "Thank you, I shall wear it tomorrow. Oh, look, there is Miss Shelby and Eugene."

The couple waved and crossed the grass. Eugene's silver-gray eyes twinkled. The peach color in Miss Shelby's cheeks was high. "Daphne, we have had the greatest fun. And a group of gypsies has camped at the edge of the fair, can you believe our good luck? Will you not come with us to hear them play?"

"Of course. Who could refuse such a treat?" Daphne said. "You do not mind, do you, my lord?"

"Certainly not. Lead the way, Miss Shelby."

The four walked to the far side of the fair, chatting about their experiences. When Daphne got to the part about the conjurer performing various tricks with cards and balls, Eugene snorted. "Child's play," he muttered, but no one heard him over the music the gypsies were playing.

They secured a place in front and watched the gypsies, whose colorful skirts swayed as they danced and twirled their tambourines. Miss Shelby seemed much taken with them. She was the only one besides Eugene to notice that some of the members of the gypsy troupe were bowing as they passed Eugene. It was done subtly, so that it could be interpreted by a casual observer as part of the dance, but the wide-eyed gypsies paid homage to the Egyptian manservant as they passed.

The music stopped, and a young male gypsy held his cap out among the crowd for anyone who wished to throw in some coins. Lord Ravenswood tossed several in, earning him a tug of the boy's forelock.

"Daphne, I had the most wonderful telling of my fortune by one of the gypsy ladies earlier. Over there," Miss Shelby said, indicating a worn tent bearing a sign that read "Fortunes Told."

Daphne looked skeptical.

"Do go, dear. The woman told me I would soon be making a journey by sea! I am so excited at the very thought. Go and find out what she predicts for your future."

"If you wish to take Miss Kendall, master, I shall wait here with Miss Shelby," Eugene offered.

"All right," Lord Ravenswood conceded. "Come, Miss Kendall, you cannot miss hearing what your future holds."

She took his arm, and they walked toward the tent. "I am not sure . . . you see, my lord, when I was a child I was quite frightened by an old crone telling fortunes."

They reached the tent, and Lord Ravenswood threw back the flap to the entrance. He walked in and with a sweeping gesture, motioned her forward. "I shall protect you," he proclaimed with mock gallantry.

The tent flap closed, and they were alone in the dim light. A table with two chairs stood in the center of the tent. On top of the table lay a deck of colorful cards. No one was about.

"It appears we are out of luck, Miss Kendall," the earl said. "Bother, I shall not be able to play the part of rescuing knight after all."

Daphne's eyes adjusted to the low light. The whiteness of the earl's cravat gleamed in the darkness. "Perhaps the gypsy will return in a moment. Look, I wonder if she uses those cards to predict the future."

Lord Ravenswood glanced at the deck. "They resemble some that Eugene fiddles with."

They both looked down at the top card. It depicted a man and a woman dressed in ancient garb facing each other, each holding a gold-colored cup. A winged lion hovered above them, and the Roman numeral two was at the top of the card. The couple appeared to be pledging their troth to one another.

Daphne raised her head to find Lord Ravenswood staring at her intently. The smoldering flame she saw in his eyes startled her. She returned his gaze wordlessly, her heart suddenly pounding. The promise of intimacy she often felt when she looked into his dark eyes was there now, weaving a web that contained only the two of them.

Seconds passed in silence. Daphne began to think he would kiss her. Her whole being seemed to be filled with waiting.

"Miss Kendall . . . I . . ." his voice was low, and he appeared at a loss for words.

"Yes," Daphne whispered, sensing his hesitation. "What it is, my lord?"

He closed his eyes for a moment, and when he opened them, she could see the distance was back in their depths. "I merely wanted to thank you for coming with me today and to tell you how much I have enjoyed this outing."

She dropped her lashes quickly to hide the hurt. For a moment she had allowed herself to hope he would share his thoughts, his feelings with her. It seemed, however, that his lordship was struggling with some inner demon.

Or perhaps she was merely mistaken in thinking he held any finer feelings for her. "It is I who must thank you for escorting Miss Shelby and me," she told him, her voice wooden.

Neither spoke as they walked out of the tent. Daphne shaded her eyes from the sun, which seemed uncommonly bright after the dimness of the tent.

It was the sun's brightness, she told herself, that caused the hot sting of tears to form behind her eyes. Mortified, Daphne held herself rigidly in check, turning away from the earl and blinking back the tears before they could fall.

"Oh, there you are," Miss Shelby's voice rang out. "What did the gypsy say?"

Daphne was able to turn a composed face to her companion. "She was away from the tent. I am no wiser than before about what my future holds."

"What a shame, dear!" Miss Shelby exclaimed. "The woman had a gift, I tell you. I found her fascinating. Should you wish to return later and try again?"

Daphne indicated she did not.

Eugene's sharp eyes looked from his master to Miss Kendall. He tried to discern whether or not he and Miss Shelby's plan to use the fair to bring the two together was working. From the dismal expression on Miss Kendall's face, and his master's stiff countenance, his hopes were not high.

At that moment Lord Guy and Elfleta Blenkinsop approached them. Miss Blenkinsop was dressed in a white muslin gown with pink ribbons. She carried a dainty white parasol over her shoulder. A young maid trailed behind her.

Lord Guy was all in cornflower blue. No pom-poms decorated his boots, Lord Guy having decided he was quite bored with them. He had told himself his decision to leave off wearing them had nothing to do with Brummell's censure.

Lord Ravenswood bowed to Elfleta, clearly surprised to see her. "Miss Blenkinsop, your servant. I had no idea we might have the pleasure of your company." He raised an inquiring eyebrow at Lord Guy.

All the joy of the day disappeared for Daphne as she listened to Lord Guy's implausible explanation of how they had desired the amusements of a country fair. She noticed Miss Blenkinsop moved to stand possessively next to Lord Ravenswood, and when the group strolled through the village green, Elfleta rested her hand on the earl's arm.

The fact that Miss Blenkinsop made thinly veiled comments insulting the entertainments offered, declared she could not be tempted to partake of any of the foul-smelling food, and pulled her skirts to the side if any of the country people came too close, was little consolation for Daphne.

The suspicion that some understanding lay between the earl and Miss Blenkinsop grew in Daphne's mind until her head ached.

Miss Shelby and Eugene had dropped behind the party and were talking quietly, each wearing an expression of frustration.

This forced Daphne to walk alongside Lord Guy, whom she greatly disliked. She could barely speak with him after his cowardly behavior at the Egyptian Hall, and confined her answers to his forced pleasantries to monosyllables.

After some twenty minutes, Eugene broke away from Miss Shelby to hasten to Lord Ravenswood's side. "Master, it grows late. If you are to keep your promise to return Miss Kendall home before the sun sets, we must leave now."

Elfleta glared at the manservant. Turning beseeching eyes to the earl, she said softly, "I hoped we might go to the Star and Garter. 'Tis fashionable, you know."

"She's right," Lord Guy chimed in. "Only fashionable place around for miles."

Lord Ravenswood ignored the fop. "Miss Blenkinsop, much as I would like to oblige you, I fear I must excuse myself. I have given my word to Miss Kendall to safely have her home before dusk."

Elfleta's hazel gaze swung to Daphne, and her lips formed a hint of a pout. She considered digging in her heels, but decided against it. Lord Ravenswood's manner toward her had been a trifle chilly. Not that she expected, or indeed desired, any warm attentions from him. She simply wanted nothing to interfere with the earl's call on her father in the morning. Therefore, she smiled sweetly and dropped a demure curtsy. "Until tomorrow, then."

Lord Ravenswood watched with a mixture of misgiving and relief as Lord Guy led Miss Blenkinsop and her maid away.

Throughout the course of the ride back to Mayfair, the four were subdued. Eugene and Miss Shelby sat together on one side of the carriage, maintaining a conversation in low voices.

This left Lord Ravenswood and Miss Kendall seated on the other side of the vehicle. In contrast to the older couple, each of them kept their gaze fixed at the passing scenery.

A heavy melancholy descended on the earl. Miss Blenkinsop's arrival at the fair had the air of a contrivance. Lord Ravenswood frowned. But surely she was too weak-brained for scheming. That fact was what held his interest. Perhaps he was making too much of her behavior today.

Or maybe his feelings for Miss Kendall caused his doubts. He had to admit she had a powerful effect on him. Alone in the gypsy fortune-teller's tent, he had been assailed with a desire to taste her lips again. To kiss her the way he had at the Pelhams' ball. He had refrained from doing so with only the strongest effort, reminding himself for what seemed the hundredth time that day that he was soon to be betrothed to another.

Anthony sighed impatiently. Did he not know his own mind?

"My lord?"

Anthony realized Miss Kendall was addressing him. He turned to face her across the short distance of the seat. "I am sorry, I did not hear you."

"I asked if you would be taking Mihos home with you tonight."

Anthony's mind raced. Here was his opportunity. He could take the cat with him, and the connection Mihos represented between him and Miss Kendall would be broken.

He could offer for Miss Blenkinsop in the morning and not see Miss Kendall again. That way, she would not be able to wreak havoc with his senses the way she was doing now, looking at him with that sincere, earnest expression in her beautiful green eyes.

"I think I shall wait if it is all the same to you."

The minute the words were out of his mouth, Anthony blinked in consternation. What was he about? Devil take it, he was just like his father! He was a fool, ignoring his carefully executed, sensible plan to find the perfect countess because of a pretty face.

He barely acknowledged Daphne's agreement to keep Mihos a little while longer. He folded his arms across his chest for the remainder of the drive home.

When the coachman brought the vehicle to a halt in front of Miss Kendall's town house, he alighted, intending on seeing her inside.

Daphne stayed him with a hand. "Please, my lord, do not trouble yourself. Miss Shelby and I are quite capable of walking up the steps unassisted."

He made no objection and motioned for Eugene to remain in the carriage, much to the manservant's annoyance. Bowing over Miss Kendall's hand, Anthony said, "Thank you again for a charming day."

She nodded and ran lightly up the steps, Miss Shelby behind her. The older woman turned to wave at Eugene while the earl waited for Cramble to open the door.

Once he saw they were inside, he climbed back into the carriage only to see a lecture about to tumble from the Egyptian manservant's lips. "Not a word, Eugene. I shall hear not a word."

Inside the town house, Daphne dismissed Cramble. She wanted nothing but to lie upon her bed and review the day's events. Perhaps she would be able to make some sense of Lord Ravenswood's puzzling behavior.

"Leonie, I am feeling weary and wish to refresh myself. Will you excuse me?"

Miss Shelby's kind eyes reflected concern. "Of course, dear. Are you certain you would not benefit from a comfortable coze?"

Daphne pressed her companion's hand before moving toward the stairs. "Thank you, no. Do not fret. I shall come about after I have rested."

Miss Shelby looked doubtful. "Very well, dear. I shall go down to the kitchens and discuss dinner with Hamish before the evening grows too late, and the bottle too low, for the man to speak coherently. After that I shall be in my bedchamber if you need me."

Daphne nodded and then climbed the steps. Gaining her bedchamber, she flung open the door. She was so absorbed in her thoughts regarding the earl, it took a moment before her surroundings registered.

Then her jaw dropped.

Chapter Eleven

As he had done with Lord Guy's room, Vincent Phillips had completely overturned Daphne's bedchamber. Lacy shifts, silk stockings, and gloves lay strewn about the room. The doors to the wardrobe were open, and Daphne's gowns had been cast into a heap beside it.

Worst of all, Biggs was gagged and tied to the bedpost, her eyes wide with fear. Daphne gasped in alarm. "Biggs! Oh, your poor hands—"

She got no further. Rough hands wrenched her arms painfully behind her back and held her. An arm grabbed her around her middle and pulled her backward up against a hard male chest. A harsh voice demanded close to her ear, "Where is the cat?"

Despite the tone, Daphne felt a flash of recognition at the sound of the voice. Too stunned at the rapidly unfolding events to immediately reply, she remained silent.

"Where is the cat, Miss Kendall?" the intruder demanded harshly at her ear.

Wildly Daphne looked about. Mihos crouched on top of the tall wardrobe, his tail switching angrily as he watched the scene. "There. On top of the wardrobe," she indicated with a nod of her head.

The man looked up. As if in answer, Mihos hissed and bared his teeth at Mr. Phillips.

Daphne cried out in pain as the housebreaker twisted her arms.

Outside in the hall, her hand raised to knock, Miss Shelby

heard her cry of distress. About to throw open the door to lend her aid, she froze when she heard a man's voice.

"Do not play games with me, Miss Kendall!" He threw Daphne onto the bed and stood over her menacingly. Biggs moaned.

Daphne lay on the bed rubbing her arms. She stared up at the intruder, her mind a whirl.

Suddenly her mouth dropped open. Mr. Phillips! Although he was masked, Daphne recognized him. The combination of his startling blue eyes and his brown hair with its blond streaks identified him. That was why his voice had sounded familiar! But it would not do to let him know she had perceived his identity.

"I-I am not trying to deceive you. I do not know what cat you are talking about. Mihos is the only cat I have."

Vincent Phillips leaned over her. Daphne shrank into the mattress. "The stolen cat statue," he growled.

Listening outside the door, Miss Shelby clutched her throat, terrified.

Comprehension dawned on Daphne's face. "The one Miss Shelby—"

"Ah, now we make progress on saving your life, Miss Kendall. Yes, the one Miss Shelby has."

Daphne stared at him, confused. He must mean the cat Miss Shelby had been accused of stealing. But what could he want with the duchess's ivory cat figurine?

In the next second a moan, followed by a thud, could be heard coming from the direction of the bedchamber door. Vincent Phillips swung his head around to find its source. Daphne seized the opportunity to scamper off the bed and run for the fireplace. Her hands were reaching for the poker when he caught up with her, grabbing her wrists.

"Let me go!" Daphne demanded. "Miss Shelby does not have the cat, and neither do I."

"I have searched her room as well and know she does not have it. Where is it?"

"I do not know—stop!" Daphne shouted when Mr. Phillips

pushed her up against the side of the fireplace and held her pinned.

At that moment, Mihos flew from the top of the wardrobe to the fireplace mantel next to Vincent Phillips's head and let out a tremendous, menacing roar. "Grraow!"

Startled, Vincent jumped away from Daphne. She darted to the side and grabbed the poker. Raising it above her head, she meant to strike him on his head, but instead her blow fell heavily on his shoulder.

He clamped a hand over the wound in pain. "Jade!"

Daphne raised the poker again but felt sick. Violence of any sort was abhorrent to her. She was not sure she could strike him again. "I tell you I do not know what happened to the cat. We believed someone in the duchess's house might have stolen it." Even now, Daphne was loath to name Lord Guy.

Mihos roared again from his position on the mantel.

"What the devil is that animal?" Vincent asked, staggering a bit and darting a leery glance at Mihos.

"Never mind. Get out of my house, else I shall summon the watch." She had every intention of doing just that regardless, but desperately wanted him to leave. She feared she would not be able to hold him off much longer.

Vincent, indeed, could have wrested the poker from Miss Kendall at any time he chose. Frustrated, though, and believing neither woman had the Bastet statue, he turned and hurried toward the window. Climbing down the outside wall, he was more determined than ever that he must find Eugene. He was certain only the manservant knew where the priceless statue was located.

Almost to the ground, Vincent jumped and landed awkwardly, twisting his foot. Cursing, he limped away.

Seeing him go, Daphne sagged against the wall in relief. All at once she began to shake. The poker slipped from her nerveless fingers, and she shut her eyes.

A muffled noise reminded her of her lady's maid's position. "Oh, Biggs! Here, let me untie you. Are you all right?"

She removed the gag from the woman's mouth first. The

maid took in great gulps of air. "Miss, I've never had anything so frightening happen to me in all my life."

"Pray you will not again, Biggs," Daphne said. She untied the woman's hands and then sat back. "What happened?"

"He surprised me, miss. One minute I was arranging your blue gown in the wardrobe and the next he was tying me up. Imagine a housebreaker in broad daylight," said the clearly scandalized abigail.

Daphne noticed Biggs was rubbing her hands and reckoned they ached abominably. "Do not concern yourself with setting the room to rights. Have one of the maids arrange things under your direction. I must find Miss Shelby and see to the servants."

Rising, Daphne crossed the room and opened the door to find her companion slumped unconscious on the floor. "Leonie!"

Biggs hurried to her side bringing a vinaigrette. Daphne thanked her and waved the pungent scent under Miss Shelby's nose. The older woman moaned and opened her eyes.

"Daphne, dear child. Oh! Oh! I heard a man's angry voice . . ." Miss Shelby struggled to sit up.

"Do not worry. I am fine. 'Twas a housebreaker, but Mihos and I triumphed," Daphne assured her. "Come, let us get you to bed." She assisted Miss Shelby to her feet with Biggs's help.

"Daphne, I had just come from the kitchens and was going to ask if you wanted a tray sent up to your room. When I went to knock on the door, I heard a man's voice—"

They reached Miss Shelby's bedchamber, and at the sight of it, the older woman shrieked. Vincent had done his work even more savagely in this room.

Fearful Miss Shelby would faint again, Daphne hurried her to the bed and helped her lie down. "Leonie, I am sorry you must try to rest among this chaos, but I do not wish to waste time ordering another chamber made up."

"No, you must not trouble the maids," Miss Shelby said weakly. "I do not have many things. It will not take long to put them in order. If I could just lie here a moment."

"That is exactly what you must do," Daphne told her.

Turning to the waiting Biggs, she said, "Please go take care of yourself. I shall attend Miss Shelby." The maid nodded and left the room.

Daphne righted an overturned chair. She did not know how much Miss Shelby had heard outside the bedchamber door before she fainted. Had she heard Mr. Phillips mention her name? Not for the world would she have dear Leonie believe herself to be at fault for this evil deed. Therefore she told her companion an altered version of the encounter with Vincent Phillips—not even mentioning she knew the identity of the villain—then said, "May I ring for some tea for you, Leonie?"

"That would be welcome, dear. And for you as well. You have sustained a terrible shock. How brave you are! I declare I cannot conceive of what the burglar thought he would gain from my bedchamber. But, there, such persons cannot be relied upon to think sensibly."

Daphne told the startled maid who answered her bell what had occurred, and ordered tea and sandwiches. Though she doubted she could get anything past the lump in her throat, she wanted Miss Shelby to have sustenance. The glad thought that her companion had evidently fainted before hearing Mr. Phillips speak of her was a source of great relief.

Over the next hour the two women drank tea and nibbled their food. Another maid came in and, above Miss Shelby's protests, tidied the room.

By the end of this time, Daphne felt Miss Shelby considerably recovered. "Leonie, I am going to leave you now. I want to reassure the servants all is well."

The older woman reached out and squeezed Daphne's hand. "Thank you, dear. Thank you for everything. You are a good girl." Tears formed in Miss Shelby's eyes.

Daphne patted her hand. "Goose! What would I do without you? Shall I send Folly in to bear you company?"

Miss Shelby's brows came together. "No, perhaps not tonight. He might startle me in my sleep."

Daphne nodded. "Very well. I shall see you in the morning. I believe I shall make an early night of it. Rest well, Leonie."

Miss Shelby managed a smile before Daphne left the room.

Alone, Miss Shelby lay quietly. It was obvious dear Daphne was not going to mention that it was she, Leonie Shelby, who was responsible for this brutal attack. The girl was so thoughtful, so very concerned with the comfort of others.

Tears rolled unchecked down Miss Shelby's cheeks as she thought of the horror of the evening. This was the thanks Daphne was to receive for taking in a lonely old woman who had been accused of thievery. It was more than Miss Shelby could bear.

Why the thief wanted the ivory cat figurine, Miss Shelby could not conceive. It did not matter. What if the man returned? All that was important was keeping Daphne safe. And she was not protected as long as someone wanted that cat figurine badly enough to break into the house and threaten its mistress.

Miss Shelby dried her eyes. She waited until she felt the household was abed before rising and pulling her old portmanteau out of the armoire. While packing it with a few meager items, she thought of Eugene. Would he think ill of her for leaving like this?

Tears flowed down her cheeks anew. How silly of her to have fallen in love with him. Why, at her age, she should be thinking of nothing but retiring to some tiny cottage in the country, not still indulging in dreams of romance and travel.

Even so, she hoped Eugene would understand why she felt she must leave. For a moment she considered sending him a note, but not being able to determine a way to accomplish this tonight without arousing suspicion, she put the idea aside. She would leave a missive for Daphne. Surely the girl would relay the information to Lord Ravenswood and his servant.

Besides, she reasoned forlornly, Eugene had never spoken of love to her. Perhaps he would not be as distressed as she thought at losing her company.

Miserable, Miss Shelby closed the portmanteau and sat down at her small desk. She pulled out pen and paper and began to write. Minutes later she slipped out of the house undetected. She had not even dared to say good-bye to the dogs, who were no doubt snoring away in the library. Nor would she see Mihos again.

Swallowing the despair in her throat, Miss Shelby clutched her portmanteau and walked away into the darkened London streets to begin her journey.

Daphne prepared herself for bed. Her chamber was once again in pristine order, thanks to the efficiency of the maids.

After double-checking the latch on the window, Daphne blew out her candle and climbed into the four-poster. Her long red hair spread out on her pillow, and she gazed up at the canopy.

Mihos hopped onto the coverlet and padded toward her, letting out a low "Grraow." Daphne smiled at him and began stroking his head absently. The cat curled up at her side.

What a day it had been. There were so many unanswered questions. Why had Vincent Phillips desired the ivory cat figurine enough to break into her house? How on earth had he learned about Miss Shelby and the stolen figurine in the first place?

The blackguard. And to think she had been pleasant to him at the museum and on the street! She had even invited him to call upon her on the morrow. What should she do now? She had not been able to bring herself to report the incident to the authorities, fearing Miss Shelby would somehow be dragged into the bumblebroth.

Perhaps in the morning she would send word to Lord Ravenswood and ask him to call. Maybe he would know what to do.

Thoughts of the earl reminded her of the pleasure she had experienced with him at the fair. Images came into her mind of his brilliant smile and his dark eyes.

She bit her lip anxiously, though, when she remembered being alone with him in the gypsy's tent. Her cheeks burned at the remembrance of how tears had formed in her eyes when she thought his lordship might kiss her, and then had not.

Uncomfortable, Daphne shifted positions. She must stop this nonsensical thinking about Lord Ravenswood. It was obvious Miss Blenkinsop's company rated higher than hers in the earl's opinion. The proprietary air with which Miss Blenkinsop regarded him spoke volumes.

Fighting tears, Daphne addressed the cat. "Well, Mihos, you and I will be parting soon."

The cat watched her closely, a grave expression in his amber eyes.

"Unless I am mistaken, the earl has found a countess for Raven's Hall. He will declare himself to Miss Blenkinsop and then take you away to live with them. I-I shall miss you."

At these words Mihos stretched out a paw to Daphne's chin in the same affectionate way he often did with Lord Ravenswood.

The small gesture of love was too much for Daphne. Holding the cat close, she allowed her tears to flow.

Unaware of the perils befalling Miss Kendall and her companion, Lord Ravenswood shut himself in his library upon his return from the fair.

He did not indulge himself in drink as he had on Saturday. Rather, he contented himself by drumming his fingers on his desk and staring morosely into the fire. He managed to pass a few hours this way with little variation.

A treacherous part of him wanted to go to Miss Kendall. He felt inexplicably drawn to her this evening.

But a mocking voice inside his head asked, what do you have to offer her? The decision has been made to ask for Miss Blenkinsop's hand in marriage. Any further association with Miss Kendall would be pointless.

Hard on the heels of these depressing ruminations came the memory of Miss Kendall's sweet face. Of her bewitching green eyes. Her pink lips. Then his mouth hungered for hers, and the desire to go to her became strong once again.

Round and round his thoughts went like children on a carousel.

At an advanced hour, the door to the library opened, and Eugene walked in to stand in front of the desk. "Master, you refused dinner. You have been sitting here alone for hours. How can I serve you?"

The earl looked up at the older man's somber countenance. All at once Anthony realized that despite his meddling ways, the manservant genuinely cared for him.

"Thank you, Eugene, but there is nothing I require tonight. Tomorrow, though, you may wish me happy."

Eugene's eyebrows rose almost into his turban. Hope soared in his chest. "Wish you happy? Is that not the phrase used to congratulate someone on a betrothal?"

Anthony nodded.

Eugene clasped his hands. "I knew you would see the light, master. Miss Kendall is everything a woman should be. Intelligent, kind, generous, beautiful—"

Lord Ravenswood scowled. "What nonsense are you talking, Eugene? It is Elfleta Blenkinsop whom I have chosen to be my bride. I shall call on Mr. Blenkinsop in the morning. I have already indicated to Miss Blenkinsop and her mother that I will do so." He gave a short bark of a laugh. "No doubt, if I do not appear, Mrs. Blenkinsop will come looking for me."

Eugene leaned forward, his hands gripping the edge of the desk. "But, master, only think! Miss Blenkinsop is lifeless. A mere fashion dummy. She cannot converse, she has no sparkle, no mind. Not to mention a body like a pole. Do you really want to share a bed—"

"That is quite enough, Eugene!" Lord Ravenswood snapped, rising to his feet. "I am going to marry Elfleta Blenkinsop. Nothing can stop me, I tell you. I shall not require your assistance this evening. Good night."

An openmouthed Eugene watched his lordship march from the room. The manservant's shoulders slumped. It appeared defeat was at hand.

Then his eyes narrowed. Despite his master's convincing words, Eugene detected a reluctance on the earl's part. Was there still time to stop the betrothal?

It was too late tonight to confer with Leonie. But speak with her he must. He would go to Clarges Street first thing in the morning. Together they would come up with a plan.

Eugene's lips curved in a small smile. He climbed the stairs to his room to begin his nightly prayers. Thank the gods he had Leonie. His wise lady. What would he do without her?

Daphne entered the breakfast room a few minutes past eight the next day. She wore a pretty morning gown of willow-green muslin. Biggs had woven the green ribbon with the flowers embroidered on it that Lord Ravenswood gave her through her dark red hair.

As soon as she seated herself, Holly, Folly, and Jolly presented themselves at her feet, acting the part of her adoring slaves. Of course, one had to feed slaves, as the scamps well knew.

Slipping them scraps under the table, Daphne drank chocolate and managed to eat a muffin before retiring to the drawing room.

Mihos had been pacing, as was his custom when agitated, but when Daphne entered, he stopped and swaggered over to her eagerly. "Grraow!"

Daphne chuckled. "Yes, I have brought your plate of kippers. Terrible for you to have to wait, but I know you cannot like dining with the dogs."

She placed the plate on the floor by the sofa, sat down, and watched Mihos attack the food.

James limped into the room to tend the fire. "Mornin', miss. I see you're spoilin' that striped devil again."

"Not a bit of it, James. Mihos has proven not only to look like a tiger, but to have an appetite like one. We simply must keep up his strength."

James smiled as he went about his work.

Daphne glanced at the clock. Was it too early to send a message to Lord Ravenswood to call on her? She wanted to tell him of the break-in. No, she shook her head slightly. Better to wait a little while.

"Has Miss Shelby been down yet, James?"

The footman paused. "No, she hasn't, miss. Odd that. Miss Shelby usually feeds the dogs real early-like."

"Leonie is probably sleeping late after the contretemps of last night. As for the dogs, oh, those miscreants. I have been feeding them when I come down as they always behave as if they are starving! The wicked, wicked creatures."

James laughed. Daphne opened a fresh copy of *The Times* and began to read. Mihos had finished eating and was licking a paw and using it to clean around his whisker pad.

This comfortable scene was shattered moments later when Biggs burst into the room. "Miss! The most dreadful thing."

Daphne's heart jumped in her chest. She rose, and the newspaper slipped out of her fingers onto the floor. "What has happened?"

Mihos looked in alarm from one to the other.

"Miss Shelby had not yet rung for anyone to help her dress, so I went along and peeped into her room. Just to make sure she was all right, what with everything that happened last night," the maid explained.

Daphne nodded encouragingly.

Biggs took a deep breath. "You can imagine how I felt when I saw her bed all made up like she never slept in it! I found this letter addressed to you, miss, propped on the fireplace mantel."

Daphne accepted the missive with shaking hands. She ripped it open and read silently.

Dearest Daphne,

It seems I have brought Bad Luck down upon your undeserving head. You were too considerate of my feelings to say so, but I know last night's terrible events were all My Fault. You should never have taken pity on me and taken me into your household, although I shall forever be Grateful that you did. Please try to think of me Fondly, and if you should have the occasion to speak with Eugene, relay my Deepest Thanks for his friendship. I fear I shall never see anyone I love again.

Yours, Leonie.

Daphne stood there, blank and very shaken. "She has run away," she told the waiting servants. Daphne was loath to reveal the intelligence that the housebreaker had been after an ivory figurine Miss Shelby had been accused of stealing. " 'Tis a misunderstanding."

James came to stand by his mistress. "Where could she have gone, miss?"

"I never heard Miss Shelby speak of any family. Did you?" Biggs inquired.

Daphne pressed her fingers to her temples. "She does have family, but I cannot believe she would return to them. I gained the impression they mistreated her."

She dropped her hands in dismay. "Heavens, I must find her. Miss Shelby cannot be left to think she is not wanted. James, bring around the traveling coach. Biggs, pack a bag for me, and bring my dark green cloak."

"But, miss, where are you going?" Biggs asked.

"I am not certain yet. I need a few minutes to think. When I have decided, though, I want everything to be ready. James, you shall accompany me."

"Yes, miss." Both servants hastened away to do their mistress's bidding.

At that moment the doors to the drawing room opened, and Eugene stood on the threshold. The manservant bowed. "Good morning, Miss Kendall. I have come to see Miss Shelby."

Mihos dashed across the room to greet Eugene, who bent and stroked his head. "Hello, little tiger, I am flattered by your attention."

"Eugene!" Daphne exclaimed, coming to meet him. "How glad I am to see you. We desperately need your help." She handed him the letter Miss Shelby left. "Leonie has gone."

"Gone?" he asked, his voice rising in shock. Daphne motioned to the letter, and the manservant bent his turbaned head to scan the lines.

"No, no, my wise lady," he muttered, agony plain in his voice. He glanced up sharply at Daphne. "What does she mean when she speaks of last night's events?"

Quickly Daphne outlined their confrontation with the housebreaker, whom she recognized, and her belief that Miss Shelby must feel responsible for the incident. Eugene listened intently, then asked, "This Mr. Phillips kept asking for the ivory cat figurine? That is the one Miss Shelby was falsely accused of taking from the duchess?"

"Yes—" Daphne stopped and tilted her head consideringly. "Well, Mr. Phillips never actually said 'the ivory figurine.' I just assumed that was what he meant. His exact words were that he wanted the 'stolen cat statue.' "

Eugene froze. "What did this Mr. Phillips look like?"

"Tall, very blue eyes, brown hair streaked heavily with blond."

Eugene closed his eyes in dread.

"What is it?" Daphne demanded. "Have you thought of something? You must tell me, Eugene."

The manservant opened his eyes. His calm expression belied his inner turmoil. "Perhaps Mr. Phillips was sent by the duchess. We may never know, and at this time it does not matter. Miss Shelby must be found."

"Exactly my feeling," Daphne said fervently.

"We need more information. You can help, Miss Kendall, by going to Miss Shelby's room and seeing what she has taken with her."

Daphne wanted to protest, but nodded and hurried from the room.

Once she was gone, Eugene turned his back to the door. The cat looked at him raptly. The manservant said, "Mihos, center your energy with mine. We will use our powers to find Leonie."

"Grraow," the cat agreed softly.

Eugene raised a hand to touch the eye-pin in his turban and concentrated with all his might. The cat sat tall next to him, his tail wrapped around his paws, his striped body swaying slightly.

The clock ticked away the seconds in the quiet room. Eugene breathed deeply and steadily. Slowly a picture came into his mind of Leonie sitting in a gypsy camp, talking with the fortune-teller from the fair.

She was with the gypsies.

Eugene dropped his hand and sunk into a chair. Mihos hopped up on the sofa and lay down watching him.

Eugene sat deep in thought. Thank the gods Leonie was safe. But for how long? Who was to say the gypsies would allow a stranger to stay among them?

He rained a number of curses down on his own head. All of this was *his* fault. When Miss Kendall had described Vincent Phillips, Eugene knew at once he was the thief in the museum in Baluk. The man sought *the Bastet statue*, not the ivory cat figurine!

Phillips must have remembered his face from that day in Baluk when Eugene had taken the Bastet statue, then traced him to London and somehow found him.

Eugene jumped to his feet in agitation. He recalled the feeling he had as he and Miss Shelby had been talking at the Egyptian Hall. The sense of being watched. Eugene would wager Phillips had been spying on them, and something they said led him to believe Miss Shelby had the statue of Bastet.

Everything fit together.

Eugene felt a stab of guilt. If only he had not taken Bastet, Leonie would not be in trouble today.

But no, that line of reasoning was senseless, he decided. He had been guided to take the Bastet statue by a higher power. If he had not done so, Lord Ravenswood would not have met Miss Kendall, nor he Leonie, and heaven only knew what would have become of Mihos.

An urgent need to find Leonie seized him. His mind worked at a great speed. He did not want to wait to relay the events to Lord Ravenswood. His stuffy master would wonder how he knew Miss Shelby was with the gypsies, and precious time would be wasted while the earl questioned the theory. And there lay the additional danger that he would not be convinced.

Ordinarily, Eugene judged, Miss Kendall would stop and question his statement as well, but right now she was not thinking logically. Her emotions were ruling her head. She could be persuaded to take him to the gypsy camp. Leonie might need Miss Kendall's assurance as well as his own to convince her to come home.

If they left right away, they would not be slowed by Lord Ravenswood.

Eugene walked to the window and stared out. Leaving Town without his master brought an even bigger dilemma. The code of honor by which he lived demanded he remain at his master's side. In all the years he was with Lord Munro, Eugene had never left him, nor had he been parted from Lord Ravenswood.

Eugene leaned his forehead against the glass and closed his eyes. His honor demanded he remain with his master. His deep regard for Leonie commanded him to go to her and bring her back where she belonged until he could make her his own.

Miss Kendall reentered the room. "Eugene, she has taken only the gowns she had when she came to me. Everything I purchased for her has been left behind."

The manservant turned from the window. "I know where she is, Miss Kendall."

Daphne gave a glad cry and crossed the room to lay her hand on the white sleeve of his tunic. "Tell me, Eugene. She is safe?"

He nodded, but cautioned, "For the moment. She is with the gypsies we met at the fair." Eugene's face was set. His decision was clear. "We must go at once."

As he had predicted, Daphne did not question his knowledge. Instead she said, "I have all at the ready. But should we not send word to Lord Ravenswood? I believe he would want to know what has happened, perhaps even accompany us."

"If I may beg a pen and paper, I'll write a brief message to Lord Ravenswood and ask one of your footmen to carry it. But we shall not wait for a reply."

Daphne had moved to a desk at the side of the room. At these words, though, she turned back to the manservant. "Eugene, I am not comfortable leaving without giving Lord Ravenswood the facts and allowing him a chance to reply. Besides, he may be able to assist us."

"I am afraid Lord Ravenswood is not available just now," Eugene lied, knowing his master would not call on Mr. Blenkinsop for another hour or more. But he could not run the risk of anything interfering with their immediate departure.

Daphne was uncertain. She laid out the pen and paper neatly on the desk and asked, "Where is he? Cannot we send word he is needed urgently?"

Eugene took a deep breath, feeling trapped. In order to get his wise lady back, he must tell Miss Kendall the painful truth. Otherwise she would send for the earl.

"It would be awkward. You see, he has gone to ask Mr. Blenkinsop for his daughter's hand in marriage."

Daphne's face paled. She clutched the back of the desk chair. Eugene hastened to her side, mentally cursing the distress his words were causing her.

"I see," she whispered. "Certainly the earl must not be disturbed."

She blinked, then swallowed hard, struggling to keep her composure. The effect of Eugene's words was shattering. Although she had judged the earl about to offer for Miss Blenkinsop, somehow hearing it confirmed extinguished any spark of hope she had left.

"Ah, Biggs, just in time." Daphne moved away from the desk to accept the green cloak and a small traveling valise the maid handed her. "Tell James I wish to see him."

The maid bobbed a curtsy and left the room.

Daphne glanced back at the sofa where Mihos lay, and paused. She put down her cloak and bag, and walked over to the cat. "I believe the time has come for us to part, Mihos."

The striped cat raised his head and stared into her eyes.

She reached out and scratched the top of his head, an action sure to please. "Remember I told you last night our time together was near an end? Well, it seems I was right. You must go home to Lord Ravenswood now."

Mihos raised a paw and began to stretch it out in the direction of Daphne's chin, but before he could do so, she grasped it gently and gave it a quick little kiss.

She rose and saw James standing in the doorway. She gave orders for him to assign another footman the task of safely returning the cat to Lord Ravenswood immediately. James nodded and hastened away.

Whirling around to face Eugene, Daphne lifted her chin, tears sparkling in her eyes. "As soon as your note is written, we shall leave. I shall await you in the coach." She picked up her cloak and bag, and hurried from the room.

Eugene crossed to the cat. Mihos had risen to a sitting position and stared after Daphne. "You must not worry, little tiger. You have a job to do. It is your duty to guard Bastet while I am gone."

Mihos sat a little straighter.

Satisfied with this answer, Eugene walked over to the desk. He sat down and tried to compose his thoughts. An inner torment gnawed at him, and he stared down at the blank paper.

All of a sudden, his expression lightened. Perhaps all was not lost. Perhaps there might still be a chance for his master and Miss Kendall. He carefully chose his words and began to write.

Chapter Twelve

About an hour later, Lord Ravenswood stood in the hall of his town house, dressed in a dark blue coat of superfine and buff-colored pantaloons.

He had deliberately delayed paying his call on Mr. Blenkinsop until the morning was advanced, correctly surmising that Miss Blenkinsop was not an early riser.

However, it was apparent that, at least for this morning, the girl had woken some time ago. While breakfasting, Anthony had received a note from Mrs. Blenkinsop, saying they awaited his promised call with the greatest of anticipation.

Frowning into the hall mirror, his lordship's mood could best be described as resigned. He would go to the Blenkinsops and have done with the matter once and for all.

If the truth were told, at the moment his thoughts dwelled more on Eugene's failure to attend him that morning. This unprecedented negligence raised his curiosity, as well as his ire. Mrs. Ware said Eugene had come into the kitchen for tea earlier and then left the house by the back door. When questioned, none of the other servants knew of Eugene's whereabouts.

Anthony decided he would deal with Eugene later. Giving a final adjustment to his cravat, he accepted his hat and stick from Pomfret and moved toward the front portal. The butler opened the door to a day that matched the earl's mood. The weather was cloudy and dismal.

Just as Anthony prepared to step outside, a familiar growling meow and raised voices came from the hall behind him. He turned back at once.

The source of the altercation was a footman in Miss Kendall's livery, who struggled with a twitching, jerking, covered basket. The servant had one hand at the bottom of the container, and the other pressed firmly down on the wicker lid. Angry protests emitted from the basket.

The young man looked up at the earl's appearance and bowed. "My lord. I 'ave your cat and a message for you."

Anthony handed his hat and stick back to Pomfret before addressing Daphne's servant. "You may put the basket down."

The footman appeared greatly relieved as he complied with the request. He placed the basket on the floor and then jumped away as if in fear of attack from the occupant.

Instantly Mihos's head appeared through the top of the basket, followed by the rest of his body. Hopping out onto the tiled floor, the cat gave a disgusted shake of first one, then the other hind leg. He saw the earl and trotted over to rub against his boots. Anthony bent and scooped the animal into his arms.

"Lor'," the footman was moved to say. "It's plain 'e likes you, sir. We weren't so lucky at Miss Kendall's. As soon as we gots the basket out, it was like 'e knew 'e was about to be trapped. 'E flew off, runnin' all over the 'ouse. Took 'amish, the cook, that is, and Mrs. Biggs and me almost an 'our to get 'im in that there basket."

Anthony's mouth twisted in a grin at the picture the footman painted. *But stay a moment. Why had Miss Kendall sent Mihos to him?* "Did you say you have a message for me?"

"Oh, yes, my lord." The footman fished around in his pocket. "Miss Kendall says it's time to return the cat to you, but your servant, Eugene by name, sent you this." He handed the earl a folded square of paper.

Eugene? The manservant was at Miss Kendall's? Anthony shifted Mihos and the letter to one arm, reached into his coat pocket, and handed some coins to the footman. Pomfret led the young man away.

Alone in the hall, Anthony walked over to a side table and gently deposited Mihos on the shining wood surface. "What is going on, Mihos? Where is Eugene, and what possessed

Miss Kendall to return you? Have you done something unpardonable?"

"Grraow," Mihos denied, his tail flicking.

"Watch that bowl," Lord Ravenswood told him, struggling to open the missive and mind the cat. "It is very special to me, as it features a likeness of Raven's Hall."

The cat rubbed his jaw against the bowl's rim, and the earl elbowed him away.

Finally, having gotten the paper open, he gazed down at Eugene's painstakingly printed letter.

Master,

I beg a thousand pardons for leaving you like this. Terrible things have happened to Miss Kendall and Miss Shelby. I fear for their very lives. I shall do my humble best to save them.

Your servant, Eugene.

P.S. We are with the gypsies from the fair.

Anthony read the note twice. Shock held him motionless, and apprehension squeezed his heart. "What on earth am I supposed to make of this cryptic message?"

Mihos paid him no attention. He was intent on sniffing the inside of the bowl.

The earl pounded a fist on the table, startling Mihos, and making the precious bowl jump a few inches toward the table's edge. "The devil! Damn Eugene for not explaining the predicament clearly. Are Miss Kendall and Miss Shelby in real danger?"

Or was this one of Eugene's machinations? God knew, he and Miss Shelby could take fancies into their heads that any person of sense would condemn as ridiculous.

What was he to do now?

His heart told him to speed to Miss Kendall's aid.

He glanced at the hall clock. The Blenkinsops were waiting for him, his mind argued. He was already dressed for a call, not for riding. Surely he would not be above a half an hour at the Blenkinsops, then he could ride out to the area around High

Jones to locate the gypsy camp and find out what the deuce was going on.

The cat watched the play of expressions across Lord Ravenswood's features. Then he let out a low growl and stared at him in what Anthony viewed as a challenging manner.

The earl hesitated, for some reason unable to put his rational plan into action. Should he waste valuable time going to the Blenkinsops first? What if Miss Kendall were in real danger?

His glance fell on the picture of his ancestral home portrayed on the Chinese bowl. He had chosen Elfleta Blenkinsop carefully as the best countess for Raven's Hall. All that mattered was the future of Raven's Hall. Not the fleeting feelings Miss Kendall evoked in him. The earl shrugged. Granted, he must admit his feelings for her had persisted beyond what they ought.

But Raven's Hall would live on for eternity. His tender regard for Miss Kendall would fade away, would it not?

He turned toward the front door, intent on completing his mission at the Blenkinsops before haring off to High Jones.

A loud crash stopped him. Mihos stood on the wood table, staring at Lord Ravenswood.

Anthony looked down at the shattered remains of the Chinese bowl. He passed a hand across his forehead and moaned.

"Pomfret!" he shouted. The butler appeared immediately. "Have this mess cleared away."

Pomfret's face registered horror at the destruction. "Shall I try to have the bowl pieced back together, my lord?"

"No," the earl said. " 'Tis not necessary."

"Grraow!" Mihos agreed.

Anthony ignored him. "Have the grooms send around my fastest horse as quickly a possible."

"Yes, my lord," Pomfret said.

The earl took the stairs two at a time, Mihos scampering after him. Reaching his chambers, Anthony quickly changed into riding clothes, cursing Eugene for not being there to help him.

Once dressed, he moved to his desk and scribbled a hasty note to the Blenkinsops, begging their pardon for his rudeness.

He explained an emergency obliged him to leave Town, and he would call on them upon his return. He folded and sealed the letter, and in his hurry left it on his desk.

He recalled the letter halfway down the stairs. He paused just long enough to instruct the housemaid polishing the banister to fetch it from his room and see to its delivery.

Mihos reclined on his lordship's bed. With no one about, and little for him to do, amber eyes fixed on the last item the cat had seen in motion.

He stretched, then crept across the bedcovers. With a bound he leaped to the desktop and pounced on the folded scrap of vellum. Velvet paws batted the paper onto the floor, across the carpet, and to the edge of the bed. Apparently tiring of the game, Mihos gave the paper one final swipe, propelling the missive entirely out of sight.

Tail high, the tiger-striped cat then strolled out of the room, mounting the stairs to the servants' quarters in search of Eugene's bedchamber.

Not many moments later the housemaid entered his lordship's room. Over lunch that day she confided to the downstairs maid that she feared their master had gone off his hooks, ordering delivery of nonexistent letters.

Rain fell in sheets outside the coach in which Daphne and Eugene traveled. Neither occupant made an attempt at conversation. Eugene was busy blaming himself for Miss Shelby's departure. Daphne concentrated all her energies on not bursting into tears at the mental image of Lord Ravenswood going down on one knee in front of Elfleta Blenkinsop.

When they reached the village of High Jones, Eugene alighted first. "Please stay in here where it is dry, Miss Kendall. I shall question the villagers until I find which direction the gypsies took."

"Thank you, Eugene," Daphne said.

It did not take long to learn that the gypsy troupe had left the village in a southwesterly direction. Eugene returned to the coach, and they rambled along the road pointed out to them for another hour. At last they spotted the gypsies camped over to the side, their ramshackle caravan half-hidden among the trees.

Again Eugene instructed Daphne to remain inside the coach. He was already thoroughly wet, so there was no need for her to ruin her clothes.

After five minutes Daphne grew impatient. She wiped the window glass with her gloved hand, and saw Eugene speaking with a gypsy man.

She could tell the conversation was not going well. What if Eugene had been wrong? What if Miss Shelby were not with the gypsies at all? Daphne frowned, recalling she had not really inquired as to how Eugene knew Miss Shelby's whereabouts.

Unable to remain idle any longer, Daphne wrapped her green cloak closely around her and opened the coach door. The sweet smells of the country met her nostrils. Even as she stepped down, the rain slowed to merely an annoying drizzle. She carefully adjusted the hood of her cloak to protect the precious green ribbons Lord Ravenswood had purchased for her at the fair.

James, acting as their driver, made as if to climb down from the box to assist her. She waved him away. Stepping closer, she realized that Eugene and the gypsy were indeed involved in an argument.

"I tell you there ain't no woman by the name of Leonie Shelby here," the gypsy man said.

Eugene's expression was tight with strain. "I know she is here. Take me to her now, or it will be the worse for you."

The gypsy man's gaze traveled to Daphne, and he eyed her appreciatively. He turned back to Eugene and sneered. "Want a fight, do you?"

Daphne gasped. She laid a restraining hand on Eugene's white-clad arm. Addressing the gypsy, she said, "If you please, I am searching for my companion, Leonie Shelby. Do you have any information that might help?"

The man leered at her. "If it be a companion you want, I'll be glad to fill the position."

Daphne shrank back in disgust from the man's blackened

teeth and filthy attire. Eugene, however, stepped forward menacingly.

The sound of hoofbeats interrupted the trio. The horse came to a halt a few yards away, and Daphne's green eyes widened in astonishment. A drenched Lord Ravenswood gazed anxiously down at her. "Miss Kendall, are you all right?"

"Y-yes, my lord," she stammered. "However did you catch up with us?"

Lord Ravenswood removed his hat from his head, emptied the accumulated rainwater, and put it back on. "As you can see, I have ridden through hours of rain to find you. Horses, of course, are always quicker than coaches."

He turned to Eugene. "I shall speak with you later regarding that reprehensible letter you sent me. Where is Miss Shelby?"

Eugene looked uncomfortable at Lord Ravenswood's mention of his enigmatic message. But he did not waste time dwelling on his master's irritation. The letter had brought his master, which was his goal. "Master, that is what this man," he said, pointing derisively at the gypsy, "will not tell us."

Lord Ravenswood transferred his gaze to the gypsy, who eyed his fine clothes and horse with seeming disdain. The man said, "I ain't telling no swell nothing, either."

The earl dismounted and glowered at the man. "I am going to give you one opportunity to tell me where Miss Shelby is before I have you and the rest of your troupe thrown off my land. Yes, you may well look surprised. I am the Earl of Ravenswood, and you are camped on the edge of my property."

The gypsy did not hesitate. "Over there in that tent," he said, and pointed. "She be with Mary Tucker, her what can tell the future." He promptly spit over his left shoulder.

The trio from London crossed the camp, while various members of the gypsy troupe bowed in turn before them. When they arrived at the indicated tent, Lord Ravenswood threw back the flap. Miss Shelby sat with another woman at a table. The gypsy was probably in her sixties, but still a very handsome woman. She looked up and smiled knowingly. "Ah, you are here at last."

Miss Shelby jumped up, fluttering her hands. "Eugene! Daphne! Oh, my lord!"

Eugene stepped forward and took her hands in his. "Wise lady, you frightened us all."

"Indeed, Leonie," Daphne said. "I have rarely been so overset. How could you think yourself not wanted and loved? How *could* you leave us?"

Miss Shelby blushed at all the caring attention given her. "But, I thought . . . with that dreadful housebreaker . . . oh, it is all my fault—"

Eugene cut off the flow of words, giving her a gentle shake. "It is not your fault! Never think that again."

"Would someone tell me what is going on here?" Lord Ravenswood asked.

"It is of no importance any longer, is it, Leonie?" Daphne asked, a hint of steel in her expression. Now that Lord Ravenswood was betrothed to Miss Blenkinsop, Daphne did not want to involve him further in her difficulties.

Miss Shelby was outnumbered. Tears of gratitude came into her eyes, and she hugged Daphne. "I do so want to come home. Not," she added hurriedly, turning to look at the gypsy woman, "that I have not enjoyed my time with you, Mary, and I learned much." Miss Shelby made hasty introductions all around.

Mary Tucker's gaze lingered on Eugene for a moment before she gave a little nod of her head. "All will work out well for you, Leonie. You have a special gift."

Then she turned and regarded Daphne and Anthony. "Ah, you will have three fine sons. But only one daughter. Take care you do not spoil her, my lord." She shook her finger at the earl.

Daphne felt heat flood her face. She waited for Lord Ravenswood to explain they were not married, indeed, that he had only that morning become engaged to another, but his lordship remained silent.

The gypsy woman laughed and shook her head. "Remember I said how it would be. I left the card picturing the couple pledging their troth to one another for you to find in the tent. Did it not tell you something?"

Daphne noticed a heightening in the earl's color. Fortunately

Miss Shelby chose that moment to gather her things and begin thanking her hostess. Eugene lifted Miss Shelby's portmanteau, and the foursome took their leave and began to make their way back through the gypsy camp.

Eugene and Miss Shelby moved a little distance ahead. Daphne turned to the earl. "My lord, I must thank you for your assistance."

The earl waved his hand dismissively. "I am only happy to see you and Miss Shelby safe. Later an explanation as to what this was all about would not be amiss."

Daphne suddenly realized the color was still high in Lord Ravenswood's face. What she had taken for embarrassment was clearly something else. "My lord, are you quite well?" she asked.

For an answer he stopped walking and swayed alarmingly. In the next instant he lay sprawled out on the ground at her feet. "Anthony!" Daphne cried, in her distress using the earl's given name.

She crouched down beside him, cradling his head in her arms. His forehead was burning hot.

He looked up into her eyes. "Those ribbons are dashed pretty in your hair, Miss Kendall," he said.

Then he fainted.

The earl was too ill to travel all the way back to Town. Obtaining directions to Raven's Hall from the gypsies, Daphne instructed James to tie his lordship's horse to the back of their coach. The Hall lay a mere three miles to the south. Eugene easily picked up his master and carried him into the coach.

Lord Ravenswood regained consciousness a few times during the trip, but did not seem aware of his surroundings. In Eugene's opinion his lordship was suffering a recurrence of the fever he had endured in Egypt. For lack of space, Eugene sat on the backseat beside the earl to guard his master from bumps and jolts. Miss Shelby and Daphne sat opposite, with Daphne twisting her fingers together and never taking her gaze from Lord Ravenswood's flushed face.

As they pulled into the drive of Raven's Hall, Daphne was

relieved to realize the rain had stopped. Although anxious about the earl, she could not help but be curious about his home. She took a minute to look out the window. "How lovely," she cried when the building came into view.

Raven's Hall was done in the elegant Palladian style. The mellow stone glowed warmly under the setting sun. The large park surrounding the house was meticulously cared for, and Daphne could make out a wide stream with a Palladian bridge spanning across it farther away down a hill.

No sooner did the carriage wheels cease turning before Daphne said, "I shall make our presence known, Eugene. James must hold the horses, for no one has come to do so."

The manservant nodded. "The estate has been undergoing restoration, Miss Kendall. I do not expect there are many hands in the stables or very many to staff the house as yet."

This prediction proved to be true. The front door was opened by a petite woman in black, rather than a butler. Silver curls peeped out from under her large cap. Her small hands rested protectively on the large bunch of keys at her waist, which identified her as the housekeeper.

She eyed Daphne warily. "Yes?"

"I am Miss Kendall. Lord Ravenswood took ill unexpectedly, and as we were nearby, we brought him here."

The woman's eyes rounded with concern. She turned from the door and called, "Byron! Byron! Master Anthony is home and needs help. Come quickly!"

A pleasant-faced man with gray hair appeared and rushed to help Eugene carry his lordship upstairs. The housekeeper hastily introduced herself as Mrs. Violet Tinkham.

Mrs. Tinkham scurried ahead to a large bedchamber. They carried the earl inside, making sure the sheets were turned back on the bed before laying him down. "Byron, be sure to keep his neck straight," she said. "The poor dear, he's burning with fever. I'll fetch his nightclothes."

"If you show me where his things are kept, I shall care for my master now," Eugene said imperiously.

In unison, Mr. and Mrs. Tinkham glared at him. Violet Tinkham looked like a small soldier ready to defend her field.

She informed Eugene that she and Mr. Tinkham—Byron—had been at Raven's Hall for more than twenty-five years. Her husband's position as house steward gave him precedence, she did not doubt.

Daphne stood near the door with Miss Shelby. A knot tightened in her stomach at seeing the earl stretched out on the large bed. Fearing that an argument as to whom should care for the patient was about to break over their heads, Daphne tried to diffuse the situation. "Mr. and Mrs. Tinkham, this is Eugene, Lord Ravenswood's manservant. He was with the earl in Egypt and nursed him through a previous fever. Is that not so, Eugene?"

"Yes. For many days and nights I tended him," the manservant informed them proudly.

Mrs. Tinkham's face softened a trifle at this devotion, but she was not prepared to relinquish the reins. "Byron, will you see to the ladies while I take care of Master Anthony? Mr. Eugene can remain here in case I need help."

Eugene's lips pressed together, but realizing Mrs. Tinkham held sway at Raven's Hall, he resigned himself to the role of assistant.

A short while later Daphne wandered around the opulent blue and gold drawing room done in a classical style. Its warm richness, marked by beautiful works of art, velvet- and silk-covered furniture and a painted ceiling, was a contrast to the cool, classical hall with its plain stone walls and geometric black-and-marble floor with Adam's pattern, *a la grecque,* running diagonally across the surface.

Daphne and Miss Shelby enjoyed a delicious supper and retired to the drawing room afterward. Miss Shelby sat on a blue velvet sofa while Daphne walked about the room, pausing once or twice to examine a piece of the earl's fine collection of porcelain.

She could not help but admire the elegance of Raven's Hall. She judged Lord Ravenswood had worked very hard on the estate. Miss Blenkinsop was a lucky girl, indeed. Daphne felt all the strength drain from her body at this depressing thought. She sank into a chair across from her companion.

"Daphne, dear child," Miss Shelby said. " 'Tis been a long day, and you look exhausted."

"I confess, I am tired," Daphne admitted.

"You must go up and rest, but before you do, you must know how thankful I am that you came after me. I daresay I was not thinking clearly when I ran away. I am not used to having people care about me, you know. But when I saw you and Eugene and the earl come through the entrance of Mary Tucker's tent, I was all but overwhelmed by happiness."

Daphne rose and hugged Miss Shelby. "Thank goodness we found you, Leonie." Her brows came together. "Though how Eugene knew where you were, I cannot say."

Miss Shelby remained silent on that point. "Well, dear, we still have the problem of the housebreaker. And now Lord Ravenswood is fighting a fever."

The two ladies turned as the door to the drawing room opened, and Eugene entered. Daphne asked, "How is Lord Ravenswood?"

"He is still battling the fever," Eugene said wearily. "I only came down for a moment to say good night."

"Oh, dear," Miss Shelby said.

Daphne bit her lip. "Perhaps Miss Shelby and I should return to Town in the morning. I have no wish to be a burden on the household, and I am sure Miss Blenkinsop would want to know her fiancé is ill."

"What?" Miss Shelby cried. "His lordship is betrothed to Elfleta Blenkinsop?" Her blue eyes nearly started from her head.

Eugene did not address the question. He turned to Daphne. "I am hopeful this fever will be of short duration, and believe you and Miss Shelby should remain here. Lord Ravenswood, I know, would not like to think that you and Miss Shelby traveled such a distance with only James's protection."

Daphne was too tired to argue. "Very well. We shall make no decisions tonight."

Eugene smiled and bowed to Daphne. He then raised Miss Shelby's hand to his lips, bringing a blush to that lady's cheeks.

"Do not worry, wise lady, all is not lost," he whispered before leaving the room.

The tenderness in his gaze was comfort enough to send Miss Shelby into a deep, restful sleep.

In a pretty pink and pale green bedchamber just next door, Daphne tossed and turned. The mental image of Lord Ravenswood proposing to Miss Blenkinsop returned and warred with the memory of the warmth in his gaze just before he fainted.

Readjusting her pillow for at least the tenth time, Daphne told herself the warmth came from his fever and not from any fondness for her.

With this disheartening thought, she finally fell into an uneasy sleep, wondering what the coming day would bring.

Chapter Thirteen

The next morning, Daphne awoke rather late. A maid named Sadie brought her chocolate and a roll, then helped her into a jonquil muslin gown, chattering about how brightly the sun was shining after all the rain.

Daphne thanked her, then went down the hall toward Lord Ravenswood's room. There, she encountered Eugene. "Good morning. How is the earl?" she asked anxiously.

The older man had circles of fatigue under his eyes. "In the night my master was restless, but about an hour ago, the fever broke, and he is asleep."

Daphne felt her spirits lift. "That is good news, Eugene. I am sure Lord Ravenswood will be grateful for your good care."

Eugene snorted. "Mrs. Tinkham would not let me near my master! I sat uselessly in a chair at the edge of his bed all night, while she bathed his head and persuaded him to take liquids. She is a managing sort of female."

Daphne suppressed a chuckle. "Will you try to get some sleep for yourself now that his lordship is out of danger?"

Eugene sighed. "Yes, I must. May I ask you to tell Miss Shelby I will speak with her later today? I would find her myself but—"

"I shall tell her," Daphne interrupted. "Off with you, and please do not get up until you are refreshed."

Eugene nodded his thanks and moved away.

Daphne hesitated outside of the earl's door. For some non-sensical reason she wanted to see for herself that his color had returned to normal and that he rested peacefully.

Chiding herself for being silly, she turned and retraced her steps to her room and took out her cloak. Running lightly downstairs, she found Miss Shelby and gave her Eugene's message.

"It appears to be a lovely day, Leonie. Such a change from yesterday. I mean to inquire after James and then explore the grounds. Will you come with me?"

"No, dear, you run along," Miss Shelby said. "I shall pass the time in Lord Ravenswood's excellent library until I have a chance to speak with Eugene."

Daphne nodded. She sensed Miss Shelby and Eugene had much to talk about.

She was not to know just how many topics were covered when Eugene ran Miss Shelby to earth in the library. It was late in the afternoon. The shadows were growing long and candles had been lit. Miss Shelby sat reading in a comfortable gold-and-white-striped chair in front of the fire.

"Oh, Eugene, here you are at last," she said, putting aside her book.

The manservant sat down nearby in a matching chair. "I am sorry not to have spoken with you earlier, Leonie. I was awake all night, and after I slept today, I wanted to make sure my master was properly cared for before coming to you."

"How is Lord Ravenswood?" Miss Shelby asked with concern.

"Much better," Eugene said. Then he leaned forward. "We do not have much time. I have thought of a plan."

"Heavens," Miss Shelby exclaimed, "never say the earl has truly affianced himself to Miss Blenkinsop."

Eugene smiled with satisfaction. "No, he was to call on her father yesterday morning, but he told me he did not take the time to do so. He rode directly out to find us, as I had intended."

Eugene explained what had transpired the morning after Miss Shelby's disappearance and about how he had written a dramatic note to which his master could not help but respond. Miss Shelby clapped her hands with glee over the tale.

"What I am thinking now," Eugene said, "is that you and I

must make an excuse and return to Town, leaving Miss Kendall and Lord Ravenswood here alone. Naturally, once back in London, I shall be certain Miss Blenkinsop learns they are at Raven's Hall together."

Miss Shelby nodded eagerly. "Excellent. But what reason shall we give for going back without them? Daphne was saying only last night that she wished to return to Town."

Eugene thought hard. "It might be best not to tell her we are going. Instead we shall escape and leave a letter telling Miss Kendall we wanted to report the break-in at her town house to the authorities. We believed she would prefer to remain here until Lord Ravenswood is well. It is not much of an excuse, and we shall not be going to the authorities, but it may answer."

Eugene spent a moment ruefully contemplating the fact that this would be the second time he had left his master. He decided the end justified the means.

He looked up and was startled to see tears glistening in Miss Shelby's eyes. He reached over and grasped her hand. "What is wrong, wise lady?"

"Oh, Eugene," Miss Shelby said miserably. "It is my fault that awful man broke into Daphne's house, and now all of this." She spread her hands expansively.

Eugene was assailed by a terrible wave of guilt. He gripped the arms of his chair. Leonie thought it was the ivory cat figurine Mr. Phillips sought, when, in fact, it was Bastet.

As he gazed into Leonie's kind blue eyes, Eugene realized how very much he loved her. Her pain hurt him. He must tell her how he had taken the Bastet statue and why, and pray that the uncommon knowledge and understanding she had always exhibited in the past would serve him now.

"There is something I need to tell you, Leonie." He drew her over to a sofa and sat close to her while he explained about his quest to be free, about Bastet's guidance, and about Vincent Phillips's desire to wrest the statue from him for evil intentions.

Through it all, Miss Shelby listened intently, asking an occasional question and holding Eugene's hand.

At last, the story complete, Eugene squeezed her hand and said, "So you see, Leonie, I cannot beg you to share my life until I am free of my obligation to Lord Ravenswood, and Bastet is returned to the museum."

Miss Shelby's eyes glowed. "Did you say you would want to spend your life with me?"

Eugene nodded. "I love you, my wise lady, and want to protect you always."

Miss Shelby felt a surge of pure joy. "And I love you, Eugene. But do you only wish to protect me?" she asked coyly.

Eugene's earnest expression brightened, and his face creased into a sudden smile. "No, Leonie. There is much more." He leaned forward and pressed his lips tenderly to hers.

Daphne knocked on Lord Ravenswood's door about six o'clock that evening. A maid answered and informed Mrs. Tinkham of her presence.

The housekeeper appeared at the doorway. "Yes, Miss Kendall?"

Daphne wished she could dispel the suspicious look in the woman's eyes. "I wanted to inquire as to my host's condition before dinner."

"He is tolerable. The fever broke this morning, and after he rested I was able to convince him to take some porridge."

"Tinky!" Lord Ravenswood called. "Tell this silly maid I may get up. The goose is nigh to tears because I want to leave my bed."

Mrs. Tinkham whirled around and fled to her patient's bedside. "I shall do no such thing, Master Anthony. You have a visitor, so I suggest you get back under those bedcovers and make yourself respectable."

Daphne flushed. She had not thought she would be able to see his lordship at all, much less be given access to his bedchamber. But here was Mrs. Tinkham leading her into the masculine room, muttering, "Take care not to tire him."

Lord Ravenswood's dark brows rose when he saw her. He wore a paisley banyan and a frustrated expression. Daphne curtsied. "Good evening, my lord. How are you feeling?"

The earl scowled. "Like the veriest blockhead. I do not know how a little rain could have made me so ill."

Daphne smiled tentatively, although her heart pounded at the sight of the handsome earl propped in bed. She noticed his complexion no longer looked flushed—in fact, it was paler than usual. "I shall take that to mean you are recovering. When one is strong enough to be grumpy, it is always a good sign."

Mrs. Tinkham chuckled. "You have the right of it, Miss Kendall." She sounded almost friendly.

"Am I to be taken to task by the two of you, then?" his lordship asked mockingly.

Daphne found it impossible not to grin. There was something warm and enchanting in his good humor. "I shall not keep you, my lord. I only wanted to inquire as to your progress before going downstairs to dine."

Lord Ravenswood shot a playfully ferocious look at Mrs. Tinkham but addressed Miss Kendall. "One can only improve so much when one is being starved. I daresay you, Miss Kendall, will be treated to a fine capon or even some roast beef while I am forced to sip thin gruel."

Mrs. Tinkham twitched the bedclothes into place and began to fuss over her charge's pillows. "Don't be ridiculous, Master Anthony. Broth is not gruel, and you are still weak."

"I ask you, Miss Kendall," he said with the air of someone done a great injustice, "how is a man supposed to regain his strength on broth? Can I persuade you to have your dinner sent up on a tray so I might at least *see* food, please?"

Discerning the light of amusement in his lordship's eyes, Daphne laughed.

"Booberkin," said the one who had known his lordship from his cradle. Mrs. Tinkham's sharp gaze went from Lord Ravenswood to Miss Kendall. She seemed to like what she saw. It was past time for Anthony to bring home a bride in the housekeeper's opinion, and while this Miss Blenkinsop he spoke of earlier sounded biddable, Mrs. Tinkham shrewdly judged the girl would never make Anthony happy. "I'll have Byron set up a table by the fire, and you two can eat there."

Before anyone could respond to this statement, Mrs. Tinkham sped from the room, leaving Sadie in attendance for propriety.

Daphne felt uneasy at the thought of taking her dinner with the earl under these circumstances. "My lord, I never meant to intrude on your peace this way. I shall go and tell Mrs. Tinkham that I shall dine downstairs."

Lord Ravenswood leaned forward and caught her hand. "Are you joking, Miss Kendall? Without you, I would not be getting a meal, and I confess, I am weak as a kitten. You would be doing me a great favor to remain."

Daphne withdrew her hand from his. It trembled from his touch, and she reminded herself sternly that the earl had no romantic interest in her. Still, she supposed there was no harm in sharing a meal with him. "Very well. I shall stay."

Soon enough they found themselves comfortably seated by the fire at a table laden with chicken, vegetables, bread, and wine. Their main topic of conversation was Raven's Hall.

"I very much enjoyed wandering the grounds today, my lord. The gardens are especially beautiful."

Anthony sipped his wine. "Thank you. Capability Brown is the artist who designed them. He had definite ideas as to how nature should look."

Daphne pulled apart a piece of bread. "I noticed there are few horses in the stables, other than workhorses, that is."

"True. One of my tasks before I can finally return home is to replenish the stables. Tattersall's ring is the only place to find good horseflesh."

Anthony laid down the fork. His voice grew sad as he reflected on the past. "You met Isabella, Miss Kendall. The woman did a thorough job of ruining the estate with her willful, selfish spending. My father indulged her to the bitter end, and yet she left him.

"After he died and I returned, it made me ill to see what had become of my home. The gardens and hedges were wild and overgrown. The tenants lived in poverty, and their houses barely stood upright. All the farm buildings were dilapidated, for the estate had been badly managed for years. And that fact, combined with Isabella's constant draining of its funds, brought a once rich property to its knees. Initially I had to sell off the horses and many of the furnishings to keep things going until I began making money in Egypt."

Daphne was thoughtful. "How terrible for you to have to take on the responsibility of restoring the estate. It must have been a daunting proposition, indeed. I admire the way you obviously prevailed. Raven's Hall is a place of great beauty and peace and prosperity."

Anthony studied Daphne carefully. Her words, her tone of voice, and her expression appeared to reflect her honest opinion. "Those are the very qualities that I have been striving for, Miss Kendall. Keeping the estate in good heart is an everlasting job. Unlike my father, I shall not allow any intelligent schemer—no matter how pretty a face she possesses—to destroy Raven's Hall in my lifetime."

At these words something clicked in Daphne's mind. She suddenly felt the need to be alone with her thoughts.

She placed her napkin on the table, and rose. "My lord, you must forgive me for keeping you from your rest. I fear Mrs. Tinkham will give me a scold should you suffer a relapse."

Anthony stood as well and gazed at her steadily. "On the contrary, Miss Kendall. The meal and your company have revived my strength. I believe that in a day or so more I shall be ready to return to Town. May I beg your indulgence until then?"

Daphne wanted to tell him she would stay with him forever. She wanted to tell him that she loved him and yearned to be his partner in life, in love, in caring for this marvelous house and its grounds and people. "The day after tomorrow will suit me fine, my lord."

She curtsied to him and nodded to Sadie, then quit the room. Anthony sank back down in his chair and stared into the fire for a long time after she left.

Daphne sought her bedchamber. Gaining that room, she crossed to the window and drew the curtains back to gaze out into the darkness.

His lordship's words regarding his stepmother and Raven's Hall had been an awakening experience that left her reeling. His family's ordeal with Isabella had obviously left Lord

Ravenswood suspicious when it came to women. Hence his pursuit of a quiet, compliant bride and his subsequent choice of Elfleta Blenkinsop.

But what of love? Was the earl prepared to sacrifice love and instead choose a tediously submissive woman because he feared any lady of intelligence and spirit might turn out to be another Isabella?

But he had it all wrong. A lady who loved him would cringe from deception. Was he not putting himself more at risk by not choosing to make a love match?

Daphne signed and let the curtain fall. Though this new insight helped her understand Lord Ravenswood better, it did not change anything. The earl had set his course and offered for Miss Blenkinsop. It seemed no amount of love or understanding on her part could change that fact.

She must begin distancing herself from him. She would begin tomorrow. If only she had not agreed to stay another day.

The next morning Daphne ate a hurried breakfast brought to her room on a tray. Her willow-green muslin gown had been cleaned and pressed while she slept, and she scrambled into it with Sadie's help.

When she was ready, and without even stopping at Miss Shelby's door to say good morning to that lady, Daphne went down to the kitchen. She begged the startled cook for some bread and cheese, for she planned on spending the day outdoors. Avoiding the earl might be cowardly, but Daphne felt quite desperate. She could not endure another cozy meal with the gentleman she loved while the specter of his engagement to another hung over her head.

A few minutes later she was armed with a basket that contained enough food to keep her from starvation for several days. Daphne stepped outside into the sunshine and began walking to the far side of the estate.

Having spent a restless morning in bed, Anthony felt well enough to dress by mid-afternoon. However, struggling into an acorn-brown coat and leather breeches, even with the aid of a footman, the earl felt drained of energy.

He no sooner sat down in a high-backed chair by the fire resting when Mrs. Tinkham bustled in. "Master Anthony, what have you done?"

"Merely gotten dressed, Tinky, nothing worthy of your censure," Lord Ravenswood teased.

Little Mrs. Tinkham stood before him with her hands on her hips. "I shan't allow pretty Miss Kendall to visit you today if you don't take care of yourself properly."

Anthony raised a brow at her. "How do you propose to keep me from her?"

Since this was exactly the direction Mrs. Tinkham wished the conversation to take, she sat down in the chair opposite him. "I am glad to hear you are adamant about seeing her."

Realizing his folly, the earl heaved a sigh. "Begad! I suppose it is too late now to claim I am in a devilish bad condition after all, and must be left in total quiet."

"What you are suffering from most is a want of sense, Master Anthony, and that's plain enough," Mrs. Tinkham said. She folded her hands in her lap. "Now, tell me why you are prepared to offer for Miss Blenkinsop when you really want Miss Kendall."

Anthony looked mulish, then remembered how long Tinky had been at Raven's Hall. "Miss Blenkinsop is, well, not particularly strong-minded. She will be a compliant wife."

Mrs. Tinkham's mouth fell open. "Is that what she has to offer?"

"Well, yes. But she is from good family and has a large dowry as well," Anthony said, feeling very much on the defensive. "We do not wish for another Isabella here, do we?"

Mrs. Tinkham was much struck by this statement. She remained silent for a moment, then leaned forward in her chair. "Master Anthony, Miss Kendall is nothing at all like Isabella."

"She is intelligent, Tinky, just like my stepmother. Clever women are dangerous." Even as he said the oft repeated words, the theory rang hollow in his own ears.

"Stuff!" the housekeeper said roundly. " 'Tis a lady's *character* that you must look to in order to judge whether she is capable of the kind of behavior Isabella displayed. From what I have seen, Miss Kendall is a *lady*; she is kind to all, and caring. Look how concerned she was for that heathen man-servant of yours! Besides which, you love her, do you not?"

Lord Ravenswood made as if to protest, but found he could not. It was true. He loved Daphne Kendall. Good God. He raised a hand and rubbed it across his forehead. "You have figured out a lot in a short period of time, Tinky."

Mrs. Tinkham seized the advantage. "Well, I've known you all your life, haven't I? And even though I don't know Miss Kendall very well, I know a girl in *love* when I see one."

Lord Ravenswood snapped to attention at these words. He remembered how Daphne had responded to his kiss at the Pelhams' ball. She was not the type to respond to his passion unless her affections were engaged. Why, now that he thought about it, the sort of grasping he most feared was as foreign to her nature as caviar to pigs!

He rose to stand firmly on his feet. "Where is Miss Kendall?"

"Cook says she has gone outdoors. Now, Master Anthony, just because you have finally come to your senses does not mean you should wander the estate looking for her in your condition!"

Lord Ravenswood flashed her a boyish grin, just before closing the door behind him.

It was easy enough for Eugene and Miss Shelby to slip away from Raven's Hall without anyone being the wiser. They hired a vehicle and reached London late that afternoon.

"I shall start the rumors going about Lord Ravenswood and Miss Kendall. The underbutler next door is the neighborhood gossip." Eugene told Miss Shelby outside of Daphne's town house in Clarges Street. "Wait for me here, and I shall call on you later and apprise you of any developments."

Miss Shelby clung to the sleeve of his white tunic. "Oh,

Eugene, I do hope we have done right in leaving them in the country alone."

"They are hardly alone with that dragon, Mrs. Tinkham," he said dryly. He raised her hand to his lips and kissed it warmly. "Soon, Leonie, soon, we shall be together. Would you like to see Egypt?"

Miss Shelby smiled, then chuckled outright. "Oh, yes, Eugene. You know I long for travel. Remember Mary Tucker told me I would soon be going on a sea journey."

"She is knowing, but not like you, my wise lady," Eugene told her, and then took his leave.

Miss Shelby let herself into the back of the house and was promptly greeted by three exuberant dogs. She patted them each in turn, asking, "How would you like to live with Daphne and Lord Ravenswood in the country?"

Lord Ravenswood felt tired and hungry. He had spent two hours riding about the estate, looking for Miss Kendall without success. Coming up to the Palladian-style bridge, which spanned a wide stream, he dismounted. After leaving his horse to graze, he stretched out under a leafy tree at the water's edge and allowed the gentle sound of the stream to lull him to sleep.

That is how Daphne found him an hour later.

Strolling across the bridge, she saw his supine figure and let out a cry of distress. Thinking he had collapsed, she rushed across the bridge and dropped down to his side on the grass. Her heart jumped in her chest. She reached out a hand and felt of his forehead. Thankfully it was cool.

"My lord, can you hear me? Are you all right?" she asked urgently.

For an answer Lord Ravenswood slowly opened his brown eyes and gazed into her anxious face. Then he leaned forward and swiftly caught her in his arms. He lowered his head and kissed her, his mouth moving over hers and devouring its softness.

Caught off guard, Daphne returned his embrace, giving herself freely to the passion of his kiss.

Then, despite the intensity of desire, Daphne suddenly

remembered Lord Ravenswood was engaged to Miss Blenkinsop. She wrenched herself away from him and sprang to her feet.

"How dare you, my lord?" she demanded. Fearing she might at any moment burst into tears, she turned and began a swift march across the bridge.

He caught up with her before she made it halfway across. "Daphne! Please! Wait a moment."

She continued on her way, so he darted in front of her and grasped her by the shoulders. "Daphne, I beg your pardon. You see, I have been out searching for you all day, and I grew so tired that I had to stop and rest. When I woke and saw your dear face above me, well, I could not restrain myself. I admit, you had reason to think me perfectly mad."

Daphne lowered her gaze in confusion. She had to calm her disordered thoughts and could not do so with him looking at her with that gentle, concerned, *loving* expression. In her confusion, she found refuge in righteous anger. "Mad, my lord? No, I think playing fast and loose with my affections would be a more accurate description."

"Whatever can you mean?" he asked at once.

"You are betrothed to Elfleta Blenkinsop! And yet you embrace me, kiss me—"

He gripped her shoulders more tightly. "I am *not* engaged to Miss Blenkinsop. How could you think—Eugene! I shall strangle him," he pronounced grimly, his arms falling to his sides.

Daphne wondered if she should feel some guilt for the relief she felt. "You are not betrothed?"

The earl ran a hand impatiently through his dark hair. "No. In truth, I was going to offer for the chit Tuesday morning. Then I received a letter from Eugene—maybe I will not strangle him after all—saying you were in danger. I rode out to find you instead of going to her house."

One dark red curl lay across the whiteness of her shoulder. He picked up the tempting spiral and idly drew it between his fingers. "I have been a fool, Daphne."

"How do you mean, Anthony?" she asked him softly. A bright spot of hope began to grow in her.

His brown eyes sought hers. "When Mihos first came to live with me, every time he stretched out his paw to my chin in a gesture of affection, I thought he was going to rip my nose off. I based this assumption on the way Isabella's cat, Brutus, had behaved. When I met you and saw how attractive and intelligent you were, I did not want to care for you, fearing you would use those qualities against me, the way Isabella did with my father."

Daphne laid a hand against his cheek. "What made you realize I would not?"

"You are not at all like Isabella." The earl swallowed hard. "You care more for people than things, and you are never cruel. And, while my father loved Isabella, she did not return his passion. You do love me, do you not, my heart? For I love you madly."

A smile of pure joy lit Daphne's face. "Yes, Anthony, I love you."

Then she was in his arms. His kiss sent swirling bursts of ecstasy coursing through her. She felt as if she could not get close enough to him, and savored every moment his mouth was on hers.

Several minutes later he reluctantly drew away and asked, "Why did you send Mihos back to me? I thought we had agreed you were to keep him for some time longer?"

Her fingers stroked his hair. "I thought you were going to marry Elfleta."

He pulled her against him and whispered into her hair. "You are the only lady I shall ever marry, my heart. I love you. Will you have me?"

Daphne looked at him and pretended to consider. "I do not know. Do you think Mihos will get along with Holly, Folly, and Jolly?" Her teasing look was unmistakable.

"God help us," the earl muttered, before he claimed her lips again.

* * *

Because of Mihos, Elfleta Blenkinsop never received Lord Ravenswood's note telling her he had been called out of Town on an urgent matter.

Therefore on this, the second day after the earl was to call, Elfleta sat in her drawing room. She was beside herself with fury. How dare he treat her thus?

Also in the room, Mrs. Blenkinsop had alternately questioned and berated her daughter regarding the entire affair, making Elfleta even angrier.

The knocker sounded and a few minutes later, the butler ushered Lord Guy into the room. He was full of the gossip Eugene had spread all about Lord Ravenswood and Miss Kendall being alone together at the earl's estate. Lord Guy prayed he would be the first to relate it to the Blenkinsops. He got his wish.

"What's that you say!" Mrs. Blenkinsop shrieked upon hearing the account.

Elfleta gasped, shaken by the strongest emotion ever felt in her young life.

Lord Guy was all apologies. "Dear me, I thought you ladies would know. His lordship's behavior is disgraceful, Miss Blenkinsop. Disgraceful! Your goodness has been sorely used."

Elfleta called up the few brain cells at her command and thought furiously. Despite the fact that the earl had not formally made her an offer, she had been too puffed up with conceit to keep quiet about her expectations. Several members of the ton were made privy to the knowledge that she was shortly to announce her engagement.

Elfleta needed a fiancé. Fast.

She turned her hazel eyes toward Lord Guy and allowed a few graceful tears to fall.

Happy for the chance to play at being the gallant, Lord Guy whipped a lace handkerchief from the pocket of his celestial blue coat and handed it to her with a flourish. "Were you mine, I would never treat you thus."

"You would not?" Elfleta asked him tearfully. She gazed up at him adoringly, her hazel eyes huge in her face.

"Never!" Lord Guy cried, throwing himself into his role for all he was worth. "Only give me a chance to prove myself."

"Yes, oh, yes, I shall marry you," Elfleta breathed.

Lord Guy's eyes popped in his head. Before he could absorb what had happened, Mrs. Blenkinsop was wishing the couple happy and calling her reluctant husband into the room to join in the congratulations.

When Mr. Blenkinsop hinted at the size of his Elf's dowry, Lord Guy began to relax. The happy thought of all that money soon had him envisioning a new wardrobe full of coats in every shade imaginable. Tailors from Hyde Park to Charing Cross would be begging for his custom.

Lord Guy would not have been so sanguine had he known his future mama-in-law was even now casting a stern eye over his dress. She determined on the spot to educate him as to the proper way a gentleman should present himself to the world.

Wedding plans were the last thing on one lady's mind. Miss Shelby sat in the drawing room of Daphne's town house and worried about Eugene's safety. Something told her Mr. Phillips might easily have learned where Eugene lived and would break into Lord Ravenswood's house. What might happen if he did not find the Bastet statue? Would he lie in wait for Eugene?

As the minutes ticked by, Miss Shelby's premonition of danger grew stronger. Coming to a decision not to wait for Eugene, she placed a shawl about her shoulders and hurried downstairs. With a footman to accompany her, and Folly for extra protection, she ventured out into the dark streets.

Halfway to Upper Brook Street, she encountered Eugene headed in the same direction. Folly barked a greeting.

"Leonie, what are you doing out? It is not safe," Eugene said.

Miss Shelby wrapped her shawl tighter about her shoulders. "I had a bad feeling."

Eugene touched a finger to his eye-pin. Then he looked at her. "You must go home. I shall take care of this—"

"No, Eugene! John and Folly and I will come with you. I insist!"

Seeing she could not be swayed, Eugene reluctantly agreed.

They hurried through the dark streets. When the earl's town house came into view, Folly broke away from them and ran toward the back of the house. Miss Shelby and Eugene looked at each other, then followed him. After they rounded the corner, a startling sight, and still more startling sounds, brought them to a standstill.

Vincent Phillips clung to the ledge of an open window on the second floor, his beaver-trimmed greatcoat ballooning out around him. Mihos perched in the window frame, roaring at the intruder.

While they watched, Vincent held on with one hand and tried to push the cat out of the way with the other. In a lightning-fast motion, sharp claws ripped through the flesh of the hand clutching the ledge.

Giving a loud cry, Vincent fell to the ground heavily, clutching his injured foot. Folly raced to the spot and commenced a furious barking and showing of teeth.

Miss Shelby found her voice. "Run for the watch, John."

"You!" Vincent shouted at Eugene. "I'll get the Bastet statue from you yet!"

Miss Shelby quieted Folly, who continued to hover menacingly over the thief.

"No you will not," Eugene said calmly, moving to stand guard over Vincent's supine body. "Bastet represents the beneficent powers of the sun and is the goddess of joy. She will not be used for evil."

Two enforcers of the law came at a run around the corner. "What have we got here?" one man asked.

"A common housebreaker," Eugene replied.

At that moment Folly's fondness for beaver apparently overcame his scruples and Miss Shelby's training. The dog lunged for the pocket of Vincent's greatcoat, which was trimmed in his favorite fur.

The material ripped, and out fell the ivory cat figurine Vincent had stashed there, planning to foist it off on a sailor for cash on his way to Philadelphia.

Miss Shelby gasped in recognition. "That belongs to the Duchess of Welbourne!"

"Caught with stolen property, eh?" one of the watchmen said.

"Yes," Miss Shelby promptly replied. "And this is the Earl of Ravenswood's town house the man was trying to break into."

"Off to the roundhouse he goes, then." The two men carried a protesting Vincent away, saying they would call on the earl tomorrow for a statement.

Miss Shelby patted Folly's head. "What a good dog. You have redeemed yourself." Folly favored her with a wide doggie grin and wagged his tail.

Eugene looked up to the open window, where Mihos had all the while been watching the proceedings. "Good work, little tiger." Mihos turned to the delicate business of washing his paws and paid no further attention.

Eugene placed an arm about Miss Shelby's shoulder. "Come, it is time I walk you home."

Hours later Eugene stood alone in a darkened room. At the far end of the chamber, a light began to glow. Soon the ebony body of a woman with a cat's head came into view. She sat upon an intricately carved golden throne with many live cats sitting at her feet.

"You have done your duty, Eugene," she said. Her voice seemed to come to him from a great distance. "I am pleased."

Eugene dropped down to his knees in front of her. "My goddess, I am ever grateful for your benevolence."

Bastet raised a hand. Cupped inside her palm was an eye-pin similar to the one Eugene wore in his turban. The pin seemed to catch the light and reflect it toward Eugene's pin until a single beam formed between them. Eugene remained motionless.

Bastet spoke again. "You are free now, Eugene. Free."

"Grraow!"

Eugene sat bolt upright in bed, his heart pounding in his chest. Mihos stood on the bed next to him.

It had been a dream, Eugene thought. Only a dream.

Or had it?

Eugene threw off the bedclothes and rushed to the armoire. Before going to bed, he had made sure the Bastet statue was safe in its hiding place. His hands brushed aside the clothes inside, and he looked down.

The folds of burgundy velvet lay empty on the bottom of the armoire. Eugene slowly reached for them and held the soft material in his hands.

Having served her purpose, Bastet was gone.

Eugene sank to his knees, tears of happiness running down his cheeks.

Epilogue

A month after their wedding, The Earl of Ravenswood and his countess, Daphne, reclined on their bed at Raven's Hall. The sounds of Holly, Folly, and Jolly barking and cavorting outside reached their ears through the open window.

Anthony had, and not an hour before, used his body in many talented ways to show his blissful bride how much he loved her. Daphne thought it scandalous that her husband had taken her to bed in the middle of the day. But, she decided smiling lazily, she would soon grow accustomed.

While her husband went to pour her a glass of iced lemonade, kept cool in the bucket he had thoughtfully brought to their room earlier, she reached over to the bedside table and picked up a late wedding gift. Seeing her busy at her task, he perused his mail.

"Well," he said, opening a letter, "here is another note from William Bullock."

"Have they cleared up the mystery yet?" Daphne asked, pulling at the wrappings of the gift.

"No. As far as anyone knows, the missing Bastet statue simply reappeared in the museum in Baluk."

"Maybe someone had a guilty conscience," Daphne offered.

The earl put the letter aside and brushed his lips across his wife's naked shoulder. " 'Twill always be a wonder. Like the softness of your skin."

Daphne nudged him away. "Darling, please, I am trying to open this present."

Lord Ravenswood sighed and picked up another letter. "Here is one from Eugene and Leonie."

Daphne looked up eagerly. "Oh, how are they? I confess, I cannot wait for them to visit, although I am happy they were able to travel after their marriage. Your gift to them was most generous, Anthony."

"Eugene deserved a reward for all his years of faithful service. It seems they are now on their way from Egypt to Turkey. They have not stopped traveling since they wed," Anthony remarked. "I, on the other hand, prefer to stay right where I am." He reached for his wife again, but she evaded him.

Daphne finally succeeded in unwrapping the gift, whose giver had not been identified. She pushed the paper aside and lifted a small, odd-shaped lamp from the box.

"Look at this," she said to Anthony, a perplexed frown on her face.

The earl pulled back the sheet covering his wife. "Hmm, yes, I should be delighted."

"Oh!" Daphne giggled, and wrapped her arms around her husband, welcoming his kiss. The lamp fell from her fingers to roll unheeded off the bed.

The soft thud woke Mihos, who reclined on a chaise across the room. The striped cat jumped down and swaggered over to where the lamp lay on its side.

He sniffed it with a great show of feline disdain. Then, with his tail held high, he turned and strolled out of the room.

LANTERNS

*Romance and intrigue abound in this latest installment
of the Sanguinet Saga
by beloved Regency romance author*
Patricia Veryan.

Miss Marietta Warrington is the backbone of
her family, now that her endearing but reckless
father has gambled away the family fortune.
Reduced to renting the dower house of
Lanterns, an abandoned estate, Marietta and
her sister are scrambling to save every penny as
they struggle to find suitably well-heeled hus-
bands. Then Marietta discovers a stranger
named Diccon living among the ruins of
Lanterns, and he takes her heart by storm. Is the
handsome and mysterious Diccon the smuggler
he appears to be, or is he the gentleman
Marietta has been praying for?

Published by Fawcett Books.
Available now wherever books are sold.

Love Letters

Ballantine romances are on the Web!

Read about your favorite Ballantine authors and upcoming books on our Web site, LOVE LETTERS, at **www.randomhouse.com/BB/loveletters**, including:

♥What's new in the stores
♥Previews of upcoming books
♥In-depth interviews with romance authors and
 publishing insiders
♥Sample chapters from new romances
♥And more . . .

Want to keep in touch? To subscribe to Love Notes, the monthly what's-new update for the Love Letters Web site, send an e-mail message to
loveletters@cruises.randomhouse.com
with "subscribe" as the subject of the message. You will receive a monthly announcement of the latest news and features on our site.

So follow your heart and visit us at
www.randomhouse.com/BB/loveletters!

THE SAVAGE HEART
by Diana Palmer

Meet the extraordinary, mysterious, handsome Matt Davis. He's a loner, a maverick, a man who depends on his wits, his hard-won personal wealth, and his stunning physical prowess to handle anything that comes his way.

Anything, that is, until Tess Meredith storms into Chicago . . . and into the deepest recesses of Matt's lonely heart. Tess is no stranger . . . and she's more than a match for him. When one of her friends is accused of murder, Tess turns to Matt for help. And she means help, for she insists on being his full partner in an investigation that quickly turns deadly dangerous . . . and brings this remarkable pair to an admission of love they have fought since their first meeting.

From Mary Jo Putney comes
the New York Times *bestselling*

ONE PERFECT ROSE

a tale of star-crossed romance
in a special keepsake hardcover edition
available only from Fawcett Columbine Books.

Stephen Kenyon, Duke of Ashburton, has always taken the duties of privilege seriously—until he receives shocking news that sends him fleeing from his isolating life of extreme wealth and status. Eventually he finds safe harbor with the theatrical Fitzgerald family, whose warmth and welcome he has always craved. But his greatest longings are piqued by the lovely Rosalind Jordan, a wharfside foundling who has grown into an enchanting and compassionate woman.

Can Stephen succumb to his one perfect Rose, given the secret that propelled him into her arms to begin with? Can Rosalind resist a man who fulfills her wildest dreams because he may never be hers?

Passionate . . . compelling . . . powerful . . .

Now on sale wherever books are sold.

Romance Endures in Columbine Keeper Editions!

"A delicious stew of crime, passion,
high fashion, and tragic love."
—*Affaire de Coeur*

From Sally Beauman,
the bestselling author of *Lovers and Liars*,
comes a new tale of international intrigue
and fatal passion.

DANGER ZONES

A reclusive designer of originality and passion, Maria Cazarès is a legend shrouded in mystery. When the fashion glitterati assemble in Paris to breathlessly await the new Cazarès collection, a long-buried secret resurfaces and tragedy strikes. Two journalists, Rowland McGuire and Gini Hunter, pick up the scent of an unfolding scandal that will converge with the desperate search for an innocent girl who has disappeared. And at last, some blood red truths will be revealed....

**Published by Fawcett Books.
Available wherever books are sold.**